Chapter

THE THIRTEENTH CLIENT

Shelmore, then three-and-twenty years old, had been in practice as a solicitor for precisely six months, and, probably because he had set up in his own native city of Southernstowe, the end of that period found him with exactly twelve clients on his roll. His line was the eminently safe one of conveyancing and the clients were profitable ones; he knew enough of his profession to know that his first half-year's experience was satisfactory and promising. Another fledgling, lower down the street, a former fellow-articled-clerk, admitted at the same time as himself, who had gone in for police-court practice, was doubtless having livelier times, but not making so much substantial gain; his office, perhaps, was more crowded, but Shelmore preferred the dignified quiet of his own, wherein he and his clients talked of nothing less important than the transference or acquisition of real estate.

In a youthful fashion he was somewhat proud of that office. At the street door there was a beautiful, highly-polished brass plate, engraved in the very best of taste: Francis D. Shelmore, Solicitor; at the head of the stair leading up from it there was a smaller one, similarly inscribed, on an oak door; within that door, in the dark room liberally provided with all the proper show of papers, parchments, and japanned tin boxes, sat Shelmore's one clerk, an astute, sharp-eyed, precocious youth named Simmons Hackdale; within an inner door, duly covered with green baize, sat Shelmore himself, in a private office very neatly and tastefully furnished and ornamented.

Whenever one of the twelve clients came, Shelmore was always busy, and the client was kept waiting a little, the time of waiting being adjusted by the clerk in accordance with his own estimate of the client's value and importance. But, in plain truth, Shelmore had a lot of time on his hands, and it was a good deal to his credit that he spent some of it in improving his own knowledge of law, and some in giving a gratuitous course of legal education to his—unarticled—clerk. Shelmore, having been a bit of a precisian since boyhood, kept exact hours. He arrived at the office at exactly ten minutes to ten every morning; at ten minutes to five every afternoon he prepared to leave it. He was preparing to leave it now—a certain Wednesday afternoon in the last week of what had been an unusually fine September, He had tidied up his desk and put away his books and assumed his hat and overcoat; his umbrella, tightly rolled, stood ready to his hand; close by it lay the Times, neatly folded, to be carried home to his aunt. Miss Olivia Chauncey, with whom he lived, in an old-fashioned house in the oldest part of Southernstowe. He stood by the window, fitting on his gloves with meticulous precision; thus engaged, he looked out on the scene beneath and in front; he had gone through that performance every afternoon for six months; it would not have disconcerted him if he had been assured by some infallible prophet that he would go through it every afternoon for many and many a long year to come. It was all part of what he wished and liked—a well-ordered, calm, systematic life routine, in, which tomorrow should be as today.

Yet, at that very moment, had Shelmore but known it, things were stirring close by, which were not according to any routine of his, and were going to break in upon the regularity of his daily life. As he stood there, looking unemotionally out of the window, he saw something which, if it did not exactly excite him, at any rate interested him. The block in which his office was situate was a corner one. It commanded views of a good bit of the centre of the old city, and in particular a full prospect of the front of the ancient Chancellor Hotel. And what interested Shelmore was the sudden appearance of a girl at the entrance of the court-yard of the Chancellor—a girl, who, for a second or two stood on the curb, looking doubtfully and inquiringly around, as people look at unfamiliar things and scenes. She was a tallish girl; she was slim and willowy; he had a convinced idea that she was young and pretty; she was smartly dressed; she was a stranger. He wondered about her without knowing why he wondered: then, as he saw her look round again, hesitate, and suddenly cross the street in his direction, he formulated a theory.

"She's in some perplexity," mused Shelmore. "Wants to know something."

The girl disappeared from view amongst the folk on the sidewalk, and Shelmore, the last finger of his gloves being adjusted, picked up the neatly rolled umbrella and the equally neatly folded Times, and prepared to quit the scene of his daily labour. But before he had opened the green baize door, he heard voices in the clerk's room. He paused: the green baize door opened, and Simmons Hackdale's sharp-eyed face appeared, and his hand held out a card.

"Young lady," said Simmons, laconically. "Wants to consult you."

Shelmore took the card mechanically and stared at the neat script. Of course this was the girl he had just seen from his window. And this that he was staring at would be her name—Miss Cynthia Pretty, St. Meliot's, Camborne. Camborne! Why, Camborne was a good two or three hundred miles away, in Cornwall! What... he suddenly looked up, nodded at his clerk, and, drawing off his gloves and removing his hat, turned to his desk, as to a refuge. But being there again, his eyes went to the door...

He got a general impression of Miss Cynthia Pretty as Simmons Hackdale showed her in. She was tallish, and she was slim and willowy, as he had thought at first, and she was undeniably attractive. He was not sure whether her hair was gold—deep gold—or whether it weren't a bit reddish; he was uncertain, too, about her eyes, whether they were blue or whether they were violet—anyway, the lot of her, put together, lighted up the office. And she was young—perhaps nineteen, perhaps twenty; he couldn't tell; certainly she was very young. And suddenly he felt very young—and a little small—himself. For at sight of him, Miss Cynthia Pretty let out an involuntary exclamation.

"Oh!" she said, pausing between the door and the desk. "Are—are you the Mr. Shelmore whose name is on the door downstairs. You are? Oh! Well, you look so awfully young to be a solicitor. And it's a solicitor I want."

"Perhaps I'm older than I look," answered Shelmore, recovering his wits. "And I assure you I'm very wise! Will you sit down and tell me—"

His client dropped into the easy chair to which he pointed, and let her hands fall together in her lap. She gave him another critical inspection.

"You look a bit clever," she said. "And anyway, you're a man and a lawyer, and that's what I want. I'm in a mess, Mr. Shelmore!—at least, I don't know what to do. As you see from my card, my name's Pretty—Cynthia Pretty. I live near Camborne, in Cornwall. I'm half-proprietor of a famous tin mine there. The other half belongs to my partner, Mr. James Deane. Mr. Deane is also my guardian and trustee and all that sort of thing, under my father's will, because, you see, I'm not yet of age—I'm only nineteen. I'm telling you this as a sort of preliminary to the really important business. Well, that's just this—Mr. Deane and I have lately been travelling about. Not together—separately. He's been in the North of England—he's fond of old places, antiquities and so on. I've been staying with an old school friend at Bath. Mr. Deane and I arranged to meet here, at the Chancellor Hotel, Southernstowe, today—this afternoon, to be exact. We were to stay here a few days, to look round; then we were going on to Dover, and to the continent—Holland and Belgium, and perhaps Germany. Well, I got here, not half-an-hour ago, from Bath, with all my luggage, and drove straight to the Chancellor. They'd got a room booked for me

4

right enough—Mr. Deane booked it when he arrived here on Monday—that's the day before yesterday. But Mr. Deane himself isn't there!—he's clean disappeared!"

"Disappeared!" exclaimed Shelmore. "How? Why?"

"Don't ask me," replied his caller. "I don't know! That's what the girl clerk in the office, across there, says. The landlord wasn't in, and I couldn't get much out of her—she isn't very brilliant or illuminating. But that's what she says—that Mr. Deane came there on Monday, some time, and disappeared mysteriously during Monday night, and they've never seen him since. And—and I thought I'd better consult somebody at once, and so I came out and looked about for a solicitor, and I saw your name, and—well, that's just where it is."

"How old is Mr. Deane?" asked Shelmore.

"Sixty-three last June," answered Miss Pretty. "Any reason why he should disappear?"

"Goodness, no! What reason should there be?"

"Not knowing him, I can't say. Any financial reasons?"

"Mr Deane is a wealthy man. He and I, as partners, are both wealthy."

"An domestic trouble now? Is Mr. Deane married?"

"He's a widower. His wife died when I was a little girl."

"Any sons or daughters?"

"He's neither. I've hoard him say that he hasn't a relative in the world."

"A contented sort of man? No worries?"

"I should say, having known him all my life, that Mr. Deane hadn't a care or a trouble. He's a very sunny-natured, bright-tempered man."

"And you can't think of any reason whatever why he should disappear?"

"Not one! Not the ghost of a reason! I know he was looking forward awfully keenly to this tour on the continent; and, the last letter I had from him—here, in my bag—he promised faithfully to be waiting for me at the Chancellor today at four o'clock. He's the sort of man who's most punctilious about appointments. And I'm just certain, Mr. Shelmore—there's something wrong."

Shelmore picked up his hat.

"I'll go across with you to the Chancellor, Miss Pretty," he said, "I know Belling, the landlord—we'd better see him at once."

"He was out when I was there," remarked Miss Pretty. "And I don't see what he can know about it any more than that Mr. Deane's not there since Monday night."

"Mr. Deane may have left a message with him of which the girl in the office knows nothing," suggested Shelmore. "Anyway, Belling's the man—and there he is just going in."

He led his new client through the courtyard of the old hotel, and past the office to a private room, wherein the landlord, a cheery-faced, middle-aged man, was just taking off his hat and overcoat. He made Miss Pretty a polite bow and gave Shelmore a comprehending nod.

"I've just heard of Miss Pretty's arrival and her enquiries about Mr. Deane," he said, drawing chairs forward for his visitors. "I see you've not been long in seeking legal advice, miss!—but let's hope there's no need for that. Still, it's a fact, Mr. Shelmore. I don't know anything about Mr. Deane. He's not here—and I don't know where he is."

"Just tell me what you do know," replied Shelmore. "Miss Pretty is naturally anxious about him—she's afraid something may have happened."

"Well, sir, Mr. Deane looked to me the sort of man who could very well look after himself," answered the landlord, as he took a seat opposite his callers. "But I'll tell you everything I know. Mr. Deane arrived here, from London, I understood, on Monday

5

afternoon, about four o'clock. He booked a room for himself—number seven. Then he booked a room for his ward. Miss Pretty, who, he said, would be here on Wednesday—number eleven. Here, of course, is Miss Pretty, and the room is all ready for her. But where's her guardian? Well, all I can tell is this: Mr. Deane's luggage was taken up to his room. He went up there himself, and had some tea sent up. He came down to dinner at seven o'clock, and dined in just the usual fashion. After dinner, he came to me in the bar-parlour and asked if there was any particular amusement in the place. I told him we'd just opened a new picture house, the first thing of its kind ever known in Southernstowe, and that it was well worth seeing. He said he'd go. He went. He came back about ten o'clock, or a little after. He asked me to join him in a drink. He had a whisky and soda in this very room—Mr. Deane sat in that very chair you're in, Mr. Shelmore. We talked about the picture house, and the money there was in that industry nowadays. Then he observed that he'd seen a very handsome lady at the picture house, who occupied what, he said, was evidently a place of honour, and seemed to be some local celebrity. I told him that that would be Mrs. Champernowne, the Mayor of Southernstowe. He was much interested in that, he said that though he'd heard of ladies being mayors before, he'd never actually seen one in office. I told him that Mrs. Champernowne was a very smart, clever woman, proprietress of one of the biggest businesses in the city, that since her coming to Southernstowe twenty-odd years ago, she's always taken a vast interest in civic affairs, and that this was her second year of office as chief magistrate. We talked a while about women's share in politics and municipal life, and then about eleven o'clock, he said he'd get off to bed. We said good-night at the foot of the stairs—and that, Mr. Shelmore, was the very last I saw of him! Never seen, nor heard of him since!"

"But—your people?" suggested Shelmore.

"Ah, to be sure!" asserted Belling. "The chambermaid—she saw him last."

"Under what circumstances?" enquired Shelmore.

"Well," replied the landlord, "a few minutes—perhaps ten minutes or a quarter of an hour after he'd gone upstairs, he rang the bell for her, and asked for a glass of hot milk. She came down and got it for him; when she went back with it, Mr. Deane, according to what she told me next morning, was in his pyjamas and dressing gown, sitting in an easy chair and reading a book. He asked her to bring him some China tea and a dry biscuit at seven o'clock sharp next morning. She bade him good-night and went away, leaving him there sipping his hot milk, and reading his book-and there you are!"

"There he was—late on Monday night—anyway," remarked Shelmore. "Well-but let's get to seven o'clock, Tuesday morning. What about that?"

"Seven o'clock Tuesday morning, the chambermaid took up the tea and biscuits," continued Belling. "There was no response to her knock, so she went into the room. There was no one there. She thought Mr. Deane had gone to the bathroom, so she set down the tea and went away. But presently she took hot water there. Still he wasn't there. And we've never seen or heard of him since. As I said before, the last person who ever saw him in this house was the chambermaid, late on Monday night, when, apparently, he was about to get into bed—ready for bed, anyway!"

"Did the chambermaid notice if the bed had been slept in?" enquired Shelmore. "I mean on Tuesday morning?"

"Oh, yes! I asked her about that. It had. Certainly it had—I went up there myself afterwards and saw that it had."

Shelmore glanced at Miss Pretty. She was listening intently to the conversation, and already a puzzled look was fixing itself on her face. Suddenly she put a question to Belling, in prompt, direct fashion.

6

"When did you first miss my guardian?" she asked.

Belling gave Shelmore a smile which seemed to suggest that a man would more readily understand the situation than a woman.

"Well, miss," he replied, turning to his questioner, "probably not until the morning was well advanced. We had a good many guests in the house yesterday morning, and I was very busy. It was, I should say, about eleven o'clock before it suddenly struck me that I hadn't seen Mr. Deane about. Then I made enquiry of the chambermaid, and heard all that I've told you. She, of course, thought the gentleman had risen early and gone out for a walk before breakfast—so many gentlemen do."

"That means that his clothes had gone with him!" said Miss Pretty, sharply. "He wouldn't go out in his pyjamas! But did no one see him go out?"

"Yes," observed Shelmore, rising from his chair, "that's it!—did no one see him go out? Because he must have gone out between last thing at night and first thing next morning. But there's only one thing to do. Belling—we shall have to consult the police. I see your telephone's in the corner. You don't mind if I ring up the City Hall? There's no time to be lost in an affair of this sort."

He crossed over to the telephone… within a couple of minutes he turned to his companions. "That's all right." he said. "Mellapont's coming over himself—Superintendent Mellapont."

WHAT ABOUT THE BED?

There presently strode into the landlord's private parlour a man, who, had he been in plain clothes instead of in a smart, tightly-fitting, black-braided blue uniform, would have been set down by nine people out of ten as a Life-Guardsman in mufti. A very tall, heavily-built man, with a keen, determined face, he turned a sharp, enquiring glance on Miss Cynthia Pretty in the same second wherein he nodded, half-carelessly, to Belling and Shelmore.

"Evening, Mr. Belling—even, Mr. Shelmore," he began. "What's all this?—gentleman disappeared from the Chancellor? This young lady's guardian, eh? Yes?—well. What are the surface facts, now?"

He dropped into a chair and sat, listening attentively, while Shelmore briefly explained matters. Then he turned alertly on the landlord.

"Why didn't you put yourself in communication with me, Mr. Belling, as soon as you missed this gentleman?" he asked, with something of judicial severity in his tone. "It's a good deal more than twenty-four hours since you missed him, and this is the first I've heard of it!"

Belling spread out his hands and shook his head.

"That's all very well, superintendent," he retorted, "but if you'd been in this business as many years as I have, you'd know that hotel guests do strange things! The only notion I had at first was that this gentleman had gone out for a walk, gone further than he intended, got breakfast somewhere, and would turn up for lunch at the usual time. I took the trouble to go up and look at his room, and saw that the bed had been slept in—that confirmed my first idea. Then, later, when he didn't come in, and as the day—yesterday—wore on, I got another idea—that Mr. Deane probably had friends in the neighbourhood, and had gone to breakfast with them, and was staying on for the day with them. As the day passed, I got more certain that the second was the right idea—friends. You see—"

"A moment," interrupted Mellapont. He turned to Miss Pretty. "Has your guardian any friends or acquaintances in Southernstowe or neighbourhood?" he asked. "I mean—to your knowledge?"

"To my knowledge, no," replied Miss Pretty. "Indeed, I'm quite sure he hadn't. Mr. Deane had never been in Southernstowe before Monday, and he knew no one here, nor near here. We talked a good deal about Southernstowe when we were making our holiday plans. He wanted to see the cathedral, and the old walls, and the old churches and houses here—if he'd known anybody here or hereabouts I'm confident he'd have mentioned it. I know this—he'd never been in this part of England before."

"That seems to settle your second theory, Mr Belling," remarked Mellapont. "But you were about to observe—"

"I was only going to say that Mr. Deane's absence seemed to fit in with what he'd told me about his ward coming," said Belling. "He'd said that Miss Pretty wouldn't arrive until Wednesday afternoon. Very well!—he'd until Wednesday afternoon to do as he liked—no engagement that could keep him in. What more likely than that, if he had friends—I say if, mind you—in this place or neighbourhood he should stop with them until it was time to meet Miss Pretty. I think I was justified in thinking that. I've often had gentlemen come here, book a room, have their luggage put in it, stroll out to see somebody, and never come back for one, two, or three days. That's what I thought about this case—gone off to see somebody, and stopped."

"Theory!" said Mellapont. "Now let's get down to plain fact. Thee plain fact is that Mr. James Deane was in his bedroom, number seven, at the Chancellor Hotel at eleven o'clock on Monday night, and that at noon next morning he was gone. Now then, when did he go? Monday night or Tuesday morning? Mr. Belling!—let me have a word or two with the chambermaid we've heard about—fetch her in."

Belling left the room, and Mellapont, with a glance at the door, bent forward to Miss Pretty.

"Would your guardian be likely to have a good deal of money on him?" he asked, quietly. "Ready money?"

"Yes!" replied Miss Pretty, promptly. "He would! He'd have a lot on him. You see, we were going on the continent. Besides, he always had a lot of money on him when lie was travelling about—I've travelled with him before, often."

"And valuables, now? Watch, chain—that sort of thing?" suggested Mellapont. "Good jewellery?"

"He'd a lot of very valuable jewellery on him," said Miss Pretty. "It was rather a weakness of his."

"H'm!" murmured Mellapont, with a glance at Shelmore. "Ah!—it's as well to know that much, eh, Mr. Shelmore? Monday, as you'll remember, was quarterly fair-day, and there are always some queer characters about, and they hang on in the place until late next morning. However—but here's the chambermaid."

Belling came back, ushering in a young woman who looked curiously and enquiringly at the people awaiting her, but chiefly at the superintendent, who, on his part, gave her a keen, appraising glance as if estimating her quality as a reliable witness.

"Mary Sanders," said the landlord. "She it was who saw Mr. Deane last."

"Just so," assented Mellapont. "And that was—what time, Mary?"

"Just after eleven o'clock, Monday night, sir," replied the chambermaid, readily.

"When you took him some hot milk, saw him evidently ready to go to bed, and got his order for tea at seven o'clock next morning?"

"Yes, sir."

"And at seven o'clock next morning, when you went, he wasn't there?"

"No, sir."

"So he never drank the tea you took up?"

"Oh, no, sir!—the tea was never touched."

Mellapont became silent and remained silent for a full minute. The chambermaid, a self-possessed, alert-looking young woman, watched him steadily. Suddenly, he bent forward, looking hard at her, and whispered rather than spoke his next question.

"What about the bed, Mary? What about the bed?"

The chambermaid started and flushed a little.

"What—what do you mean, sir?"

"I mean—had the bed been slept in, Mary!—had the bed been slept in? Come, now, with your experience as a chambermaid, eh? But—I see you've got some idea of your own on this very important point. Out with it, Mary!"

The chambermaid smiled a little, glancing covertly at her master.

"Well, sir," she said. "I certainly did think something when the gentleman didn't come in before breakfast, and I'd looked more closely round the room, and more particularly at the bed. I think he'd got into bed, but he hadn't stopped in bed! I think he'd got out again pretty quick."

Mellapont slapped his hands on his knees and looked slowly and significantly from Belling to Shelmore and from Shelmore to Miss Pretty.

"She thinks he'd got in bed and had got out again pretty quick!" he said, in a sort of dramatic stage aside. "Ah! And what made you think that, Mary?" he went on, turning again to the chambermaid. "You have reasons?"

"Well, sir, when I looked more closely at it, the bed didn't look to me as if it had been slept in all night," answered Mary. "There was just one dint in the top pillow. The sheets were quite straight and uncreased. It was just as if the gentleman had got into bed, bethought himself of something, got up again, and never gone back."

Mellapont slapped his knees again.

"Admirable!" he exclaimed. "Admirable! Mr. Deane went to bed and immediately got up again! Now Mary, you're evidently a girl who keeps her eyes open. When you took Mr. Deane his hot milk where did you set down your tray?"

"On the dressing table, sir, close by where he was sitting in an easy chair, reading."

"Did you notice anything on that dressing table? You did, of course. What, now?"

"Well, sir. I couldn't help noticing—they were there in the middle. A gold watch and chain, a diamond pin, and some rings—diamond rings, I think."

"He wore two diamond rings—valuable," murmured Miss Pretty.

"Just so," said Mellapont. "And now, Mary, were these things on the dressing table when you went in next morning?"

"Oh, no, sir!—there was nothing there! Except brushes and combs and that sort of thing. No valuables, sir."

Mellapont turned and nodded two or three times at Shelmore.

"Nothing could be plainer." he said, in a low confidential voice. "Mr. Deane got up, dressed himself, even to the putting on of his jewellery, and went out—that night! Mary!"

"Sir!"

"I take it that you have charge of the corridor, or passage, or whatever it is, in which the bedroom number seven is situate?"

"Yes, sir. It's the first floor. There are six rooms—numbers three, five, seven on one side; four, six, eight on the other."

"What time did you go off duty that night?"

"Usual time, sir—half-past-eleven."

"Now, then!—did you ever see Mr. Deane leave his room?"

"No, sir—certainly not!"

"Supposing he'd wanted anything after you went off duty—who'd he have got it from?"

"Kight, the night porter, sir. Any bell from the bedrooms is answered after eleven-thirty by Kight."

Mellapont turned to Belling with a wave of his hand.

"Now—Kight!" he commanded. "Kight!" Belling nodded to the chambermaid. "Send him here, Mary," he said. "At once." When the chambermaid had gone, silence fell in the private parlour. It was largely caused by the behaviour of Mellapont, who folded his arms across his broad chest, turned his face towards the ceiling and, fixing his eyes on some real or imaginary spot, seemed to lose himself in profound meditation. He only came to earth again when a stockily-built man in a green apron entered the room and looked enquiringly at Belling.

"The superintendent wants to ask you a question or two, Kight," said the landlord.

Mellapont turned on the night porter—less critically than on the chambermaid. He put his first question with seeming carelessness.

"You're on duty from eleven-thirty to seven, aren't you, Kight?" he asked.

"No, sir! Eleven o'clock at night to eight o'clock in the morning."

"Half-an-hour's difference one way and an hour's the other, eh? All right!—anyway you were on duty on Monday night?"

"As usual, sir."

"Do you know Mr. Deane—the gentleman in number seven?"

"Yes, sir. Saw him say good-night to Mr. Belling when he went upstairs Monday night."

"Did you ever see him come down again that night?"

"I did not, sir."

"Nor early next morning?"

"No, sir."

"Never saw him at all during the night?"

"Never set eyes on the gentleman, sir, after I saw him go upstairs."

"Could he have come down and gone out without your seeing him?"

"It's hard to see how he could, sir. In fact, in an ordinary way, impossible."

"Why, now?—why impossible?"

"Well, sir, the guv'nor there'll understand. You see, this old courtyard outside makes a sort of main passage through the house, from front to back. There's a front entrance to it, as you know, into the High Street; there's a back entrance into Sepulchre Alley. Both entrances are closed at eleven o'clock, when I come on duty: it's my first job to close them. Half-way up the courtyard I've a little room, the door of which is always open. If anybody wants to get in during the night—late travellers, motorists, cyclists, and such-like—they have to ring me up from outside. Same way, if anybody wanted to go out, I'd have to open a door for 'em. Though, to be sure, there is a way out without bothering me—if anybody knows it."

"Ah, there's a way out without bothering you, is there, Kight?" said Mellapont. "And what's that, pray?"

"Well, sir, in our back entrance into Sepulchre Alley there's a sort of wicket door in the big one. It's just kept on the latch. Anybody inside the hotel can let himself out by that door. But—he couldn't get in again without ringing for me."

Mellapont turned to Shelmore with a convinced nod.

"Mr. Deane let himself out by that door!" he said. "Good! Now—when? Kight!"

"Sir!"

"On Monday night, between eleven o'clock, and up to Tuesday morning at eight o'clock, were you ever away from your little room in this courtyard. Gone away in any other part of the house?"

"I was, sir—twice. I keep a supply of liquors in my room, sir, for night consumption. I took a whisky and soda up to number fifteen, second floor, at a quarter to twelve—gentleman had come in by a very late train. He kept me talking a few minutes."

"And the other occasion?"

"I took a cup of coffee and some biscuits to number five at six o'clock in the morning, sir. That was a motoring gentleman, who wanted to be off early."

"And on both these occasions you'd be away upstairs for a few minutes, eh?"

"Only a few, sir."

"Still, it would be possible for anybody to come downstairs, unobserved, during those few minutes, and let himself out by that wicket door into Sepulchre Alley?"

"Possible, sir," agreed Kight, with a grin, "but—not very probable. It would mean, anyway, that whoever did it knew the house, and the wicket door and Sepulchre Alley. And I understood that this gentleman was a total stranger."

Mellapont rose from his chair.

"All the same," he said, turning to Belling. "I'm convinced that Mr. Deane, after retiring on Monday night, immediately got up again, dressed, came down, and let himself out while Kight was in number fifteen! The questions now are—where did lie go, and where is he? That's my job! I'm going to start on it straight off. Mr. Shelmore, you come with me to my office. Miss Pretty, let me advise you to settle down and get some dinner, and to be no more alarmed or anxious than's natural—I'll do my best. Now, Mr. Shelmore."

Shelmore only lingered a moment to tell Miss Pretty that he would send his aunt. Miss Chauncey, to call on her that evening, and then followed Mellapont out of the hotel. The Superintendent tapped his shoulder.

"Mr. Shelmore!" he whispered. "Don't you be surprised if this turns out to be a bad case! Robbery, and maybe murder?—aye, murder! And I'm handicapped. As you know, owing to that big coal strike in South Wales, all our regular police have been dragged off there to help, and I've nothing but special constables at my disposal—civilians. However, I must do what I can, and the first thing is to comb out the city for this unfortunate gentleman. Mr. Shelmore!—I smell murder!"

With this dark prediction on his lips, he led Shelmore into the police station beneath the ancient City Hall, and through a vaulted ante room, where, all alone, a tall, athletic, smart-looking young man was just fastening on his sleeve the striped badge of a special constable.

Mellapont strode quickly across the room and gave its solitary occupant a hearty smack on the badged arm.

"The very man I most wanted to see at this moment," he exclaimed. "Come into my office!—come, both of you. You know Mr. Hackdale, Mr. Shelmore?—Mr. Hackdale's the most reliable of my specials—just the man for this job."

Shelmore knew John Hackdale well enough. He knew him as being under-manager at Champernowne's Drapery Store, the big establishment owned by the clever woman who at that time was Mayor of Southernstowe: he knew him also as the elder brother of his own clerk, Simmons Hackdale. But he knew more of him—as did most natives of the city. He knew that John Hackdale and his brother Simmons had been left orphans when one was seventeen and the other ten, unprovided for and practically friendless, and that the elder, by his own unaided efforts, had kept the two of them, clothing, feeding, and educating the younger until Simmons was old enough to do something for himself. He knew, too, that John Hackdale, now a young man of twenty-six, had the reputation of being a pushing and an ambitious fellow, and that he was looked upon at Champernowne's as the mainspring of the business, and as being its real controller, in spite of the fact that there was above him a nominal manager.

"Of course I know Mr. Hackdale," he answered, as they passed into the superintendent's office. "It would be odd if anybody didn't know everybody in a place as small as Southernstowe, superintendent."

"Ah, well, you see, I'm not a native!" said Mellapont, with a shy laugh. "My two years here haven't made me familiar with the smallness of the place, even yet. But now let's tell Mr. Hackdale chat's occurred—he's the main man amongst my special constables, and he can talk to the rest. Just give me your close attention for five minutes, Mr. Hackdale."

John Hackdale listened quietly while Mellapont told him the story which had been elaborated in the landlord's parlour at the Chancellor. Shelmore watched him while he listened, and thought to himself that John Hackdale was fitted for something better than a draper's counter, however long and big and wide that counter might be. Unlike his brother Simmons, who was meagre and sharp-featured, and had a good deal of the fox or ferret look about him, John was a tall, well-built man, handsome of face, and with an air of quiet reserve in eyes arid lips that would have stood him in good stead, thought Shelmore, if he had gone in for professional work—his own, for instance. He had the barrister look—Shelmore mentally pictured him in a wig and gown. And that he had something of legal acumen was proved by his first remark.

"What do you think of that, now?" asked Mellapont, making an end of the story. "How's it strike you?"

Hackdale looked slowly from one man to the other.

"It strikes me like this," he answered. "Whatever the young lady may think, her guardian has been in Southernstowe before."

"Aye?—and what makes you think that now?" demanded Mellapont, eagerly. "What?"

"Obvious!" said Hackdale. "He knew all about the wicket door in the entrance to Sepulchre Alley. To my knowledge that wicket door's been there—well, ever since I was a youngster. When I first earned my living as a shop boy, I've carried many a parcel into the Chancellor by that door."

"Good!" said Mellapont. "So you think—"

"I think Mr. Deane knew Southernstowe, and somebody in Southernstowe," replied Hackdale, "and that he took it into his head, suddenly, to go out and see that somebody, late as it was. That he never returned is a matter which—"

He paused, glancing meaningly at his companions.

"Well?" said Mellapont, sharply. "Well?"

"Which needs closely enquiring into," concluded Hackdale. He paused again, looking still more meaningly and narrowly at the superintendent. "I suppose, as he was travelling about, he would have money on him—and valuables?" he suggested.

"Lots!—according to all we've just heard," asserted Mellapont.

"It was quarterly fair-day, Monday," remarked Hackdale. "As you're aware, a good many of the riff-raff—drovers, hangers-on, and the like—stop about the town overnight, sleeping out, many of them. If Mr. Deane went out at midnight, say to some house on the outskirts—"

"Just what I've been thinking!" exclaimed Mellapont. "Well, the only thing is to search and enquire and make the thing public. There's one advantage of being in a place as small as this-any rumour'll be all over the spot in an hour. Make it known, Hackdale—you too, Mr. Shelmore. Hackdale, I suppose you're going on your beat—north side of the city, yours, isn't it? Drop the news wherever you go—somebody, surely, must have seen or heard something of this man."

"I don't know," said Hackdale, doubtfully. "Ninety-nine out of every hundred of Southernstowe people are in bed by ten o'clock. During this special constable business, I've scarcely met a soul in the streets after that hour."

He nodded to Shelmore and went out, pausing in the outer room to say a few words to a couple of fellow special constables who had just come in and were preparing for their voluntary duties. Then, leaving the police station, he went out into the street and turned down a narrow lane that ran along the side of the City Hall. At the end of that lane there was a small square, set round with old, half-timbered houses; in one of these, a boarding house, kept by two old maiden ladies, Hackdale lodged with his brother Simmons. He wanted to see Simmons now: Simmons was the likeliest means he knew of for noising anything abroad: Simmons, at a word, would spread the news of Deane's strange disappearance all over Southernstowe in half-an-hour.

Hackdale opened the door of the boarding house and walked into a square, oak-wainscotted hall, lighted from the centre by a swinging lamp. Beneath this lamp stood a man in immaculate evening dress, who was carefully brushing an opera hat. He was a tall, well-built man of sixty or thereabouts, who had been strikingly handsome in his time, but who now bore something of the appearance of a carefully-preserved and skilfully patched up ruin. This was Mark Ebbitt, whom Hackdale knew both as a fellow lodger and as manager of the newly established picture house; he also knew that in his time Ebbitt had been an actor, and that his career had not proved over successful; indeed, Hackdale remembered him, on his first coming to Southernstowe, as having been in the down-at-heel and frayed-linen stage. But now he had blossomed out again, and as manager of a flourishing place of amusement was revelling once more in purple and fine linen.

The two men nodded familiarly, and Hackdale paused on his way to his own sitting room.

"Heard any news?" he asked.

"Not an atom, my boy," replied Ebbitt. "Have you?"

Hackdale told him of what he had just heard; Ebbitt, carefully adjusting the opera hat in front of a mirror that hung over the fireplace, listened without any great show of interest.

"That must have been the stranger I noticed at our show on Monday night," he remarked. "Tallish, Spanish, grey-bearded chap, in a brown tweed suit: I noticed, too, he'd got a damned fine diamond in his cravat! Um!—Well, if elderly gentlemen with jewels like that on 'em will go walking abroad at midnight in country towns—eh?"

"Well, just mention it to anybody you come across tonight, will you?" suggested Hackdale. "Publicity—"

"My boy, the whole thing'll be all over the town before supper time!" declared Ebbitt; "Lord bless you! if the poll-parrot upstairs took it into her head to fly out of window, do you think all Southernstowe wouldn't know it in five minutes? Publicity?—trust country-town tongues for that!"

He wrapped a white silk muffler round his throat, gave the opera hat an extra tilt over his right ear, and swaggered out, and Hackdale, opening a door on the left of the hall, walked into the parlour which he and his brother shared as a sitting room. Simmons was there—the remains of his tea-supper before him, but he himself deep in a big law-book, on either side of which he had firmly planted an elbow. From between the knuckles which pressed against his temples, he looked up at John.

"Here's a nice job for you, Sim," said Hackdale. "Just suit you. You're going out, of course?"

"For a bit," answered Simmons, questioningly. "What's up?"

"This is up," replied Hackdale. He sat down, keeping his hat and coat on, and told his brother all about it. "So, if you're going to drop in at the club, mention it—mention it anywhere. Tell everybody you meet."

Simmons nodded. His sharp eyes grew thoughtful.

"That would be the girl who came to Shelmore this afternoon, just as we were leaving," he remarked. "Shelmore went out with her. Name of Pretty—Miss Cynthia Pretty."

"Anything like her name?" asked the elder brother. "Was she pretty?"

"Top hole!" declared Simmons. "Swell, too. Card said she lived in Cornwall, but I'll lay a fiver to a penny she didn't get her clothes in those wilds! London make—from top to bottom."

"Good lad," said Hackdale, approvingly. "Always cultivate your power of observation, Sim, and you'll do! Well-I'm off on my beat. See you at breakfast."

A small packet which he knew to contain sandwiches, and a flask in which he had stored a supply of weak whisky and water, lay on a side table; stowing these away in his pockets, Hackdale nodded to his brother and left the room. But instead of going out of the house by the front door, he went through a passage to the back-yard, and there released his dog, a pure bred Airedale terrier, known to the neighbourhood as Martin; with this valuable assistant at his heels he turned back towards the City Hall, and went off towards that part of Southernstowe which was just then under his charge.

Mellapont had reason when he spoke of the smallness of the city whose police arrangements he superintended. So old that its people boasted of it as being the oldest settled town in England; famous as possessing one of the most ancient of English cathedrals: interesting and notable to all lovers of archaeology and its ways, Southernstowe was utterly insignificant in point of size. A square half-mile held all there was of it, within its ancient and still well preserved walls, at any rate: you could walk in and out and all round it within an hour. It had but three streets; one, High Street, ran across it from east to west; another, North Bar, ran from High Street to the walls on the northward; the third, South Bar, ran from the centre of the town to the southern extremity. Out of these streets meandered, to be sure, almost aimlessly, various alleys, courts, and passages, but they were so narrow, and their entrances so often veiled by modern frontages, that only the inhabitants knew of them; in many cases they had no name.

Hackdale's beat lay on the north side of the city. Out there, once the walls were passed, there was a district of residential houses—mansions and villas standing in private grounds, with open country beyond. The principal people of the place lived up there; professional men, merchants, well-to-do tradesmen. His own employer, Mrs. Sophia Champernowne, the mayor, had a big place that way, Ashenhurst House, where she lived with her brother, a queer, apparently shiftless, do-nothing-at-all sort of amiable, well-dressed person, commonly known as Mr. Alfred. What Mr. Alfred's surname was, neither Hackdale, nor anybody else knew—he was just Mr. Alfred. All that anybody knew about him was that when Mrs. Champernowne first came to Southernstowe, twenty years before, and bought up a decaying business which she speedily transformed into a first class, up-to-date equal-to-London and Paris drapery store, Mr. Alfred came with her, and had been with her, as parasite or satellite, ever since.

Hackdale was not very far from the gates of Ashenhurst House when a man suddenly came across the road and hailed him. In the light of a neighbouring lamp he recognised the man as one James Bartlett, a well-known figure in Southernstowe. Bartlett had been a man of substance in his time, but a fatal passion for betting on one hand, and for strong drink on the other, had reduced him to the position of a loafer who lived from hand to mouth. But loafer and ne'er-do-well though he was, he had a confident manner and a ready tongue, and he lost no time in saying his say, as he accosted John Hackdale under the lamp.

"Hullo, Mr. Hackdale," he said, familiarly. "Doing a bit more special constabling, eh?—Well, I daresay you'll do it as well as the regular police, what? But what's this I hear, Mr. Hackdale, about a gentleman being missing from the Chancellor? It is so, is it?—aye, well, maybe I could tell a bit about that."

Hackdale, who would not have wasted one minute of his time on Bartlett in broad daylight in a Southernstowe street, had no objection to talk to him in a lonely place under cover of partial darkness. He whistled his dog to him and halted.

"What could you tell?" he asked, half contemptuously.

"Well, I don't mind telling you," answered Bartlett, with a marked emphasis on the personal pronoun. "You're a cautious young fellow, and can keep your tongue still—if need be: I'm not a fool myself, Mr. Hackdale. But it's this—I was out, latish, Monday night, up this way—been to see somebody; never mind who. And just as I got within North Bar about midnight, I met a strange gentleman. Tallish, thinnish man, grey beard—very well dressed; I could see that. He stopped me—wanted to know something. Eh, Mr. Hackdale?"

"What did he want to know?" asked Hackdale, vaguely convinced that something important, something which would, somehow, affect himself, was coming out. "What?"

Bartlett tapped the special constable's arm, and lowered his voice to a whisper.

"He wanted to know where Ashenhurst House, Mrs. Champernowne's was!" he answered. "Just that!"

Hackdale remained silent. It was Deane, without doubt, that Bartlett was talking of. What did Deane—a stranger—want with Mrs. Champernowne, at midnight? However...

"Did you tell him?" he asked suddenly.

"I did! Why not?"

"Did he go that way?"

"Straight ahead!—after giving me five shillings."

There was another silence, during which Hackdale did some hard and quick thinking. Bartlett broke it.

"I reckon that would be the missing gentleman, Mr. Hackdale! Went up this way, seeking for Mrs. Champernowne—and has never been seen since! Queer!"

Hackdale looked round. There was nobody within sight or hearing on that quiet road. He touched Bartlett's shoulder.

"Have you mentioned this to anybody?" he asked. "You haven't?—to a soul? Look here!—don't! There's some mystery, and—well, it won't do to have Mrs. Champernowne's name mixed up with it. Keep it to yourself, Bartlett, until I see you again. And—here!"

He had loose money in his pocket—gold, silver—and, scarcely realising what he was doing, he pulled it out and dropped it into Bartlett's ready palm. Bartlett made haste to put it away with that hand, while he squeezed Hackdale's arm with the other.

"Mum is the word, Mr. Hackdale!" he whispered. "I'm your man, sir! Not a word... "

He shot off suddenly into the gloom, and Hackdale, after staring in that direction for a second or two, went slowly forward. He was dazed by what he had heard. What did it mean? He was near the grounds of Ashenhurst House by then, and he gazed at the lighted windows, wondering if anybody behind them knew... anything?

He went along, past the gates, past the grounds, and down a narrow side lane that bounded Mrs. Champernowne's tennis lawn and fruit orchard. And there, following his usual track, he turned into an old sand pit, long disused and now thickly grown over with shrubs and vegetation, across which there was a short cut to another part of his beat. But Hackdale never took the short cut that night. The Airedale terrier, plunging in amongst the undergrowth, began to growl and then to whine, and Hackdale, following him, suddenly stumbled upon a man's body... supine, motionless.

THE SAFETY PIN

Hackdale was essentially cool and calculating in temperament and disposition, and when the first thrill of his discovery had spent itself, which it did very quickly, his natural calmness in dealing with a difficult situation came to the surface. He had no doubt whatever that the body lying at his feet was that of the man who had so mysteriously disappeared from his room at the Chancellor Hotel. He had no doubt, either, that the man was dead. So much, he knew, was certain. And what was another, and to him a much more pertinent certainty, was that the man was lying dead in an unfrequented waste which lay within a hundred yards of Ashenhurst House—the private residence of Mrs. Champernowne.

There was just sufficient light—twilight—left to see what Hackdale saw, but he had the means of more accurate vision in one of his pockets. Quietly and slowly, hushing the Airedale terrier with a gentle word or two, he produced an electric torch and, turning its light on, stooped closely to the still figure. Dead, of course!—dead as a door nail, he said to himself, using the hackneyed simile. And there, in a black and congealed pool in the sandy turf, was blood. One more look, a closer one, and he saw that the dead man had been shot through the head, from just behind the ear—there was a mark there. And not shot by himself, for neither of the outstretched hands grasped any weapon, nor did any weapon lie near. Murder!—sheer murder!

Hackdale stood up, wondering when the murder had occurred. He himself had been past that very spot, about the same time, only the previous evening, and had noticed nothing. But then, he reflected, he had not had his dog with him. He would have passed the place, unsuspecting, tonight, if it had not been for the dog. But—had the man been shot there, where he lay, or had his body been dragged or carried there from elsewhere? He held the electric torch to the ground, examining its surface. All around, save for small, insignificant patches, the flooring of the old sand pit was thickly grown over with short, wiry grass, on which any footmarks were necessarily difficult to trace—Hackdale saw none. Nor did he notice any disturbance of the bushes amongst which the body lay. But they were very low, stunted bushes, there; it was quite probable that two people, wandering and strolling aimlessly about in that sand pit in the darkness would never notice things that only grew knee-high, and would not realise that they were off his short cut. And, of course, there had been two people—one was the murdered man lying at his feet; the other was the murderer. And—who was he?

He turned back to the body, and without as much as laying a finger on it, held the electric torch still closer. This was the man, of course. A tallish, thinnish, grey-bearded man, in a suit of brown tweed, of smart cut—so he had been described to Hackdale, and there all the features of the description were. The face was pressed into the sandy turf; he saw little of that, and at the moment had no wish to see more: he wanted others, Mellapont, in particular, to see everything as he himself had first seen it. He had some vague idea that when a dead body is found, no one should touch or interfere with it until the police have been called, and he was temperamentally strict in adherence to usage and custom. But suddenly, as he moved the electric torch to and fro above the inanimate figure. Hackdale saw something which, in that same instant, he knew he would touch... and not only touch but make haste to secrete.

That something was a safety pin—a curiously shaped, unusually made safety pin of bronze wire. It was pinned in the dead mans' tweed jacket, a little over the flapped pocket on the right hand side, and Hackdale saw at once how it came to be there. Either in passing through a fence, or getting over a fence, the dead man had caught his smart new jacket against a nail or some equally sharp projection, and had got a long, irregular rent in it, extending for several inches through the outer cloth rid the inner lining. And the rent had been faistened together with the safety pin at which Hackdale was now staring as he had never to his knowledge stared at anything in his life: the stare was accompanied by a jerky, involuntary exclamation.

"Good God!—that?"

Within the instant, and with a furtive glance round him, as though, even in that solitude he feared observation, Hackdale had unfastened and withdrawn the safety pin from the dead man's jacket and hidden it away in his purse. And that done, he switched off his light, murmured a word to the Airedale terrier, and turned back to the path. Before he had gone six yards he realised that he was trembling all over—the coolness which he had felt at first had vanished at sight of the safety pin. But it had got to come back—he had got to be cooler than ever. Then he remembered the flask in his pocket; its contents were meant to last him for the whole of his night's vigil, but now he swallowed them at a draught. That revived him, and with something between a sigh and a sardonic laugh he left the sand pit and went off in the direction of Ashenhurst House.

Mrs. Champernowne's residence stood in the midst of ornamental grounds—a fine, commodious, red brick mansion, big enough for a large family; far too big, Hackdale had often thought, for a single woman, her brother, and half-a-dozen servants. But Mrs. Champernownc, as Hackdale knew well enough, was a very rich woman, and could afford to do what she pleased: afford to keep up these fine gardens, and a couple of motor cars, light the house with electricity, and surround herself, as she did, with every luxury. Yet, as he made his way up the asphalted drive to the front door, the contrast between the brilliantly lighted windows of the house and the darkness and solitude of the sand pit struck him forcibly—he could not tell why. Here was light, warmth, life—there, a hundred yards away, coldness, death. Was there any link between the house and the sand pit, and if so...

His reflections were cut short by the opening of the door. A smart young woman, spick and span in her black dress and coquettish cap and apron, glanced at him smilingly and demurely: Hackdale, who cultivated politeness as a business asset, touched his cap.

"Evening, Jennie," he said, marvelling at the steadiness of his own voice. "Mrs. Champernowne in?"

The parlourmaid came a step nearer, familiar and confidential.

"The mistress is out, Mr. Hackdale," she answered. "Gone to dine with Sir Reville Childerstone—there's a dinner party there. I don't expect her back before eleven. Mr. Alfred's in, though," she added.

"Oh, well!—I'll see him a minute, then," replied Hackdale. "I suppose he's not engaged."

The girl laughed, tossing her head as much as to imply that Mr. Alfred was never engaged, and, retreating into the hall, preceded Hackdale along its length to a door which she threw open without any preparatory knock.

"Mr. Hackdale, Mr. Alfred," she announced, with the same easy familiarity that she had shown to the caller. "Wants to see you a minute."

Hackdale walked into a small, cosily furnished room, in the open grate of which a bright fire of pine logs blazed and crackled. In front of it, in the depths of a roomy lounge chair, his slippered feet to the fire, sat Mr. Alfred, an elderly, spare-figured man, wrapped in a smart dressing gown, and wearing a tasselled velvet smoking cap. He had a mild and weak blue eye, a weaker mouth, scarcely hidden by a grizzled moustache, a retreating chin, and an amiable smile. He held a large cigar in one hand, the Times in the other, and on the table at his elbow stood a decanter of whisky, a syphon of mineral water, and a half-filled tumbler. His first action on seeing Hackdale was to wave him towards these comforts.

"Hullo, Hackdale!" he said. "Glad to see you! Sit down—have a drink—clean tumbler on the sideboard there—help yourself. Turning a bit coldish o' nights, what?"

"No thank you, Mr. Alfred," answered Hackdale. "I'm on special constable duty— mustn't stop. Mrs. Champernowne's not in?"

"Dining with Sir Reville," replied Mr. Alfred. "Party there! Anything up?"

"You haven't heard any news from the town tonight?" asked Hackdale. "No? Well, there's a queer sort of business occurred at the Chancellor Hotel. A gentleman who came there on Monday afternoon has disappeared—mysteriously."

"Pooh!—run away without paying his bill!" remarked Mr. Alfred. "Usual explanation of such mysteries."

"No," said Hackdale. "He's a known man—a man of wealth. Name of—" he paused, carefully watching the other's face—"name of Deane, James Deane."

"Never heard of him!—don't know him!" declared Mr. Alfred. "Quite unfamiliar to me. Anybody in the town know him?"

"I don't think so," replied Hackdale. "There's—no evidence that anybody does. A tallish, spare-figured, grey-bearded man. I know you stroll round about a good deal, Mr. Alfred—you haven't seen such a man during this last day or two?"

"No, not to my knowledge—lots of men like that about, though," replied Mr. Alfred. "Not an uncommon type, from your description. Looking for him?"

"Everybody's looking for him," said Hackdale. "The whole town, by this time!"

"Then they can very well spare you for half-an-hour," observed Mr. Alfred, with a knowing grin. "Sit down and have a drink and a cigar."

But Hackdale said no once again, and, letting himself out of the house, went swiftly away in the direction of City Hall. He met a fellow special constable in North Bar, and, without telling him of his discovery, took him back to the police station. And there Hackdale, alone, marched into the superintendent's office, where Mellapont sat at his desk, examining a pile of documents. He shut the door, turned, and spoke two words.

"Found him!"

Mellapont leapt to his feet.

"What!—Deane?" he answered.

"Of course—who else?" retorted Hackdale. "Yes!"

"Where, then?"

"In that old sand pit behind Ashenhurst House."

Mellapont came a step nearer, staring. For a moment he remained silent.

"You—you don't mean—dead?" he asked, tensely.

"He's dead enough," answered Hackdale. "Shot through the head. And—it's not suicide, either. There's no revolver lying about."

Mellapont stared at him during another moment's silence. Then he pointed to a chair. "Sit down, Hackdale, and tell me all about it," he said. "Stop!—have you told anybody?"

"No one, so far," replied Hackdale. "It was this way... "

Mellapont listened attentively and in silence while Hackdale told of his evening's doings. At the end he put one direct question.

"You didn't examine the clothing?"

"No!" said Hackdale. "No!"

"Then you don't know whether he's been robbed or not," said Mellapont. "Probably he has! Now the thing is to get him down here."

"There's a thing should be done," remarked Hackdale suddenly, as the superintendent began bustling about. "Footmarks, you know! I couldn't trace any—close by, that is. But then I'd only an electric torch. Still, there must be some about, somewhere. Because, whoever shot him must have gone with him into that sand pit. You see?"

"Unless he was shot elsewhere, or carried there," said Mellapont. "That's to be thought of, you know."

"I thought of it—and I looked carefully at the bushes, where he's lying," replied Hackdale. "I saw no signs of his having been carried or dragged."

"No clue to anything, in fact?" suggested Mellapont.

"I got no clue to anything," said Hackdale deliberately. Nothing, he said to himself, should induce him to tell about the safety pin which lay in his purse. That was his own secret, for the time being, at any rate. "To anything." he repeated. "I don't know, of course, because he's lying face downwards, and I didn't touch him—didn't want to, until you'd seen him yourself—but I should say that most likely he's been robbed, as you suggested at first."

"Probable!" assented Mellapont. "Well—we'll get off."

Hackdale stood by while the superintendent got his available forces together, and then prepared to lead him and them back to the sand pit. Outside, Mellapont touched him on the arm.

"Chilham, the police surgeon," he whispered. "You know where he lives?—top of North Bar. Go on ahead and tell him, and ask him to come with us. May as well have him there at once."

Hackdale found Chilham in his surgery and got him out in time to join the superintendent and his men. In silence he led them out of the town, past the grounds of Ashenhurst House, and into the sand pit. Presently the glare of half-a-dozen bulls'eye lanterns was concentrated on the dead man. Chilham got down on his knees. But he only said what Hackdale already knew.

"Shot through the head from behind!" muttered Chilham. "Close quarters, too. Turn him over. Look there—front of his head shot away. The murderer must have been close behind him, and held the revolver within an inch or two of his ear."

But Mellapont, bearing in mind what he had learnt at the Chancellor, was looking at something else. It was obvious enough that Deane had been shot, murdered—now he wanted to know why. He pointed to the dead man's neckwear, a smart four-in-hand cravat.

"Diamond pin gone!" he said. Then he pointed lower. "Gold chain gone! Feel in his pockets, Watson."

The man addressed, a plain clothes policeman, dipped his fingers into one pocket after another, and suddenly looked up.

"There isn't a thing on him, superintendent! Clear sweep—not even a pocket handkerchief left!" he exclaimed. "Empty—the whole lot!"

"Just what I expected," muttered Mellapont. "Not going to be much mystery about this case, I reckon! Robbery as well as murder!—murder for robbery. Hackdale," he went on, turning away from the main group, "there's nothing more you can do here. Run down to Shelmore's private house, and tell him all about it, and ask him to get his aunt to go with him to the Chancellor to break the news to the young lady. And look here—ask Shelmore to wait at the Chancellor until I come there. We must have a look at the poor fellow's effects."

21

Hackdale went away, found Shelmore, gave his message, and, purposely keeping aloof from the police station, finished his duties for the night—by going carefully round his beat. At midnight he went home. Ebbitt had just come in, and was standing outside the door of his own sitting room, divesting himself of his cloak and muffler. He beckoned Hackdale to enter and pointed to the whisky decanter.

"Have a spot after your labour?" he suggested. "Just going to have one myself. Well, heard anything of that missing man?"

"Yes," said Hackdale. "He's been found. Murdered—shot. And robbed."

"Robbed, eh!" exclaimed Ebbitt. "Ah!"

"Wasn't so much as a pocket handkerchief on him," continued Hackdale. "And, according to our information, he'd a lot on him when he went out. Money—valuables."

"I told you I noticed a fine diamond pin on him," remarked Ebbitt. "That is, if that was the man."

"That would be the man," said Hackdale.

He drank off his whisky, said good-night, and went upstairs to his own room. He had a small safe there, set on a stand in a recess, and his first action after entering the room was to unlock it. His next was to take from his purse the curiously shaped safety pin, and to put it away in the safe's furthest corner.

Chapter

5

THE PICTURE POSTCARD

Mellapont strode up to the front entrance to the Chancellor, just as the night porter was closing the doors, and slipped inside with a sharp question.

"Mr. Shelmore here, Kight?"

"With the guv'nor in the private parlour, sir," answered the night porter, pointing down the courtyard. "Said he was expecting you, sir."

"That's it," said Mellapont. He moved in the direction indicated; then suddenly paused and turned back. "Look here, Kight," he continued, confidentially, "there's a question I wanted to put to you. You aren't the boots as well as the night porter here, are you?"

"No, sir—there's a regular boots, Marsh."

"I suppose he's not about here? He is?—in the kitchen? Fetch him here a minute, Kight, I want to see him."

The night porter went along the courtyard, turned in at a door, came back with a man who, judging from his hands and his apron, was already engaged at his job of boot cleaning. Mellapont went up to him.

"Look here!" he said. "When do you collect the boots and shoes from the bedroom doors—night or morning?"

"Both times, sir," answered the man. "Depends a good deal on how many people there are in the hotel. If it's pretty full, I go round late at night, and get a start on what there is put outside the doors. If there aren't many people here, I don't go round till say five o'clock in the morning."

"Monday night, now?—night before last?" suggested Mellapont. "How were things then?"

"House was full, sir—there wasn't a room empty. I went round, first, at half-past eleven and gathered up what there was—a good lot. Went round again for another lot when I took back the first."

"Can you remember anything about what was outside number seven?" asked Mellapont. "Think now "

"Yes, well enough!" answered the man. "There were two pairs of walking shoes there, when I went round the first time—a black pair and a brown pair. I cleaned them, with others, and took them back about—well, it would be about one o'clock in the morning. They were still there, outside the door, when I passed it again at five o'clock."

Mellapont nodded, reflected a moment, said a word of thanks to the man, and then, turning away, walked quickly forward to the private parlour. There he found Shelmore and Belling, evidently discussing the situation. Without preface he broke in upon their talk with a reference to what he had just heard.

"You may think there's nothing in that," he said, when he had told them about the two pairs of shoes, "but I see a good deal in it. When we examined Deane's body and clothing tonight, I noticed something at once which to me seemed very significant. He'd gone out in a pair of dress shoes—thin-soled, patent leather things! What do you make of that, Mr. Shelmore?—as a lawyer?"

"I'm not versed in this sort of thing," replied Shelmore. "What do you make of it?"

"Why, that he'd no intention of going far; that he knew he wasn't going off the pavement; that he knew where he was going—to some private house, close by!" replied Mellapont, triumphantly. "Let the young lady upstairs say what she likes, Deane knew this town, and somebody in it! Who? That's to be found out. The young lady may think her guardian had never been here before, and had no acquaintance here, but... we shall see! By-the-by, how is this young lady? Much shocked?"

"She was very much shocked, but she took it very well," replied Shelmore. "My aunt is with her—she'll stay the night with her."

"Your aunt is a good sort, sir," said Mellapont. "Well, we shall have to ask the young lady a lot of questions in the morning. But now," he went on, turning to the landlord, "I want to have a quiet look at whatever this poor gentleman left in number seven. You never know what you may find, and there's no time like the present. I suppose all's quiet upstairs, Mr. Belling? Then take Mr. Shelmore and me up."

Belling led the way across the courtyard to an inner hall on the opposite side, and then up a flight of oak-balustered stairs to the first floor. Opening the door of the room number seven, he switched on the electric light, whispered to Mellapont that he and Shelmore could count on not being disturbed and could lock up his room and bring away the key when their investigations were finished, and left them. Mellapont, turning the key in the lock when the landlord had gone, looked round.

"A very precise and orderly gentleman, the dead man, Mr. Shelmore," he murmured. "I can see that at once!"

Shelmore saw what he meant. Whether it had been so left by its unfortunate late occupant, or had since been tidied up by the chambermaid, the room was spick and span in its neatness. Various toilet articles lay disposed in symmetrical fashion on the dressing table: magazines and newspapers were laid out in order on a side table; the half open doors of a tall wardrobe showed garments hung on stretchers; every object in the room seemed to be in its proper place.

"What do you expect to find here?" asked Shelmore, who was feeling vague as to the reason for Mellapont's visit to this room. "Some clue?"

"You never know what you may find, Mr. Shelmore," replied Mellapont, still looking about him. "There's more to be found and seen here than we found on the man's clothing, anyway! I suppose Hackdale told you?—there wasn't a thing on him! Every pocket had been emptied—even to his pocket handkerchief. Now that last matter seems to me very odd and perhaps significant. Why rob a dead man of a thing like that!—a handkerchief! But there it is—there was nothing. Money, valuables, papers—if he had any—all gone. That reminds me—when we go down again, I want to ask Belling a question or two. But now, let's look round. These suitcases first—when you're at this game, Mr. Shelmore, always begin at the beginning. Good solid leather stuff, these suitcases—don't make as good as that nowadays."

One after the other he lifted the lids of two suitcases, which lay on a stand at the foot of the bed: each was empty.

"Methodical and orderly man," muttered Mellapont. "Put all his things away in a wardrobe and chest of drawers. Well—clothes first. Might be some letters or papers in pockets."

There were two suits of clothes and one overcoat in the wardrobe, but a search of the pockets revealed nothing. Nor was there anything in the chest of drawers but a plentiful supply of linen, hosiery and the like, all neatly folded and laid away. Mellapont turned to a leather attache case which lay on a chair close by.

"This'll be the likeliest thing in which to find papers," he said. "And luckily, it's not locked. Now, then, what have we here?"

He lifted the attache case on to a table immediately beneath the electric light, and threw back the lid; Shelmore stood at his elbow while he examined the contents.

"Papers and books mostly," muttered Mellapont. "Guide books, by the look of 'em."

He took out, one after another, several paper-bound books of the sort he had mentioned—guide books to towns, cathedrals, famous ruins, and the like. Beneath these lay a writing case, furnished with its owner's own stationery: Shelmore noticed that the address engraved on the notepaper was the same that he had seen on Miss Pretty's visiting card. In one pocket of the case were several letters, addressed to James Deane, Esquire, at various places, and all signed "Your affectionate Cynthia"—in another was a collection of hotel bills, neatly folded and docketed.

"Trace his recent movements from there, anyway," remarked Mellapont, after a glance at the dates. "Seems to have been knocking around a good deal, lately. And here, evidently, are pictures that he's collected on his travels—must have had a mania for that sort of thing, I think, Mr. Shelmore—unless he intended them as a present for the young lady—perhaps she collects them."

He pointed to the left hand half of the attache case, which was filled with packet upon packet of picture postcards, all neatly secured with indiarubber bands and ranged in order. Mellapont began to take these packets out, pointing to the fact that they were all methodically labelled. He began, too, to recite the names of the places which they pictured.

"Evidently collected these as he went along," he remarked. "Didn't the young lady say he'd gone North while she was slaying at Bath? Just so—well, here we can follow his route. Exeter. Bristol, Gloucester, Worcester, Birmingham, Sheffield, Normansholt—where's Normansholt, Mr. Shelmore?"

Shelmore, unobserved by Mellapont, had started a little at the mention of Normansholt. One of his twelve clients, Sir Reville Childerstone, of Childerstone Park, just outside the city, had some property at Normansholt, and had lately been much concerned about his conduct of one of his tenants there: he had been obliged to employ Shelmore's professional services in the matter: the name, therefore, was quite familiar to Shelmore. He glanced inquisitively at the packet of cards which Mellapont was handling.

"Normansholt?" he repeated. "Oh, that's in Yorkshire. Historical old town—famous castle and that sort of thing."

"Um!—that seems to have been his top mark," said Mellapont, continuing to turn over the carefully arranged packets. "Seems to have turned southward then. Doncaster, Newark, Peterborough, Stamford, Ely, Cambridge, London, Dorking, and so here. Good round, Mr. Shelmore!—mostly old places, I reckon—probably had a taste for antiquities. Well, I'll just glance through these letters, to see if there's anything—"

He picked up the letters which he had taken out of the visiting case, and, sitting down on the nearest chair began to skim them over. Shelmore, out of idle curiosity about a place of which he had heard in the course of professional business but had never seen, took up the packet of cards labelled Normansholt, and, releasing them from the rubber band, turned them over one by one. Normansholt, he thought, must certainly be an interesting and picturesque place. Deane had collected some twenty or thirty cards of it—views of the great Norman castle, the old churches, the various remains of antiquity. Each made a picture... but Shelmore suddenly found himself looking at a particular one with a sharply aroused sense of wonder and speculation.

This was a coloured photograph of what seemed to be an old-world nook and corner in a peculiarly old town. It depicted a sort of square, with a patch of green in the centre; out of this green rose a tall mast. All around were quaint, half-timbered houses of early Jacobean architecture. In the left hand corner of the card were the words May Day Green, Normansholt. And Shelmore knew sufficient of old English customs to know that this was a picture of a place where the old May Day revel had been celebrated aforetime, and that the tall mast was one of the last of the ancient Maypoles.

But this was not the thing that aroused his wonder and speculative faculties. In the corner of the square of houses stood one which was larger, more important looking, more picturesque than the others. From its roof and clustered chimneys, some hand, Deane's presumably, had drawn a thick pencil line to the top edge of the card—a line that terminated in an equally thickly-marked asterisk. And seeing this Shelmore felt a question spring up, uncontrollably, in his mind.

"Why?"

"Why?—yes, that was it," he repeated to himself—"why? Why out of the twenty, twenty-five or thirty picture postcards of Normansholt had Deane selected that particular one and that particular house for marking in an unmistakably distinct fashion? What was his reason? Why had he done it. Again—why?"

He glanced round at Mellapont. Mellapont was deep in the letters and the hotel bills. And, seeing that, Shelmore hastily but carefully went through his collection of cards, from start to finish, beginning with those of Exeter and ending with those of Dorking, which was evidently the last place visited by Deane before coming on to Southernstowe. Out of the entire collection not one single card was marked, with the exception of that which had aroused his wonder. And, as he put the cards back in the attache case a definite question shaped itself before him—what particular interest had James Deane in the corner house in May Day Green in the old far away northern town of Normansholt?

Mellapont suddenly rose from his chair, bringing back the letters and hotel bills to the writing case.

"Nothing there that throws any light, Mr. Shelmore," he said. "Hotel bills—nothing! And the letters—just chatty gossipy letters from the young lady to her guardian—nothing in them, except to confirm his statement that they were to meet here, spend a day or two looking around, and go on to the continent. Well, let's put all back, lock up the room, and go downstairs: I want to see Belling again."

Belling was in his parlour with the door open, evidently waiting. Mellapont motioned Shelmore inside, closed the door and sat down.

"Nothing that gives any clue up there," he said. "But look here, Mr. Belling, I want to get a bit more information from you. You're aware already that this gentleman, when found, hadn't a thing on him in the way of money, valuables or personal property. Now you had opportunities of seeing him on Monday night, and you saw that he'd both money and valuables. But—did other people?"

"Anybody could see that he'd a fine diamond pin, an expensive gold watch chain, and a couple of diamond rings on his fingers!" replied Belling. "That is, if they'd got any eyes at all, and turned them on him!"

"Aye, just so!" agreed Mellapont. "But—money? Did he make any show of money? I don't mean boastingly, swaggeringly, but—just naturally, as some men do. You know—some men pull their money out without thinking—some—"

"I know what you mean," interrupted Belling. "Well, yes, he was certainly one of the sort that are a bit what I should call careless in that way. He came into the bar a little before dinner, and asked the barmaid for a sherry and bitters—I was in there, and I noticed that he pulled out a handful of notes—fivers—openly, and picked some silver from amongst them—seemed to have a lot of money, notes and coins all mixed up in his pocket. He did the same thing after dinner, when he came to me in the bar and asked me about whatever amusements were going on. He pulled out a fistful of money, then, to pay for two cigars."

"Were there people about?" asked Mellapont.

"Several! The bar was full, both times."

"Townsfolk, or strangers?"

"Both. There were several strangers there. Men I didn't know anyway—and I think I know everybody in Southernstowe. Motorists, some of them. Others I took to be men who'd been to the fair."

"And they could see his money?"

"If they were looking at him, just as easily as they could see his diamond pin! Nothing to prevent them!"

Mellapont suddenly rose and bidding good-night to the landlord, went away with Shelmore into the deserted High Street.

"What do you think, superintendent?" asked Shelmore precisely.

Mellapont coughed discreetly, and, alone though they were, lowered his voice.

"I'll tell you what I think, Mr. Shelmore," he answered. "And I don't suppose I shall ever think anything else I think that Mr. Deane was watched, followed, murdered, and robbed by some person at present unknown, who knew that he'd money and valuables on him. That's what I think! But—I also think something else. I think that Mr. Deane, whatever he may have said to his ward, knew somebody in Southernstowe, and had some extraordinary reason for seeing that somebody on Monday night! And I'm going to move heaven and earth to find out who that somebody is!"

6

THE OPPORTUNE MOMENT

Shelmore was not the first man to whom Mellapont had made this declaration of future policy. Mellapont had already made it, even more emphatically, to John Hackdale, and Hackdale had thought about it a good deal before he went to sleep and again as soon as he awoke. All the same, Hackdale went to his work at Champernowne's next morning as if nothing unusual had occurred since his leaving it at five o'clock the previous afternoon. Nominally under-manager, with an under-manager's salary, he was in reality the mainspring of a big industrial machine.

For so small a town, Champernowne's was a big store, doing a big business. That business had all developed to its present state of commercial prosperity through the energy of Mrs. Champernowne, whom everybody knew to be a very remarkable woman. Nobody in Southernstowe, however, knew who Mrs. Champernowne really was. Twenty years before, she had suddenly appeared in the city, and before anybody knew what she was doing, had bought up a decaying, though old-fashioned draper's business, pulled the out-of-date premises to pieces, built a first class modern store, and surrounded herself with a small army of capable assistants. There were those in Southernstowe who prophesied the loss of Mrs. Champernowne's money, but Mrs. Champernowne knew what she was doing. Southernstowe though a small city was an unusually wealthy one; the people of the immediate neighbourhood were wealthy, too; aristocrats and gentlefolk, but thick as blackberries: Mrs. Champernowne proposed to bring the modes and goods of London and Paris to their very doorsteps. And, ere long, visitors to Southernstowe found themselves staring in amazement at a shop which would have done credit to either Oxford Street or the Rue de la Paix; Mrs. Champernowne and her establishment represented the last thing in contemporary fashion. And Mrs. Champernowne made money, and within ten years was reputed to be the richest woman in the neighbourhood, and possibly the wealthiest citizen of her adopted dwelling place. But she had other interests than her store. She played a considerable part in the affairs of her adopted city, gave large sums to its charities, and furthered all schemes of civic improvement, and in the end a grateful and admiring Corporation unanimously elected her Mayor. Her election and the duties consequent upon it took her away a great deal from her business, but everybody in her employ knew that whatever other engagement she had on hand, Mrs. Champernowne was always in her private office at the store every morning at nine-thirty sharp, and that during the next hour and a half she took good care to assure herself that the well-oiled wheels of her machinery were running with their usual smoothness.

At half-past ten on the morning following his discovery of Deane's dead body, John Hackdale knocked at the door of that private office and was bidden by his employer to enter. He went in to find Mrs. Champernowne seated at her desk and alone. She was writing a letter, and, as she looked up, Hackdale gave her a keen, searching inspection. A tall, plump, handsome, well-preserved woman, still on the right side of fifty, Mrs. Champernowne usually showed signs of great good temper, good humour, and general contentment with life in general. But it seemed to the under-manager that on this particular morning she looked harassed and worried, and that her usual fresh colour had somewhat faded; there were signs of anxiety about her, and when she spoke her voice was slightly irritable in tone.

"What is it, Hackdale?" she asked. "Anything important?"

"I want a few minutes' conversation with you, Mrs. Champernowne," replied Hackdale, ostentatiously closing the door behind him. "Private conversation—if you please."

Mrs. Champernowne's pen stopped dead in the middle of a line, and she looked more closely at her visitor. Hackdale gave her look for look.

"Strictly private," he added, "strictly!" Mrs. Champernowne pointed to a chair at the side of her desk.

"Well—what is it, then?" she demanded, with some asperity. "You'll have to be brief, for I've a Council meeting at eleven o'clock—an important one."

"This is more important, much more, than any council meeting, Mrs. Champernowne," said Hackdale. He seated himself by the desk and leaned forward. "Mrs. Champernowne," he went on. "You've heard, of course, of what happened last night— that a man was found, murdered, in the old sand pit behind your house?"

"I've heard that a man was found there who'd been shot dead," replied Mrs. Champernowne, with an affectation of carelessness which Hackdale was quick to see through. "Whether it was murder or suicide, I don't know."

"Murder!" said Hackdale. "No question of suicide. The man was deliberately murdered, Mrs. Champernowne!—it was I who found him! And it was very fortunate— very fortunate indeed—that I was quite alone when I found him. Very fortunate, Mrs. Champernowne, for—you!"

The colour suddenly rose to Mrs. Champernowne's face in an angry flush. She made as if she would rise from her chair. But Hackdale went on, with a shake of the head.

"Fortunate, I say, for you, Mrs. Champernowne! For—I found something on him! Can you guess what it was? Well, then—this!"

With the last word he suddenly produced from his pocket and held towards his employer, laid on the open palm of his left hand, the curiously-shaped safety pin which he had taken from the tear in the dead man's coat. He glanced from it to the woman; it needed but the merest look to see that Mrs. Champernowne's cheeks had turned deadly pale.

"You recognise that, Mrs. Champernowne?" Hackdale continued, in a low, smooth voice. "Of course you do! Do you remember that on Monday afternoon you came to me in the drapery department and showed me a small specimen box of these pins which you said had just come in for your approval, from a man who had taken out provisional protection for their patenting, and who wanted to know your opinion of them as a business proposition? You said to me that the idea was a remarkably good one—and then you put the box in your pocket, and went home with it. How came it that I found one of these pins in that dead man's coat? Obvious! Mrs. Champernowne, all that's known about the dead man is that his name is Deane, that he came to the Chancellor Hotel on Monday, and that on Monday night late he slipped out of the hotel—without doubt to visit somebody: Mrs. Champernowne, that somebody was you!

"He was with you that night—sometime. There's a certain man here in Southernstowe, on whom I could put my finger in ten minutes, of whom Deane asked the way to your house, near midnight, on Monday. Deane found his way to your house, Mrs. Champernowne! He was with you—some time. Probably he tore his coat in your grounds, or in getting into your grounds—and you gave him this peculiarly made safety pin to fasten the torn pieces together till he could get them mended. Mrs. Champernowne, you know as well as I do that that's all—fact! Fact!"

Mrs. Champernowne, big, strong woman though she was, sat silent under all this, nervously knitting her fingers together. It was some time before she spoke, and when words came they were faltering.

"Who—who knows of—of all you've said?"

"Nobody! Not a soul, Mrs. Champernowne! Do you think I'm a fool? Nobody knows—nobody can know—unless I speak."

"Who—who is the other man you referred to?"

"That's my business, Mrs. Champernowne. Best not ask—leave him to me. I can silence him—if you make it worth while to be silent. Look here, Mrs. Champernowne, let's be practical. Nobody knows anything of what I've told you. Mellapont is firmly of the opinion that Deane was followed, murdered, and robbed—that he was murdered for the money and valuables which, undoubtedly, he had on him. So far, so good =-the police'll stick to that. But Mellapont has another theory—that Deane went out to call on somebody in the city whom he knew, and Mellapont swears he'll find out who that somebody is! Mellapont can't!—he hasn't a clue—not a single clue. I'm the only soul living that has the clue—that safety pin is the clue, Mrs. Champernowne! Make it worth my while to hold my tongue for ever, and you can rest assured that you're as safe—as if all this had never happened. I don't know what took place between you and the dead man—and I don't want to know. It's nothing to do with me. But—I can save you from an unpleasant situation. Give me what I want, and nobody will ever know that Deane went out to see you—and did see you! The episode will be—closed!"

Mrs. Champernowne was watching him as intently as she was listening.

"But—the other man?" she asked suddenly.

"I tell you I can silence him," replied Hackdale. "Easily! With money—your money, of course."

"And—yourself?" she said. "Yourself?" Hackdale drew a long breath, and, folding his arms, looked round the room. When he turned again to his employer, it was with a smile—the smile of a man who finds it vastly agreeable to be in a position to dictate terms.

"Well, Mrs. Champernowne," he answered. "I've been a very good, trustworthy, dependable servant to you—you've never once had to find fault with me that I remember. It will be in your interest to give me what I want. And that's this—your present manager, Mr. Bywater, is out-of-date and useless—he's worse than useless; he's a nuisance! Pension him off, at once, and give me the managership. Date my appointment from last January the first, and give me a thousand a year—salary to be further considered at the end of two years. Reasonable, Mrs. Champernowne!—very reasonable."

Mrs. Champernowne's cheeks were assuming their usual colour. She remained silent for a moment or two, watching Hackdale, and turning her rings round and round on her plump fingers.

"How much money will satisfy that other man?" she asked abruptly.

"A couple of hundred pounds, put in my hands, and judiciously used," answered Hackdale, with promptitude. "Ample!"

Mrs. Champernowne rose from her desk, and going over to a small safe in a corner of the room, took from it a bundle of notes and without counting handed them to Hackdale. Then she picked up a handful of papers.

"Come in and see me about the other matter at twelve-thirty,'" she said. "I must go to the Council meeting."

Without another word she left the room, and Hackdale, having put the safety pin in one pocket and the notes in another, went back to his duties. But at half-past twelve he was back. Mrs. Champernowne had just come in—and as he closed the door, she turned on him and to their business without waste of words.

"Hackdale!—you're going to play straight about this?"

"My interest is to do that, Mrs. Champernowne!"

"I know nothing—nothing—as to how or why that man was murdered," she went on. "Nothing—absolutely nothing! Still, I won't deny—to you—that I saw him that night. Why—is my business. Still—I don't want that to get out. You're sure that it can't get out through you or that other man?"

"Make yourself easy, Mrs. Champernowne! It'll not get out from either. Are you certain that nobody at your house knows?"

"Certain of that—yes! He caught me at the entrance gate—I talked with him there—a little. Never mind why. Well, this managership. I can do better than that, Hackdale. Sit down—listen. I'm going to be married—to Sir Reville Childer—stone. You expected it?—very well. This business will be converted into a limited liability concern. I can make you secretary and manager. Now for details… "

Hackdale went away from Champernownes to his dinner feeling as if a couple of inches had been added to his stature. Simmons, awaiting him in their sitting room, was quick to observe his good spirits. He looked his wonder when Hackdale, suddenly rising from the table, went over to a cupboard and produced a bottle of champagne.

"It's neither my birthday nor yours," observed Simmons.

"Never mind, my boy!" exclaimed John. "I've had a stroke of big luck this morning. Bit of a secret at present, Sim, but you'll hear all about it before long. Going to be great developments at our place, and I shall be biggest man there, Sim!"

"What'll it run to—then?" enquired Sim.

Hackdale laughed. The prospect which Mrs. Champernowne had opened out before him was infinitely better than that he had sketched for himself.

"Can't say as to that yet, my boy!" he answered. "But—big—big, Sim! Didn't I always tell you I should be top dog at Champernowne's some day. Nothing like my motto, Sim—always look after your own interest! Self first!—never mind where the other fellow gets to. You don't look round in running races—at least, if you do, some other chap'll be past you in a flash. You look after yourself at Shelmore's as well as I've looked after myself at Champernowne's, and you'll do. I'll tell you what, Sim!—now that this is coming off. I'll pay for your being articled to Shelmore, and then, if you work hard, you'll be a fully qualified solicitor in a few years. What do you say to that, Sim?"

Sim cocked his ears. His sharp eyes went to the champagne in his brother's glass. But it was still as untouched as his own; clearly John made this offer in soberness.

"I'll drink to that, John!" he said, suddenly. "Cost you a bit, you know."

"Don't mind that, my boy, as long as you do well, and it pays," declared Hackdale. "Well, here's luck to it and the Hackdale motto—'Look after Number One!' Sim, if ever I—start a crest or that sort of thing, I'll have that underneath! Never mind anybody else—self first, and hang the second fellow."

"Good!" assented Simmons, and went steadily on with his dinner. "I'll speak to Shelmore about the articling when I go back. But—I shall try to bargain with him."

"Bargain? How?" asked Hackdale.

"Try to get something out of him," answered Simmons, with a crafty look. "Suggest that he should do a bit towards it. I've been jolly useful to Shelmore! If I can screw something out of him, why not? Save your pocket."

Hackdale nodded, sipped his wine, and smiled.

"I don't think you'll let the flies settle on you, Sim!" he said, with evident satisfaction. "You know pretty well how to take care of yourself! Bargain all you like with Shelmore. You know your own interests."

"Trust me!" muttered Simmons. "Been studying 'em long enough!"

He went back to Shelmore's office at half—past two, intending to broach the subject there and then. But just as he was about to knock at Shelmore's door, Shelmore's bell rang, and Simmons responded to find his principal standing near his desk, reading a written document with an air of something very like doubt or disfavour.

"Hackdale," he said. "Miss Pretty has been here. She's a very determined young lady, Hackdale!—the sort that insists on having her own way; also, it seems that though she's not of age, she's a very large sum of money in her bank which she can spend as she likes; and though she's been in consultation with Superintendent Mellapont all the morning, and Mellapont has practically proved to her that her guardian was murdered by strangers for the sake of what he'd got on him, she won't believe it—she's got it firmly fixed in her head that Deane was followed here and murdered by some enemy. And she insists on offering a reward, and has asked me to get a bill printed and posted for her. I don't see much good in it—I firmly believe Mellapont to be right. What do you think, Hackdale?"

"What's the amount?" asked Simmons.

"She fixed it herself!" replied Shelmore. "A thousand pounds! A very wilful young lady!—she declared that if that didn't bring any result, she'd double it. I suppose we'll have to get it printed and distributed for her?"

"If she likes to do it, why not?" said Simmons.

"Seems to me waste of time and money," answered Shelmore. "However—take it over to Pemberton's, and give them instructions for printing and posting it. Something may come of it—but I'm doubtful. Still—somebody's guilty, and that somebody's somewhere."

He handed over the copy to Simmons, and the clerk, without further comment, turned away. As he went down the stairs to the street, he met an elderly gentleman coming up, and recognising Sir Reville Childerstone, told him that Mr. Shelmore was in his office, and then, for particular reasons of his own, made more haste than ever to discharge his errand.

Chapter

7

THE CREVICED WALL

Pemberton's printing office lay in a narrow alley at the back of the Chancellor Hotel, and when Simmons Hackdale hurried in at its door, Pemberton himself, one of those men who wear a perpetually worried look, stood behind the counter, sorting paper. He listened with something of an aggrieved air while Simmons explained what he wanted, and then shook his head.

"Can't get it out by tonight, nohow!" he declared. "Don't care how insistent the young lady is. Get it done and distributed and posted, too, for you by noon tomorrow, Mr. Simmons—that's the quickest I can do."

"All right," said Simmons. "No such hurry as all that, when it comes to it. What about a proof?"

"Look in when you go home this evening," answered Pemberton. "I'll have one ready for you."

Simmons hurried back to Shelmore's. He had his own reasons for hurrying. He knew that Sir Reville Childerstone was now closeted with Shelmore in his private room, and he wanted to hear what they were talking about. Also he knew how he would easily satisfy that desire. Simmons had a natural propensity for finding out every thing possible about anything or anybody, and he was not beyond eavesdropping or listening at keyholes. But there was no need to listen at the keyhole of Shelmore's room. Before Simmons had been a week in Shelmore's employ, he had discovered that the wall which separated the clerk's room from the private office was by no means sound proof. It had crevices in it—and, being merely a lath-and-plaster erection at best, the crevices in course of time had opened, and were not at all obscured by flimsy wallpaper. Indeed, there was one in particular, through which Simmons had poked his finger, so wide that you could see through it into Shelmore's room: over that crevice Simmons always kept an old overcoat hanging on his side, while, on Shelmore's, he had hung a local calendar. And now, going quietly up the stair and entering his own room with the tread of a cat: he went over to this convenient crack, held the overcoat aside, and put his ear to the wall. He had not been listening many minutes when he knew that he was getting first hand confirmation of the truth of a rumour which had been gradually spreading through Southernstowe, for some time—Sir Reville Childerstone was going to marry Mrs. Champernowne. Sir Reville was discussing marriage settlements with Shelmore, who was evidently making elaborate notes of his wishes; Simmons gathered from the conversation that the marriage was to be solemnized before long—probably before Christmas. He learnt that Mrs. Champernowne, on becoming Lady Childerstone, would give up Ashenhurst House and go to Childerstone Park, four miles outside the city. And then came personal details which, for family reasons, interested the listener much more.

"I gather that Mrs. Champernowne won't take on the mayoralty again?" said Shelmore, after a slight pause in the conversation, during which Simmons had heard the steady scratching of his employer's pen. "Or will she?"

"She won't," replied Sir Reville. "As Lady Childerstone she'll retire into private life. Done her duty, I think, Shelmore—indefatigable in her discharge of it, what?"

"An admirable mayor!" assented Shelmore. "I question if they'll find any man in the city who'll do as well as she's done. But the business? What's she going to do about that?"

"She's just come to a decision—this very morning," said Sir Reville. "She and I have just been lunching at the Chancellor, and she informed me of her settled intentions. The thing's private at present, but, of course, I don't mind telling you, as between solicitor and client, knowing that the news won't go any further. Champernowne's, Shelmore, is to be turned into a limited liability company."

"Ah!" said Shelmore. "Good idea, Sir Reville! Of course, Lady Childerstone will keep a controlling interest in it?"

"To be sure—she'll hold a majority of the shares, and, for a time at any rate, she'll act as chairman of the directorate," assented Sir Reville. "I propose to take up a considerable number of shares myself and to become a director—the business is too valuable a property to neglect, though, of course, after its conversion into a company it won't need the daily supervision which Mrs. Champernowne now gives it."

"It'll need a first rate manager," remarked Shelmore.

"He's there to hand!" said Sir Reville, with a satisfied chuckle. "Made and trained and taught all the tricks of the trade by Mrs. Champernowne herself! Young Hackdale!—smart fellow! He's to act as secretary and manager—Mrs. Champernowne proposes to give him a couple of thousand a year."

"Well, I daresay he's worth it in a big business like that," said Shelmore. "Yes, Hackdale's all right—clever man, and a pushing, hard working man. I suppose all this is to be carried out shortly?"

"At once," replied Sir Reville. "Before the marriage. So you can get on with those settlements—always well to be in time, Shelmore. Um!—well, I think that's all just now, and I'll be off. By-the-by, heard any more about this murder affair?—any fresh news?"

"Nothing," answers Shelmore. "The police—such of them as are left in the city, for, as you know, nearly the whole lot are away on this coal strike business—are making enquiries all round, but they've not resulted in anything yet. No doubt the man was murdered for what he'd got on him. But there's a curious thing about that matter which I was going to speak to you about. Sir Reville, next time we met. This man, Deane, had been travelling about in the North of England for three or four weeks before he came down here, and when Mellapont and I examined his belongings at the Chancellor we found a considerable collection of picture postcards of places he'd visited. I was much interested in seeing that one of these places was the old town where that bit of property of yours is, about which we've had so much bother—Normansholt."

"Normansholt, eh?" said Sir Reville. "Oh, been there, had he?"

"Evidently, from the number of pictures he had of it. Fine, picturesque old town," continued Shelmore. "He'd collected some striking views."

"Only been to Normansholt once, myself," remarked Sir Reville. "When I came into that piece of property there, I went down to have a look at it—had a look at the town, too, of course, while I was there. Historic place—old castle, ruined abbeys, ancient buildings—that sort of thing."

"Just so," agreed Shelmore. "Well, this man, as I say, had collected a lot, twenty to thirty, of picture postcards of Normansholt. And—this was what I'd wanted to mention to you—on one of them he'd made a conspicuous pencil mark against a certain picturesque old house. Odd—very odd, to my mind."

"Why, Shelmore?" asked Sir Reville.

"I'll tell you. There was a big collection of similar cards in his suitcase, there are four hundred in all, that he'd evidently picked up in his travels, and that was the only card that bore any mark. Why did he mark that particular card, and that particular house?" asked Shelmore. "Why?"

"Oh, I don't see anything in that!" replied Sir Reville, with a laugh. "Sort of thing that anybody might do. Probably took a fancy to the house. How do you know what the man was after? Perhaps he went up north with the idea of buying a house?—hang it, I wish he'd bought my property at Normansholt!—it's nothing but a confounded nuisance as it is—and the tenant's a confounded nuisance. I'll tell you what Shelmore, if that affair's not settled soon, you'll have to take drastic measures!"

"I've given his solicitors a fortnight in which to make an offer for settlement," answered Shelmore.

"If their client's still impenitent and defiant at the end of that time, we'll see about a writ Odd, though, isn't it, that this murdered man should have been at Normansholt and singled out a house there?—just when the place was in my thoughts."

But Sir Reville saw nothing in this but very ordinary and commonplace coincidence, and said so. He gave signs of moving, and Simmons slipped away from his crack in the wall, replaced the old overcoat, and made ready to bow the baronet out. When Sir Reville had gone, he memorized the important features of the overheard conversation. One—Mrs. Champernowne was going to marry Sir Reville Childerstone. Two—Champernowne's was to be converted into a limited liability company, and his brother John was to be secretary and manager at a commencing salary of two thousand pounds a year. Three—the murdered man, Deane, had lately been to Normansholt, in Yorkshire, and for some reason or other had marked a certain house shown in a picture postcard of that place—a circumstance which Shelmore, who was no fool, thought very odd. All right, concluded Simmons, storing these things away in his retentive memory: now he knew more, much more, than he had known at the beginning of the afternoon. And to him a day was lost unless he added to his store of knowledge.

For reasons of his own, not unconnected with the news about Champernowne's, Simmons said nothing to Shelmore that afternoon in respect of the proposed articling. At a quarter past five he left the office and went round to Pemberton's. Pemberton at sight of him pushed a damp, freshly—pulled proof across the counter.

"I can do a bit better for you," he said. "If you pass the proof now, I can print a supply off and get it distributed and posted early in the morning—get it out before breakfast-time if you like."

"The sooner the better—for the responsible party," remarked Simmons. He produced a pencil and rapidly ran over the proof. "Quite all right," he said. "No mistakes there. Then you'll get it out early—distribution, too?"

"I'll see to it," agreed Pemberton. "Shop-windows—public houses—that sort of thing."

Simmons nodded and turned away; then a thought struck him, and, re-entering the shop, he asked the printer for another copy of the proof. With this in his pocket, he went home to tea.

John Hackdale was already at the tea table, refreshing himself before starting out on his special constable duties. Simmons, entering, laid before his brother the proof of the reward bill.

"Latest!" he said, laconically.

He sat down and helped himself to tea and toast, while John, a lump of cake bulging his cheek, read the bill.

"Whose notion's that?" he demanded, suddenly. "Shelmore's?"

"The girl's," replied Simmons. "Miss Pretty. Insists on it. Came to Shelmore, said she'd piles of ready money in the bank and would spend it like water to find out who murdered Deane, and made him draft that. Shelmore?—no!—Shelmore doesn't approve of it."

"Why not?" asked John.

"Thinks it's waste of time and money," answered Simmons. "If there's anybody in Southernstowe who knows anything of Deane's movements that night, or had ever seen him, they'd have told Mellapont before now."

John Hackdale said nothing. But he was thinking—thinking of Bartlett. Bartlett the impecunious!—who would see this bill as soon as it was passed.

"When's this going to be out, Sim?" he asked presently. "Tonight?"

"No—but by breakfast time tomorrow," replied Simmons. "Why—do you think any thing'll come of it?"

"Somebody might know something," answered John, carelessly. "A thousand pounds' offer is a wonderful thing for sharpening memories!"

"And for quickening imaginations!" sneered Simmons.

John said no more. He set off for the City Hall and stayed there some little time. When he left the dusk had fallen. Instead of going northward on his proper beat he turned down into a network of alleys and courts, and, coming at last to a cheap boarding house, knocked at its door and asked for James Bartlett.

Bartlett presently appeared, a subdued eagerness in his eyes. Hackdale motioned him to follow and led the way to a quiet spot at the end of the alley. He plunged into his business without any unnecessary preface.

"About that affair the other night," he said, eyeing his man as closely as the failing light allowed. "You've kept your mouth shut?"

"Tight, Mr. Hackdale," answered Bartlett. "Not one syllable has passed these lips, sir, to a soul, except yourself."

"I know more, now, than I did when I saw you," continued Hackdale. "Found out more. That man—we needn't mention names—did want to see Mrs. Champernowne, and did see her—met her, accidentally, outside her gates, had a brief talk with her, and left her—or she left him. She knows no more than that. He must have been lured by somebody into that sand pit, murdered there, and robbed. Of course, Mrs. Champernowne knows nothing whatever of anything that happened to the man after she left him. But— you understand? She doesn't want it known that she ever saw him. She has—reasons. And—nobody but you knows—what you know. Eh?"

"I'm following you, Mr. Hackdale," said Bartlett, knowingly. "I'm taking it all in, sir."

"Then take this in," continued Hackdale. "Questions are sure to be asked—enquiries made. Don't you think it would be just as well—for everybody—if you went where you wouldn't be questioned? Come, now? Look here!—you told me one night, some time ago, that you'd relatives in America—and that if you'd money, you'd go to them. Eh?"

"And so I would, Mr. Hackdale, so I would, I'd the passage money," answered Bartlett, with obvious eagerness. "I would, indeed; I'd go—

"Listen to me," interrupted Hackdale. "There a steamer from Southampton to New York tomorrow—she'll leave about noon. If you'll be off to Southampton tonight, by the nine fifty—three train, and will promise to sail tomorrow, I'll give you a hundred and fifty pounds to take with you, and on hearing of your arrival at whatever town it is in America you want to go to, I'll cable you another hundred and fifty. Come, now—make up your mind, Bartlett. Is it a bargain?"

Bartlett suddenly thrust out his hand.

"Done!" he said. "I'll go! I've so often talked of it—amongst what friends I have—that nobody'll think it strange. Yes, I'll go, Mr. Hackdale. I'll just pack a bag, and be off to Southampton. I can buy a few things there in the morning, and catch the boat. Done, sir!"

Within five minutes, Hackdale had handed over the hundred and fifty pounds to Bartlett, made a few arrangements with him, and gone away. He had no doubt whatever that Bartlett would clear out—none.

And Bartlett went back into the cheap lodging house and began to pack his small belongings, fully intending to be off to a new world on the morrow—fully. But before he had got half—way through his task, another visitor summoned him downstairs. This was Pemberton, the printer, who held out to him a bundle of what looked like circulars, damp from the press.

"Bit of a job for you, Jim," said Pemberton. "Just distribute these amongst the shops and public houses early in the morning, and when it's done, call round on me for half-a-quid. See?"

Bartlett held the topmost bill to the light of the door lamp and read it through with unmoved countenance. A thousand pounds reward for... he suddenly thrust the bundle back into Pemberton's hands.

"Sorry—can't do it, old man!" he said, cavalierly. "I'm just going away—to visit an old friend in the country. Try somebody else."

Without waiting for comment, he turned, hastened upstairs, and finished his packing. And as he packed, he thought, and puzzled things out, and began to develop a theory. He went on thinking and developing as he walked to the station: he continued to think and to develop after he had got into the nine fifty-three.

The nine fifty-three stopped at Portsmouth at ten twenty-eight. And at Portsmouth Bartlett got out, forfeited his ticket, and went off to find a cheap hotel. By that time he had given up all thoughts of America: at present, he considered, there were better chances in England.

MISS PRETTY'S WAY

Pemberton, baulked of Bartlett's services in the matter of bill distributing, turned elsewhere. He had no difficulty in finding a substitute, there were plenty of idle men about, any one of whom were glad enough to earn the half-sovereign which Bartlett spurned. And by nine o'clock next morning every shop window in the business quarter of Southernstowe was displaying the bill, and early risers were wondering if anybody would be lucky enough to gain the thousand pounds reward.

Mellapont saw the bills as he came down from his house on the outskirts of the city and swore softly to himself. From the start out of his career in the police force he had always been wanting a case, a big case, a suitable cause celebre, and it had seemed to him that at last he had one in the Chancellor Hotel mystery. He had meant to keep it to himself, to do all the spade work himself, to have all the credit of detection and discovery for himself. He had purposely avoided the calling in of outside assistance; he did not want any sleuth hounds from the Criminal Investigation Department at Scotland Yard poking their noses into Southernstowe, or sticking their fingers in his pie—he wanted to be able to say, when the job was done, that he had lone it all unaided and by his own astuteness and ability. And now here was interference, and of the very sort that, just then, he certainly did not want. It was vexing—and when he had finished his routine duties at the police station he went round to Shelmore's office and said so, plainly. Shelmore shook his head and spread out his hands.

"Not my fault, superintendent," he protested. "I'm not sure that I don't entirely agree with you. But what can we do with a young lady who—who's about the most determined person I ever came across? Miss Pretty came here and insisted on this being done. She told me coolly that although she isn't of age, she's piles of ready money in her bank which she can draw on as she likes, and she informed me further that she'd spend every penny of it in tracking down her guardian's murderer! She's the sort of young woman who's jolly well going to have her own way, and who'll make things deuced unpleasant for anybody who tries to thwart her. I don't know if all Cornish people are like her, for I never came across any of 'em before, but she's—well, not exactly vindictive, but filled to the brim with a spirit that's—something very like revenge. Got it into her head that it's up to her to avenge her guardian—and she isn't going to mince matters, or stick at anything. She was absolutely resolved about offering this reward, and if I hadn't done the thing for her, she'd have gone out and gone to some other solicitor. If you knew her better—"

At that moment Simmons Hackdale opened the green baize door and stood aside. "Miss Pretty!" he announced.

Miss Pretty walked in with one nod to Shelmore and another to Mellapont. So far she made no display of mourning garments; on the contrary she was arrayed in her smartest clothes, and she looked very much alive and decidedly alert.

"We were just talking about you, Miss Pretty!" said Shelmore, as he drew an easy chair towards the hearth, and gave his recently lighted fire a poke. "Superintendent Mellapont regrets that we've put out that reward bill."

Miss Pretty dropped into the easy chair and turned sharply on Mellapont. "Why, pray?" she demanded.

Mellapont rubbed his chin. He was not used to dealing with self-sufficient young ladies, and he looked at this one, as a biologist might look at a new and surprising specimen.

"Um!" he said, reflectively. "Er—a little primitive, you know, Miss Pretty. In cases like the present one, it's best to leave things to us, to the police. But to wait a little, you know, before—"

"I don't see any reason at all why I should wait!" interrupted Miss Pretty. "While one's waiting, the murderer gets away. I'm not interfering with you, superintendent—you follow your methods, and I'll follow mine. My guardian was foully murdered in this city, and I'm going to know who murdered him!"

"Just so!—I quite sympathise with your feelings, Miss Pretty," agreed Mellapont, in his suavest manner. "But—in cases like this—mysterious cases—a little diplomacy is often a good deal better than open warfare. There are various ways of going to work—I prefer the—shall we call it secret, under-the-surface way? We've agreed on the fact that somebody murdered Mr. Deane—now, have you got any theory about it?"

Miss Pretty considered matters for awhile.

"I think somebody followed him to Southernstowe," she said at last. "Somebody who knew he had money and valuables on him. I think that somebody probably stayed at the hotel and followed him out. There were lots of people staying at the hotel that night, according to what I've been told. Most of them left next morning—I don't know if they can be traced or not. I suppose you police can trace and question them?"

"The thing—to my mind—is this," observed Mellapont. "Why did Mr. Deane go out from the Chancellor Hotel so very late at night?—midnight!"

"I've been thinking about that," said Miss Pretty. "I think there may have been a reason. Mr. Deane was not a very good sleeper, and I've heard him say that he never slept well in strange beds. Now, at home, he used to go for a walk late at night—just before bedtime. I think that on that night at the Chancellor he felt that he wasn't going to sleep, so he just got up again, dressed, and went out for a stroll. Simple!"

"That he went out is certain; that he was murdered and robbed is certain," remarked Mellapont. "And," he added, "it's also certain, unfortunately, that we haven't the slightest clue to the criminal's identity. Now, my idea, my belief, Miss Pretty, is that your guardian met his death at the hands of some loafer, who afterwards robbed him. But I've another belief—I feel certain that Mr. Deane knew Southernstowe and somebody in Southernstowe, and that his real object in going out was to visit that somebody—late as the hour was."

Miss Pretty shook her head.

"When we were talking over this holiday," she said firmly. "Mr. Deane remarked to me that he'd never seen Southernstowe, never been in this part of England. So how could he know it, or know anybody here? If I thought that he knew anybody here, and that he went to see that somebody that night—if I really do get, from any evidence you can bring, to think that... "

She paused, shaking her head again, and Mellapont waited.

"Yes?" he said at last. "If you ever do get to think that?—What?"

"This!" answered Miss Pretty, with a very sombre look in her eyes. "This—I'll stop in this place until I've found out who that somebody is and have it out with him or her—I will!—if it costs me every penny I have in the world! And I've got a lot of pennies."

"You believe in a policy of thoroughness, Miss Pretty?" suggested Mellapont. "Going right through with it, eh?"

"I'm going to know all and everything about what happened to my guardian and partner that night!" declared Miss Pretty. "You go on with your police work, and let me go my way!—if we can't find and hang the murderer between us, we must be poor tools! I came to see you, Mr Shelmore," she went on, turning to the solicitor, "about two

39

matters—my guardian's funeral and this inquest you said I'd have to attend. I'm going to have Mr. Deane buried here—I've settled that, and the time and place. But—this other affair?"

Shelmon looked at Mellapont and Mellapont hastened to explain.

"The inquest opens this afternoon," he said. "It will be quite a formal affair today—just identification and so on. Then the coroner will adjoin for a week or ten days. The adjourned inquest will be the thing. Perhaps, by then, we, the police, will be in possession of more evidence. I'm doing my utmost, Miss Pretty. But look here, now—if this reward bill of yours brings anybody forward, let me know! Mutual confidence, eh?—don't do anything without me. I suppose you will remain here awhile?"

Miss Pretty gave the two men a steady look.

"I'm not going one yard out of this city till I know who killed James Deane!" she said, "That's flat!"

Then she rose, and with a careless nod, went away, and Shelmore and Mellapont, left to themselves, looked at each other.

"You see?" said Shelmore, after a pause.

"I see!" answered Mellapont, drily. "Um!—I don't think anybody's going to get any small change out of that young woman! Do you say she's only nineteen?"

"Thereabouts," replied Shelmore.

"Good Lord!—what will she be at twenty-nine?" exclaimed Mellapont. "Prime Minister, I should think. Well!—but you'll let me know if anything comes of this reward offer? Don't let's get at cross purposes. United action, eh?"

"I'll let you know," said Shelmore. "If the promise of a thousand pounds, cash down, doesn't produce anything, though—eh?"

"Just so!" assented Mellapont. "It'll look as if we were never going to know anything. Still—I've my own methods. That jewellery, now—whoever robbed him of it will want to dispose of it. To track that will be one of my lines."

"Yes," said Shelmore. "But... supposing the person who took the jewellery is under no necessity to dispose of it?"

"Eh?" exclaimed Mellapont. "What do you mean?"

"I mean," replied Shelmore, "that the valuables on Deane may have been removed as a blind; to divert suspicion; to suggest that he was the victim of a vulgar murder-and-robbery, when, as a matter of fact he was murdered for set purpose and design."

Mellapont stared, comprehended, and became thoughtful.

"I certainly hadn't thought of that," he said at last. "Yes! might be. That would argue that the murderer was some person of means, education, unusual cleverness—to think of such a thing. Um! We're all in the dark. Well—we must wait."

Miss Pretty waited, during the next fortnight. She saw her guardian buried in a quiet churchyard just outside the town; she occupied herself in clearing up her affairs; she had regular interviews with Shelmore and Mellapont. But she got no news, for nothing in the shape of news turned up. The adjourned inquest came round; the coroner and his jury heard every scrap of evidence that could be produced. And after sitting all day, the jury returned a verdict of wilful murder against some person or persons unknown, and everybody went away from the court, declaring that it was the only verdict possible, and that nobody, now, would ever know who killed James Deane.

"Reckon I do know who killed he, poor man, all the same!" declared a native wiseacre in Miss Pretty's hearing, as she passed out of the coroner's court. "Do so!"

"Who, then, if so be as you knows in your cleverness?" enquired his companion. "Mortial clever, you be, for to know it, when coroner and jury don't."

"Don't call for no mortial cleverness, that don't!" retorted the wiseacre. "One 'o they pesky idle good-for-nothing's what comes moochin' round, fair days, and hangs about the place all night, him it would be as did felonious kill and slay this here gentleman—or it med be two on 'em. Sleeps out, they does, in such places as that there old sand pit. Well, he take his walk up there; they sees him, wi' his fine clothes and goold watch chain, and sparklin' pin, and they sattles him. Plain as my old stick here, that be!—don't want no crowner, nor jury, nor pleecemen, nor yet lawyers, to tell I that! I reckon I be filled wi' more o' the meat o' common sense than all they lawyers and crowners put together—all talk they be!"

Miss Pretty went away to think. She thought a great deal that night, and the next morning she called on Mellapont at the police station.

"I've changed my opinions," she said laconically, when he had given her a chair. "Completely!"

"Yes?" enquired Mellapont. "In—what way?"

"I now think that Mr. Deane did know somebody in Southernstowe, and that he went out that night with the express purpose of seeing that somebody," she said. "Probably by appointment."

"No!" declared Mellapont, with emphasis. "Not by appointment! You remember—the chambermaid saw him in his night clothes, about to retire. He got up and dressed, after that. It was an afterthought, a sudden thought, that rising and going out."

"Well," said Miss Pretty. "Anyway, he went—to see this somebody. This somebody must have lived near where he was murdered."

"There are at least sixty houses, detached houses, villa residences, mansions, lived in by people of reputation and position round there," replied Mellapont. "It's the best residential quarter of Southernstowe."

"That was where he went—to that quarter," persisted Miss Pretty. "Why don't you make a house to house visitation? If he called at one of these houses—"

"We don't know that he ever did call," interrupted Mellapont. "He may have been going to call. I don't think he ever did call, anywhere. Had he called, late as it was, the possibility is that a servant would have answered his knock or ring, and in that case, your reward would have brought that servant forward."

"Supposing he went somewhere by appointment?" suggested Miss Pretty.

"That would argue that he'd made an appointment during the evening," said Mellapont. "We have no evidence that he spoke to anyone except Belling and the hotel servants from the time of his arrival at the Chancellor to his going out of his bedroom. I think he went to call on somebody—and never got there."

Miss Pretty rose, and looked round the drabness of the superintendent's room. "Are you any further forward?" she asked abruptly.

"Honestly—no," replied Mellapont. "Not one yard further. The whole thing is more of a mystery—an unsolved mystery—than ever."

Miss Pretty nodded and went away, and back to her rooms at the Chancellor Hotel. She had told Belling that she was going to stay there indefinitely, and had engaged his best bedroom and an adjoining sitting room. In the sitting room she now sat down, and, after a prolonged spell of thinking, over a convenient piece of fancy work, she came to a conclusion. That led her to her writing table, where, with more thought, she produced the copy for a new reward bill. When she had completed it, she took it round to Pemberton's herself and made all arrangements about printing, distributing, and posting it: this time, she said to herself, she would neither consult nor trouble Shelmore or anybody else: this was her own affair.

41

By noon next day everybody in Southernstowe had read the new bill. It went far beyond the terms of the old one. Miss Pretty made three offers. She would give one thousand pounds to anybody who could prove that he or she saw James Deane after he left the Chancellor Hotel on the night of his death. She would give one thousand pounds to anybody who could tell anything about the missing jewellery. And, finally, she would give three thousand pounds to any person who could give information which would lead to the arrest and conviction of James Deane's murderer.

Simmons Hackdale was one of the first people to see this new bill, and his mouth began to water, and his hands to itch. If he could but get a clue—the slightest clue! And that very afternoon, if he had only known it, opportunity was coming his way. Shelmore called him into the private office and told him that he had an important, confidential mission for him. It was absolutely necessary that somebody should go down to Normansholt in Yorkshire and make personal inspection of Sir Reville Childerstone's property in that town: he, Simmons, should go. Next day…

Simmons went home to make ready. And, as he packed his bag, he remembered what he had overheard Shelmore tell Sir Reville about the marked picture postcard Was there anything in it?

BIRDS OF A FEATHER

Simmons, after a two hundred and fifty miles' journey, found himself and his modest kitbag in Nonnansholt at six o'clock on the following afternoon. He had never been in the North of England before, and his surroundings struck him, accustomed as he was to the South, as being gray and gloomy. But as he wandered through the old market square, looking about him for accommodation, his sharp eye spotted what seemed to be quite an up-to-date hotel, The Bear, and he promptly stepped aside, booked a room, and ordered dinner. Simmons had plenty of ready money in his pocket, and, knowing that whatever he laid out would be returned to him, through Shelmore, out of Sir Reville Childerstone's amply supplied coffers, he was determined to do himself well. If you are spending your own money, said Simmons, be frugal; if somebody else's, be lavish. This is a principal on which all officials are brought up, from big-wigs in Whitehall to the servants of obscure town corporations.

He was halfway through his dinner in the coffee room of The Bear when a waiter ushered in a smart, alert looking young gentleman of his own age, whose eyes were full of polite enquiry. The waiter indicated Simmons, who had written his name and address with a flourish in the register downstairs, and the young gentleman, doffing his somewhat rakish hat, came forward, smiling widely.

"Mr. Hackdale, from Southernstowe?" he suggested, coming up to Simmons. "Mr. Simmons Hackdale?"

"That's me," replied Simmons, regardless of grammatical niceties. "You've the advantage of me, though."

"Mr. Swale, Swilford Swale—of Pike and Pilkins, Mr. Hackdale," said the caller. "We heard from Mr. Shelmore this morning that you were coming down today to inspect this property of Sir Reville Childerstone, and, feeling sure you'd be here at The Bear, I thought I'd just drop in and give you a welcome to the old town—never been here before, I suppose, Mr. Hackdale?"

"Never, nor anywhere near it," answered Simmons. "Very kind of you, I'm sure, Mr. Swale. If you'd been a bit earlier, I'd have asked you to dinner. What'll you have to drink?"

Mr. Swale replied that he'd already dined, and, after some little consideration, decided to take a glass of The Bear's famous old port; Simmons, who up to then had drunk nothing, decided to join him. Mr. Swale dropped into a chair close by, and, while Simmons finished his dinner they exchanged the confidences of youth. Mr. Swale told Simmons all about Pike and Pilkin's; Simmons told Mr. Swale all about Shelmore. By the time they had had two glasses each of the famous old port they were fast friends, and had ceased to call each other mister.

"And now, what would you like to do, old man?" demanded Mr. Swale, when he and Simmons quitted the coffee room. "There's not a great deal doing in this ancient borough, but there's something. There's a theatre and a picture house, and if you care for billiards I can take you to the club. Or, as it's a fine moonlight night. I can show you round the old place, and we'll drop in at a famous pub, where the landlord's a friend of mine—he's got a drop of port that's fully equal to that we've just sampled—fully! What's your preference?"

Simmons, who had a natural inquisitiveness about anything new and unfamiliar, said that if it were left to him, he'd like to have a general look round, and Mr. Swale, pleased to act the part of cicerone, led him forth and began a systematic tour of the town. He exhibited the Market Cross, the Parish Church, the Moot Hall, the Castle, the ruins of two or three abbeys and priories, various ancient houses, and the site of the old gallows, and finally turned him round a corner into a square, from the centre of which towered a tall mast.

"That's something which, I'm given to understand, you don't often see in England nowadays, old man!" said Mr. Swale. "A real, genuine, old—fashioned maypole!—the original, antique one. There aren't many left now—don't know if you've any down your way?"

"Never seen one in my life before!" declared Simmons. "Heard of 'em, of course."

"This square," continued the guide, waving his hand around him, "is called May Day Green. They used to hold the old May Day revels here, dancing round that maypole, and so on. I've heard old residents talk about 'em—given up they are now, though I myself have seen the maypole decorated. One of the oldest parts of Normansholt this, my boy!— centuries old. There's the Maypole Inn, in that corner—that's where we'll drop in for half—an—hour. In that other corner is a fine old place—the Manor House—that with the long, sloping roofs and tall gables. There was a most extraordinary thing happened at that Manor House some twenty—two years ago—don't remember it, personally myself, but I've heard my father tell about it, many a time."

"What was it?" asked Simmons.

"Strange and mystifying disappearance of a man who lived there," answered Mr. Swale. "Sort of thing that you read about in these tales and novels—only more so. Tell you about it if you like—but let's look in at the Maypole."

Simmons followed his new found friend into an old-fashioned inn, which looked as if it had been lately transported from Elizabethan or even early Tudor days, and seemed to be a rabbit warren of cosy nooks and corners. Its landlord, to Mr. Swale's great disappointment, proved to be out for the evening, but Mr. Swale knew which particular brand of port to ask for, and, providing himself and his companion with a couple of glasses, led the way to a quiet corner in an oak-panelled room, wherein burnt a cheery fire, and suggested that as the night was still young they should make themselves comfortable.

"And I'll tell you about that Manor House affair," he added, as they settled themselves in contiguous elbow chairs. "I've often thought I'd try my hand at making a story of it, for the magazine, you know, but I'm doubtful if I've the writing trick, and besides I shouldn't know how to wind it up. Perhaps you could make something of it, old man. What?"

"Can't say till I've heard it," replied Simmons. "What's it all about—a disappearance?"

"Queerest disappearance ever you heard of!" assented Mr. Swale. "People hereabouts talk of it to this very day! Disappearance of a man who used to live in that Manor House twenty-two years ago—name of Arradeane."

"Name of what?" asked Simmons.

"Arradeane—a, double r, a, d, e, a, n, e," replied Mr. Swale, spelling it out. "Queer name, but that was it—Arradeane, James Arradeane, civil engineer."

Simmons' ears suddenly pricked and widened. Arradeane? James Arradeane? Leave off the first four letters, and you got Deane, James Deane—the name of the murdered man at Southernstowe! And—he suddenly remembered Miss Pretty and her first visit to Shelmore. She had said that her guardian, James Deane, was, by profession, a civil engineer. Could it be that he had stumbled on.

"Yes?" he said, quietly. "And—the story?"

Mr. Swale sipped his port with the air of a connoisseur and composed himself in his chair.

"I'll tell you," he answered. "Oddest thing I ever heard of!—some features of it, the features about the actual disappearance, anyway. It was like this—as my father told it. To start with, you must understand that all about twenty to twenty—five years ago, there was a big boom in coal development in this neighbourhood. It was believed that there were very rich, undeveloped seams of coal all around this town, and people began to grow rich in anticipation, and a lot of strangers came about, on the lookout for what they could get. Now amongst them was this man, James Arradeane. He was a civil engineer by profession, but he evidently had considerable private means of his own. No one ever knew where he came from, but he came, and his wife with him, and he took that old Manor House that I've just shewn you, and settled down, and let it be known openly that he was prospecting. He had some transaction with a company that was forming here; they did a lot of boring in some land they bought, just outside the borough boundary, but it didn't come to anything. According to what my father said—and he knew him well—"

"Is your father alive?" interrupted Simmons.

"Dead—these five years," answered Swale. "Well, according to him, this Arradeane was by no means dependent on his profession—he seemed to be just waiting for a likely thing to put capital into. It was well understood in the town that both he and his wife had money—my father said she was a very handsome woman; clever, too—"

"Just to get the proper hang of it, old man," interrupted Simmons again, "how old might these two have been at that time.'

"Oh, they were youngish people—under the thirties—she, at any rate," replied Swale. "He would be a bit older, perhaps. Smart couple—used to drive very good horses, and cut a bit of a dash, you understand. But it got out in the town, somehow, that they didn't hit it off, that there were differences between 'em. They'd no children, but Mrs. Arradeane had a brother who lived with them, a sort of hanger—on, you know, a chap who never did anything but loaf round and enjoy himself, at her expense, of course, and it was said that Arradeane very much objected to it and wanted to clear him out, which Mrs. Arradeane wouldn't hear of—she'd looked after this brother all their lives, though that wasn't long, and she refused to be parted from him.

"All that got to be known in the town—you can't conceal anything in a little place like this, you know, old man! And my father said that that might be the main bone of contention, or there might have been lesser ones, but anyway, it was well known that Arradeane and his wife didn't get on—the servants knew, and they talked, of course—and all of a sudden Arradeane cleared out."

"Left her?" suggested Simmons.

"In the queerest way," answered Swale. "It was the manner of the disappearance that licked everybody—the manner! To start with, this Arradeane, according to my father's story, was known to every soul in the town; he was the sort of man that makes himself popular. Well, as I tell you, he and his wife lived in that corner house, the old Manor House, which I've just shown you, with the brother I spoke of. Now, one morning these three sat down to breakfast. The servant who waited on them, a parlourmaid, said that they were quite friendly and amiable. She heard Arradeane say that he'd got to meet a couple of mining experts at The Bear Hotel at ten o'clock, and she saw him quit the house for that purpose at ten minutes to ten; she also saw him turn the corner of May Day Green in the direction of the Market Place and The Bear. From that minute to this, old man, nobody in Normansholt has ever seen that man again! The parlourmaid was the last person that ever set eyes on him—as he turned that corner! Vanished!"

"Impossible!" said Simmons. "Somebody must have seen him!"

"I tell you he was well known to everybody in this place," asserted Swale. "And this was a much smaller town twenty years ago than it is now, and now we've only seven or eight thousand people in it. Nobody saw Arradeane again: anyway, when the hunt-and-cry was raised for him, not a soul came forward who could say that he or she had set eyes on him that morning. From the moment he turned that corner he vanished utterly—just as if he'd sunk into the earth, or been snatched up into the heavens. Of course, he was not particularly missed for some hours—in fact, not till next day. He didn't go home to lunch on the day of his disappearance, nor to dinner, and he didn't turn up at night. His wife, however, thought little of that; she concluded that he'd gone somewhere out of town with the mining experts he'd spoken of, and was staying the night with them. But when she got no news of him the next day she began to make enquiries. Then things came out. He'd never been to The Bear. The men he was to meet had waited an hour for him and gone away. Nobody, as I say, had seen him. There are three railway stations in this town, small as it is—three different systems, you see, old man. Well, he'd never been seen at any one of them. He hadn't hired a trap; however he'd got away, it had been on foot. People wondered if he'd turned into the castle and fallen amongst the ruins—there are some nasty places. But although they searched here, there and everywhere, and made enquiries all round the neighbourhood, they never heard one syllable about him. Clean gone!"

"Nobody got any theory?" asked Simmons, who was quietly taking it all in and putting the pieces of his puzzle together.

"My father had one—probably a correct one," replied Swale. "It was this. Just round the corner of May Day Green there, where he disappeared from the parlourmaid's view, is what we call a ginnell—"

"What on earth's that?" demanded Simmons. "Ginnell?"

"It's what you call in English an alley, a passage," said Swale, laughing. "A narrow alley between houses—backs of houses. This particular ginnell runs down back of the Market Place to the meadows at the foot of the town. Cross the meadow and you come to the edge of a big wood that extends south-east for a couple of miles. My father's notion was that Arradeane slipped down that ginnell, crossed the meadows, behind the thick hedgerows, took to the woods, and once outside them, went clean away across a very lonely bit of country until he came to a railway line which doesn't touch us at all, and boarded a train at some small station where he wasn't known. See?"

"Good theory!" said Simmons, approvingly. "That, I should say, is what he did. But—his money?"

"Ah!" answered Swale. "That, of course, was looked into. As I said, he and his wife were people of means: they had money, both of 'em. He owed nothing in the town—sort of man who paid spot for everything. He hadn't a banker's account in the town, either: banked at Alsthford, twelve miles away. Well, it was found out, when enquiry was made about his disappearance, that two days before it happened, he drew out pretty nearly every penny of his balance—a big one—from his bank, and also took away a quantity of securities which they kept for him. Gave no reason, either. So—he carried off his money with him. Plant, old man, a clever plant!—wanted to get right away from his wife! That was about it."

"And—she?" asked Simmons. "What became of her?"

"Oh, she stopped here for awhile," replied Swale. "According to my father, after the first bit of enquiry she never made any attempt to find Arradeane. Of course, she may have known something that nobody else knew. But anyway, at the end of three months or so she sold up everything at the Manor House, and she and the brother departed—went to London, it was said. And nobody's ever heard a word of any of 'em since—not a ward.

46

But it's still talked of—of course, it was the clever disappearance that excited people's wonder—smart thing, you know, old man, to slip clear out of a place where every man-jack knew you, unobserved, and without leaving a trace! And, as I say, it would make the beginning of a rare good story—don't know if you've got any talent that way?"

"Haven't tried it yet, anyhow," answered Simmons, drily. "Might have. And all this was—when do you say?"

"Twenty to twenty—three years ago," replied Swale. "Just before I arrived into this vale of tears!"

"There'll be plenty of people in Normansholt who'll remember all three of 'em," suggested Simmons. "Must be."

"Lord bless you, old man, no end!" asserted Swale. "Lots! If the landlord had been in here, he'd have been able to tell the tale better than I've done—he knew Arradeane well enough. He'd have told it first hand—of course, I can only tell what my father used to tell me."

"Oh! well, there are a good many queer things in this world," remarked Simmons. "Hear a lot of 'em in our profession, don't we?"

"I believe you, old man!" said Mr. Swale, solemnly. "We do! Our profession lends itself to that. Ah!—if people only knew what secrets we lawyers know—eh, what? Have another port, old man?"

"Well, just one," responded Simmons. "Business to do in the morning, you know."

He did his business in the morning, had another look round the old town, and then caught the early afternoon train southward. And he went homeward absolutely certain that James Arradeane was James Deane; Mrs. Arradeane, Mrs. Champernowne; and the loafing brother, Mr. Alfred—whose surname seemed to be an unknown quantity.

TURN OF THE LADIES

Simmons' naturally acute brain, sharpened by his legal training, was busy enough as he sped towards home. That he had made a discovery he had no manner of doubt. Certain facts were obvious: he began to classify and label them. The man who disappeared so mysteriously from Normansholt was named James Arradeane, and he was a civil engineer by profession. The man found murdered at Southernstowe was named James Deane; and, according to Miss Pretty's statement, he, too, was a civil engineer. The Mrs. Arradeane of Normansholt had a brother who lived with her and was a loafer: Mrs. Champernowne of Southernstowe also had a brother who lived with her and was a loafer—and looked as if he had never been anything else. As far as Simmons could reckon things up from the story given him by his new friend Swilford Swale, the Mr. and Mrs. Arradeane of Normansholt would now be about the apparent age of Mr. Deane, now deceased, and Mrs. Champernowne, still living. Was James Deane the same person as James Arradeane? Was Mrs. Champernowne Mrs. Arradeane? Simmons was disposed to answer both questions in the affirmative.

From the very beginning of the Southernstowe murder mystery he had kept himself posted in every detail, and now, as he journeyed south, he began to remember things which, at this first hearing, had not seemed very significant, but now, in the light of what he had accidentally discovered at Normansholt, seemed very significant indeed.

He began to consider some of them as he sat in a comfortable corner of the dining car. In his pocket he had a quantity of cuttings, snipped out of the local paper, all relating to the Deane murder. He got them out and turned to the report of the adjourned inquest. Belling of the Chancellor Hotel had given evidence at that. Belling's evidence was very full; the coroner on one hand, and Shelmore (representing Miss Pretty) on the other, had extricated from him everything he could remember about his two conversations with the murdered man: Simmons now went carefully through the questions and replies. And, out of them, one fact was clearly and unmistakably to the surface—when Deane went to the picture house that fatal Monday night, he then saw Mrs. Champernowne. That was proved by the fact that when he went back to the Chancellor he asked Belling who she was, and subsequently talked to Belling about her and her office. Now then, asked Simmons of himself—did Deane, or, as he now believed him to be, Arradeane, recognise in Mrs. Champernowne the wife from whom he had run away at Normansholt some twenty years before?

Simmons thought that this was really what had happened. And if it was, it explained a good deal. It seemed to him that what subsequently took place that night was something like this—Deane, or Arradeane, after retiring for the night, suddenly took it into his head to go and see Mrs. Champernowne there and then; got up, late as it was, and went. And out of that rose more questions than one. Did Deane see Mrs. Champernowne? If so— where, and at what time? What did he want to see her about? That last question sent Simmons back to his newspaper cuttings: again he turned to Belling's evidence. Ah!— there were two or three significant questions and answers.

"What did you tell him about Mrs. Champernowne?"

"Oh—just that she was Mayor of Southernstow, and a very clever woman—very successful business woman, too, just what everybody would have told a stranger about a notable person in the city—gossip!"

"Anything else?"

"Well, I did mention that it was rumoured that Mrs. Champernowne was believed to be engaged, or about to be engaged to be married to Sir Reville Childerstone!"

That last reply seemed to Simmons to be one of great importance—he wondered how it was the coroner and his jury appeared from what followed to have paid no attention to it. But there, of course, they did not know and had no suspicion of what he, Simmons, knew. Knowing what he knew, that Deane was in all probability Arradeane and Mrs. Champernowne Mrs. Arradeane, he now saw a reason for the secret visit to her. Deane probably wanted to let her know that he was still alive, and that she was running the risk of committing bigamy.

But—the murder? Who shot Deane that night? Did Mrs. Champernowne? Did Mr. Alfred? Or were both as innocent as he was, and did Deane, as Mellapont evidently thought, fall into the hands of a gang of loafers, camping out in that sand pit, after the fair that had been held that day? That there were queer and desperate characters likely to be hanging about that night, Simmons knew well enough, and it was a plausible theory to think that Deane had fallen a victim to such folk. But, knowing what he now believed himself to know, it seemed to him that there was ground—solid ground—for suspicion about Mrs. Champernowne. Simmons was an observant young person who watched people and thought about what he saw. He believed that Mrs. Champernowne was a woman of great social ambitions. No doubt she wanted to be Lady Childerstone of Childerstone Park. And, if she was really Mrs. Arradeane and Arradeane's life stood between her and the social status she wanted, and she had the chance of ridding herself of that obstacle, unsuspected—eh?

At this stage of thought, however, Simmons suddenly remembered something which perplexed him. He had been present at several interviews between Miss Pretty and Shelmore; he had heard other conversations between them through the convenient crevice in the partition wall. He remembered now that Shelmore, wanting to be fully posted in all the details of the case, had asked Miss Pretty several questions about Deane. Miss Pretty's answers amounted to this—that Deane, accompanied by his wife, had come to Cornwall some years previously, looking out for an industrial concern in which to invest money; that he had gone into partnership with Miss Pretty's father in a tin mine; that Mr. and Mrs. Pretty were dead, and had left Deane the guardianship of their daughter; that Mrs. Deane was also dead and finally, that, as far as Miss Pretty knew, Deane had no relations and had always told her that he hadn't.

This brought Simmons up against a brick wall—to use his own simile. If Deane was Arradeane who left a Mrs. Arradeane behind him at Normansholt, who was the Mrs. Deane who accompanied him to Camborne?

"That's a stiff one!" mused Simmons. "There may be more in that little matter than I think for! What do the French say—Cherchez la femme! The devil of it is, in this case, where's one to begin the search?"

Then, with a sure instinct, he thought of Miss Pretty. After all, she was the only person handy, who knew anything about Deane's life and doings at Camborne. Some of it she knew of her own knowledge; some of it she would have heard from Deane's own lips. Miss Pretty was the person to approach and he decided to approach her.

In common with most youths of his own age, Simmons spent his evenings out of doors. Sometimes he looked in at the club: sometimes he played billiards at one or other of the various licensed houses: sometimes he dropped into the Chancellor for an hour's gossip with anybody who happened to be there. No one, accordingly, who saw Simmons walk into the Chancellor one evening soon after his return home could have deduced from that that he was after anything particular: they would merely have thought that he was loafing round as most young men, shop assistants, clerks and the like did of an evening. But on this occasion Simmons, instead of walking into the billiard room or the bar parlour, turned into a little snuggery in the middle of the ground floor, through the open door of which he could command a view of the door of the coffee room. No one was in it at that moment, and he sat there alone, smoking a cigarette and sipping a glass of port and watching. He waited until the hotel guests, then dining, began to leave the coffee room; watched until he saw Miss Pretty come out and go up the old oak stair. And then Simmons got hold of the chambermaid, Mary Sanders, who was passing his open door, and beckoned her inside the snuggery.

"I say!" he whispered, with a wink. "I want to see Miss Pretty—business, you know. Just go up and tell her that Mr. Hackdale of Mr. Shelmore's is here and wants a few words with her—there's a dear!"

Mary Sanders went upstairs; vanished in the shadows of the corridor; reappeared and motioned Simmons to advance. She took him to Miss Pretty's private sitting room, showed him in, and closed the door on his bowing form. Miss Pretty, in an easy chair by the fire, a book in her hand, stared at him. She had, of course, seen Simmons many a time at Shelmore's office, and always wondered why his hair was so red, his eyes so closely set together, and his nose so sharp. But realising that his very appearance indicated news, she asked him to sit down. Simmons sat down, set his hat on his knees, laced his bony thin fingers over its cover, and regarded Miss Pretty as a fox might regard a rabbit hole, wondering if he was going to get anything out if it.

"Yes?" said Miss Pretty. "Got a message from Mr. Shelmore?"

"Er—no," replied Simmons. "This is a private call, Miss Pretty—on my own, eh? You'll oblige me by considering anything I've got to say as strictly private and confidential, I'm sure?" He leaned forward, across his hat, and sank his voice. "Miss Pretty!" he continued, "you're very anxious to find out who murdered your guardian?"

"Well?" said Miss Pretty.

"It's a difficult case," said Simmons, certainly. "A very difficult case. A clue is hard to find—I don't think Mellapont's got the ghost of one."

"Have you?" demanded Miss Pretty.

Simmons lifted a hand and stroked his chin thoughtfully.

"I should not be averse to earning the reward you've offered," he answered. "I have my own way to make in the world. Miss Pretty, and the money would help me in the career I've mapped out for myself. Miss Pretty, will you do me the favour to treat this interview as absolutely confidential, and to answer one or two questions that I want to put to you?"

"If my answers—and silence—will help you to find out who killed my guardian, yes!" said Miss Pretty.

"I shouldn't ask for either silence or answers, if I hadn't that object in view," replied Simmons. "Well, Miss Pretty, you no doubt won't understand my questions, but believe me, they're distinct. Now, first—do you remember Mr. Deane's wife, who, I understand, has been dead some years?"

"Remember Mrs. Deane?" exclaimed Miss Pretty. "Why, of course! I knew her all my life, till she died."

"Was she of the same age as Mr. Deane? Or thereabouts?" asked Simmons.

"No—much younger. Ten or twelve years younger."

"Was he very fond of her?"

"Passionately! It was a terrible trouble to him when she died. I remember that well enough," said Miss Pretty. "I was fifteen then."

"You don't remember them coming to your part of the country?" asked Simmons.

"Oh, dear no! But I've heard my mother—and father—talk about it. Mrs. Deane was a bride. They'd just been married."

"Could you tell me the exact date of their coming to Camborne, Miss Pretty?—the year, at any rate?"

"I could—by referring to my business books, at home."

"One more question, then, Miss Pretty. Do you know what Mrs. Deane's name was, before her marriage?"

"I do!" replied Miss Pretty, promptly. "Mrs. Deane was a great reader and had a lot of books, chiefly poetry. When she died, Mr. Deane gave them to me. I have one of them here, which I slipped in my bag when I left home. There's the name—on the fly—leaf."

She picked up a slim, evidently well—thumbed volume from amongst a pile of books and magazines on the table at her side and passed it across to her visitor. And Simmons looked—and committed a name to memory.

"Nora Le Geyt," he said, musingly. "Um—sounds like an actress's name, that, Miss Pretty."

"Clever of you!" remarked Miss Pretty. "Mrs. Deane had been an actress! But—beyond her husband—nobody in our part knew that but me. She was very fond of me when I was a little girl, and I used to spend a lot of time at their house, which was close by ours. Mrs. Deane used to recite to me sometimes, and when I got older I began to wonder about her. And once, not so very long before she died—she died suddenly—I said to her one day that I thought she must have been an actress at some time or other. And then she told me that she had been on the stage before she married Mr. Deane, but she didn't want anybody about there to know of it, because Cornish people are very strait—laced, and regard the theatre as a haunt of the devil. But pray what's all this got to do with my guardian's murder?"

Simmons raised a deprecating hand. "You must excuse me, Miss Pretty!" he said, beseechingly. "We lawyers are forced to cultivate—and to insist on—secrecy. Be patient with me, Miss Pretty! I'll not attempt to conceal from you that I've a motive—vague, shapeless as yet, but undeniably there—about Mr. Deane's sad fate, and I'll work at it—yes, I'll work at it, I assure you!"

"You've something worth working for!" observed Miss Pretty, in her driest manner. "You put your hands on the man who killed my guardian and get him arrested and hanged, and there'll be three thousand pounds cash for you, Mr. Simmons. And you don't pick that up every day!"

Simmons was well aware of that, so he went away from Miss Pretty more than ever resolved to get at the bottom of the mystery. He cudgelled his brains night and day to hit on fresh plans and new manoeuvres. And on the next Sunday evening he got a brilliant idea. Like most young men in Southernstowe Simmons regarded church attendance as an excellent means of seeing the young women of the place and of forming the acquaintance of attractive ones. Happening on this particular Sunday evening to drop in at St. Gregory's where the best music in Southernstowe was to be heard, he noticed, in an adjacent seat, Mrs. Champernowne's demure parlourmaid, Jane Pratt, and remembered that in other days (once he had attended an elementary school), Jane had been one of his fellow pupils. Jane, or Jennie, as Simmons knew her, was not so pretty as she was demure, and Simmons had made up his mind to lay siege to her long before the service came to an end. He waylaid her at the porch, and after a little badinage in the churchyard suggested that he should take her for a walk, and, as Miss Pratt had no other young man in hand just then, and as Mr. Simmons was, if not a full fledged lawyer, at heart a half fledged one, and on Sundays ore a black tailed coat, a silk hat, and lemon—coloured kid gloves, she consented. Under the light of a waning moon, and in the privacy of a quiet lane that led to Ashenhurst House, Mr. Simmons and Miss Pratt became pleasantly confidential, and got on very well together—so much so that by the end of their walk they were arm-in-arm. But suddenly Miss Pratt screamed, shrinking closer to her escort's side. She pointed at a fringe of bushes and stunted trees.

"Oh! I never noticed where we were going!" she said. "That's the sand pit!—Where the murdered man was found!"

"All right!" answered Mr. Simmons, with a manly arm round Miss Pratt's slender waist. "No need to fear ghosts or anything else, when I'm about. Queer business that, wasn't it? And so near your house, what?"

"Yes," said Miss Pratt, recovering her usual equanimity. "Wasn't it? You know—I couldn't tell you if you weren't a lawyer, but I know lawyers never let out secrets—I've wondered a good deal about something I saw that Monday night. I saw Mrs. Champernowne talking to a man in our grounds at twelve o'clock! Fact! I thought it was Sir Reville Childerstone, bringing her home, but it wasn't. It was a stranger, and I've wondered—"

Simmons drew Miss Pratt to a full stop. A long and whispered conversation took place between them. It ended by his telling Miss Pratt that "Mum was the word—mum"—and they parted with a mutual understanding. Simmons went homeward something more than elated; from what he had heard he was now dead certain that Deane and Mrs. Champernowne had met on the night of the murder.

Chapter

THE GOLD WATCH

Simmons went home that night fully convinced that the secret of Deane's murder rested with Mrs. Champernowne. He was already sure beyond doubt that Deane was Arradeane, once of Normansholt; that Mrs. Champernowne was Mrs. Arradeane; that Mr. Alfred was the loafing, idle brother. There were all sorts of surmises arising out of this. Perhaps Mrs. Champernowne shot Deane with her own hand: it was not at all unlikely. Perhaps Mr. Alfred shot him—that was less likely, but still possible. Perhaps some camper out, a derelict from the fair, shot him and robbed him—to Simmons that was a very insignificant detail in comparison with the fact that, so nearly as he could reckon things up, Arradeane had seen and recognised his wife at the picture house, and had subsequently had an interview with her in her own garden. Husband and wife had met!— that was a fact. As to what happened after their meeting, Simmons was yet in the dark, though he meant to emerge into the light. But already he had another surmise, and it grew with every hour—grew until it became an obsession. Did his brother, John Hackdale, know anything of Mrs. Champernowne's secret? Was he privy to the fact that the murdered man had met Mrs. Champernowne on the night of his death? In short, was John conversant with the things that had gone on behind the rail, which so far neither policeman nor civilians had managed to penetrate?

Simmons had a name for everything, and he had a reason for suspecting his brother. In spite of his youth he was a hardened cynic. He was a sneering sceptic about altruism: nobody in his opinion ever did anything for nothing; whoever did was a fool. Whenever you saw a man suddenly advanced in station and material prosperity, said Simmons in his self communings, you could be absolutely certain that it had been in somebody's interest to advance him. And he put a question—what he called a very nasty question—to himself: Why, suddenly, without preface, on the spur of a moment, as it were, did Mrs. Champernowne lift John from an under—managership at six pounds a week to a position which, he had already learnt, was to be worth a very big salary? What was the consideration, the inducement, the quid pro quo—or quo pro quid? It was all damn rot, said Simmons, to be asked to believe that John's abilities and John's cleverness as a business man had brought about this desirable preferment: damn rot to be invited to agree to the proposition that John was the one man for the job. Simmons knew enough of the world to know that there were scores of men, hundreds of men, quite as well, if not far better fitted than John for the sort of manager-secretary to the new company who would have been glad, joyful, eager to fill it for two thirds the salary that John was to have. No!—tell all that to the marines! He knew better than to believe it. There were reasons for this sudden advancement—wasn't it significant that it had been made the very day after the discovery of Deane's dead body? John knew something! and the new post, the handsome salary, were in the nature of bribes to keep his mouth shut. But what did he know?

"That's for me to find out!" muttered Simmons as he put his key in the latch of his boarding house door. "My interest! Look after number one, Sim, old man!—number one is the closest friend you've got!"

He had been learning that precious truth from John all his life, and it had become a gospel to him: it was indeed his whole creed. He felt no gratitude to John for feeding him, clothing him, educating him, starting him in life: John had done all that, said Simmons, in his own self interest; it would never have done for Southernstowe people to be able to say that John Hackdale, smart and pushing as he was, allowed his younger brother to go about with holes in his trousers, unschooled, unlaunched in life—John knew that nothing pays so well as keeping up appearances. So at any rate argued Simmons, and he felt no compunction in suspecting John of some sort of complicity in this Arradeane-Champernowne mystery, nor in beginning to watch him closely. There was a goal in front of Simmons through which he meant to kick fortune's football, and hanging on its cross-bar was a big placard, labelled three thousand pounds.

But Simmons would not have been so comfortable in his own mind as he was after that Sunday evening stroll with Mrs. Champernowne's demure parlourmaid if he had known that within twenty miles of him there was another sly and crafty dog on the same trail as himself. Bartlett! That worthy, after reading and memorising the bill which Pemberton wanted him to distribute, had began to think rapidly. He kept his promise to John Hackdale, and went away from Southernstowe by the last train, but before that train reached Portsmouth, a short stage of eighteen miles, he had decided that he was neither going to New York nor to Southampton—let Southampton and New York go to—anywhere! For Bartlett, loafer and ne'er-do-well as he had been of late years, had, in his time, been an unusually sharp and shrewd man, and a recent devotion to rum had not quite impaired his greatness. He saw through things now. There was a secret—and he had some sort of a key to it. He had thought at first that John Hackdale had requested his silence so that no scandal or questioning should occur to vex Mrs. Champernowne, Mayor of Southernstowe. But now he saw that there was more. He was being hurried out of the way—bribed to get out of the way. A hundred and fifty cash—another hundred and fifty to come!—very good, but... not enough! By no means enough... especially in view of that reward bill. America?—no! Portsmouth, for the time being, and a snug lodging, where he could lie low and mature his plans—either for blackmailing Mrs. Champernowne or doing something towards getting Miss Pretty's money.

Bartlett stopped at a cheap hotel that night, and waking early next morning reviewed the situation and made several resolutions, largely consequent upon the fact that he had a hundred and fifty pounds in his pocket. He would take a modest lodging in Portsmouth. He would buy himself a new suit of clothes, new ties, new foot—wear. He would live quietly and be careful about his rum. He would nurse his brain and sharpen his wits. And he would get and study the Southernstowe local papers and any other newspapers in which there were particulars of the Sand Pit Murder, as the Deane affair had come to be called, and prime himself for a first frontal attack—the thing was to be armed with circumstance. Of one thing he was resolved—he was going to make money out of this, whether he got it from Miss Pretty or from Mrs. Champernowne. The money already in his pocket came from Mrs. Champernowne, of course!—not from John Hackdale. And—to use a hackneyed phrase, he muttered with a cynical laugh—there was plenty more where it came from. Blackmail money, or reward money, it was all one.

Bartlett's will power was still sufficiently strong to enable him to carry out his resolutions. He found a quiet and comfortable lodging in Portsea, in the cottage of a widow woman; he replenished his wardrobe; he cut down his rum to a reasonable allowance; his landlady knew him for a quiet, well behaved man who took his meals at the proper times, walked out a good deal, paid his bill promptly every Saturday morning at breakfast, and bought and read a multitude of newspapers. He called himself Barton there, and said he'd recently come into a little money after a life of hard work, and for a time wanted a bit of quietude. Quiet enough he was, reading his papers and snipping paragraphs out of them which he stored away in his old pocket—book. Those paragraphs were all about the Deane murder and the inquest, and there was nothing now in them, nothing much unknown to their reader and preserver. But one night, opening the

Portsmouth evening paper after his tea—supper, Bartlett read of the new offer made by Miss Pretty, and his mouth watered more than ever. Three thousand pounds! He would have handed Mrs. Champernowne over to rack, rope, knife and fire for one half of it, cash down.

Bartlett went out for his usual morning walk next day, to think things over. Should he return to Southernstowe and tell Miss Pretty what he really knew? Supposing she and her legal adviser and the police followed up the slight clue which he could give her, would he get the reward? Anyway, there was one thing he could get and at once—the two thousand pounds offered to anybody who saw Deane on the night of the murder. He saw Deane—he, Bartlett! But suddenly, and as his heart warmed at the thought of the money, he turned cold—supposing that Miss Pretty insisted on his giving proof that he saw Deane? It was easy enough for him to affirm that he saw Deane, but how was he going to prove that he did? Well, after all, it might be some proof if he also proved that John Hackdale paid him money, a lot of money, to keep a quiet tongue and go right away—but there again, perhaps Hackdale would deny that he had ever done such a thing—might indeed say that what had been done for him had been done by Mrs. Champernowne out of charity to a broken—down Southernstowe man to help him to a new start. Perhaps the best thing to do would be to go to Mrs. Champernowne at once and blackmail her, giving her the option of paying him rather than that he should resort to Miss Pretty. But—he hesitated. Not so very long before this episode, Bartlett had been in slight trouble with the Southernstowe police, and had had to appear before the magistrates, Mrs. Champernowne, mayor, presiding. He remembered the lady's stern, uncompromising manner—and he shrank from the idea of meeting her again. No! but to go to Miss Pretty, and tell what he knew. If only he had more to tell!

Bartlett's constitutional took him, mechanically, to his usual house of call—a tavern which stood in a busy thoroughfare. He supplied himself with a glass of his favourite drink, and, a tumbler in hand, stood at the bow window of the bar parlour, overlooking the crowded street and meditating anew on his plans and perplexities. And suddenly he started at sight of two people whom he, as a Southernstowe man, knew well enough. He looked and looked—and began to wonder.

The two people were a man and a woman—Kight, the night porter of the Chancellor Hotel, and Mary Sanders, the chambermaid. They were both what Bartlett called dressed up, in their best clothes, and evidently were out for the day, pleasuring. But Bartlett's sharp eyes, watching their movements across the street, saw that they were looking for something. They came along the pavement, staring at the various shops—suddenly they paused before a watchmakers and jeweller's establishment. As soon as they caught sight of it they backed away and began what appeared to be an anxious debate, which was finally ended by Mary Sanders leaving Kight and going into the jeweller's shop. She was in there some time; Kight hung about. After a while she came out and rejoined her companion; another debate followed, in the course of which Kight seemed to be expressing disapproval of something said to him; eventually, evidently on her persuasion, he went back to the shop with her; the two remained there ten minutes longer; they then came out and went away down the street together. And Bartlett, swallowing what was left of his rum, slipped out and followed them at a safe distance.

Kight and his companion walked slowly along until they came to a bank. The woman entered, Kight hung about outside. He was not kept waiting long; Mary Sanders came out again, stuffing into her handbag what looked to Bartlett like a bundle of notes. She nodded in a satisfied, re-assured sort of fashion at Kight; together they went away in the direction of the sea front, where the pleasure part of the town is. And Bartlett let them go, and turned back towards his tavern, pondering.

The comparative temperance to which Bartlett had forced himself since his coming to Portsmouth had sharpened his naturally acute senses. He was thinking hard and shrewdly now. He had read and re-read the whole thing by heart, and he was now going over the evidence given by the night porter and the chambermaid, with special recollection of what she said about seeing Deane's money and jewellery lying on the dressing table when she took him his hot milk on the evening of the murder. Now supposing... supposing...

After a few minutes quick thought, Bartlett came to a halt. He stood for a moment, appraising himself. He was decently, even well dressed. He knew that he looked eminently respectable. His nose had been inclined to redness, and his eyes to a bloodshot state when he left Southernstowe; those signs of indulgence had vanished. He knew himself, as having once been in a better position, to have a good manner and a good address; he had the comfortable consciousness of having had a superior education. And suddenly, confident of his power to play a part, he strode forward and walked boldly into the jeweller's shop which Kight and Mary Sanders had left not twenty minutes before. The jeweller, a mild, spectacled individual, stood behind his counter, examining some of his goods; further away an assistant was attending to a customer.

Bartlett went up to the principal.

"Can I have a word with you—in private?" he asked musingly.

The jeweller looked a little surprised, but he at once stepped along the counter, and opening a door at the rear of the shop, motioned his visitor to enter. Bartlett entered and gave him a look which was intended to suggest his desire for a confidential talk.

"Yes?" said the jeweller.

"The fact is," answered Bartlett, "I'm a private enquiry agent—on a very important and delicate job. You had a young woman in here just now whom I knew: I've got my eye on her. Now, between you and me, what did she want?"

The jeweller had taken stock of Bartlett. Certainly, he looked the sort of man that you would expect a private enquiry agent to be: there was that air about him. "I hope there's nothing wrong," he replied, anxiously. "If you want to know, the young woman came to sell a watch."

"A gold watch?—valuable?" suggested Bartlett readily.

"It was a gold watch, certainly," answered the jeweller. "And—yes, valuable. She told me it had recently been left to her—a legacy, you know, by an uncle. But she said that being a working woman, she'd rather have its worth than the watch itself, and she asked me to buy it."

"And—you bought?" asked Bartlett.

"I did! I gave her a thoroughly good price, too. Fifty-five pounds," replied the jeweller. "An open cheque. If there's anything wrong."

"Too late to stop your cheque," interrupted Bartlett. "I followed them to the bank. She'd a man with her—"

"I know—her husband—he came in," remarked the jeweller. "But—"

"No more her husband than I am!" said Bartlett. "Well—I'm afraid that watch is a stolen one. But I can settle that point for you within twenty-four hours. And if it belongs to the person I feel sure it does belong to, you won't be the loser. I'll guarantee that. Now—not a word to anyone till you see me about this time tomorrow."

The jeweller looked relieved. But he was obviously puzzled.

"If you suspected these people, why didn't you stop them?" he asked. "Perhaps they'll—"

Bartlett tapped him on the arm.

"That'll come after I've been here again," he said, with a wink. "I can put my hand on both of 'em at an hour's notice. They haven't the ghost of a notion that I'm on this track. Take care of the watch till you see me at this time tomorrow."

Then he went away and back to his lodging and his dinner, and that over he sat down and wrote a carefully worded letter to Miss Cynthia Pretty, at the Chancellor Hotel, Southernstowe, signing it in his assumed name of Barton. In it he said that he had an important communication to make to her in regard to the late tragedy, and would she meet him at Portsmouth Town station at ten-thirty next morning, and, in the meantime, treat his letter as being absolutely private and confidential?

Miss Pretty met him. She was eager and curious. Bartlett sized her up in two minutes, and knew that she would be a suitable gold mine to him. Suave and respectful, he gave her a brief account of yesterday's episode and conducted her to the jeweller's shop. In the little parlour the jeweller produced his purchase. Miss Pretty gave one look at it and turned pale.

"Good heavens!" she said, in a hushed voice. "Yes!—without doubt, that's my guardian's watch!"

Bartlett felt himself rising to great heights in the profession to which he had volunteered twenty—four hours previously. He turned to Miss Pretty with a warning and solemn air.

"Don't make any mistake, miss!" he said. "Be certain! After all, gold watches are all very much alike. You're sure this is the late Mr. Deane's watch?"

"As certain as I am that I'm standing here!" assured Miss Pretty. "I ought to be!—I've seen it hundreds of times ever since I was a little girl. That watch belonged to my late guardian. And you say," she continued, turning to the jeweller, "that it was sold to you yesterday by Mary Sanders, chambermaid at the Chancellor Hotel, Southernstowe? Then—"

"I didn't know the woman's name, madam," interrupted the jeweller. "She appeared to be a thoroughly respectable young person, and told me what I regarded as a thoroughly satisfactory story. But, of course, if you recognise the watch—"

"Oh, there's no doubt about the watch!" said Miss Pretty, confidently. "A good many people beside myself could identify it. What's to be done?" she asked, turning to Bartlett. "The police?"

"Certainly, miss!" replied Bartlett. "The police, of course—at Southernstowe. Superintendent Mellapont." He spoke with readiness and confidence, having already satisfied himself on the way from the station that Miss Pretty would stand to her word and pay him the thousand pounds reward for the discovery of the watch. "We must go there at once. You can make it convenient to go with me?" he went on, turning to the jeweller. "And, of course, you'll bring the watch with you."

The jeweller began to suggest inconvenience and to murmur his hopes that he wouldn't be the loser by all this. But Bartlett waved an authoritative hand.

"I told you yesterday that you shouldn't lose by the transaction," he said. "This lady will see to that—fifty pounds is nothing to her in comparison to the relief of getting a clue to her guardian's assailants. Of course you must come with us to Southernstowe you'll have to identify the young woman."

"Needs must!" responded the jeweller, and began to give instructions to his assistant. "I suppose there'll be a police court case?" he asked, as he put the watch in his pocket, and picked up his hat and overcoat. "That'll mean mere waste of time—"

"No waste of time, sir, in serving the cause of justice," observed Bartlett in his best manner. "It's a citizen's duty, that, sir, and this'll be not only a police court but an assize court affair!"

The jeweller muttered something which appeared to indicate his regret that Mary Sanders had not taken her wares elsewhere, but he accompanied Bartlett and Miss Pretty to the station and journeyed with them to Southernstowe. Bartlett had never been back to the little town since his hurried departure at John Hackdale's request. He had slunk away that night, reaching the station by back lanes and obscure alleys, but now he marched boldly up the street, conscious that many people who saw and recognised him were wondering at his new clothes, well-to-do appearance, and companionship with Miss Pretty. And in the very centre of the town, not thirty yards away from the police station, John Hackdale came suddenly out of a bank, and full upon Bartlett, Miss Pretty, and the jeweller. He stopped dead and seized Bartlett's arm.

"You?" he exclaimed. "Here? What're you—"

Bartlett shook his arm free and moved on.

"Can't attend to you at present, Mister Hackdale!" he said, with a mixture of condescension and effrontery. "Important business—give you a minute or two later on."

He marched forward, motioning his companions to follow. Hackdale, surprised out of his wits, stood open-mouthed, staring after him and them. He stared until he saw all three vanish under the portico of the City Hall and enter the police station: and then he drew a long breath.

"What the devil does that mean!" he said, half aloud. "Bartlett—who ought to be in New York!—with Miss Pretty and a stranger? And—going into the police station? What infernal tricks is he up to? Not gone!—after all! Is he going to—!"

Just then Simmons came up, a parcel of red-taped legal-looking documents in one hand. His brother seized him by the shoulder.

"Sim!" he exclaimed. "Have—have you heard anything at Shelmore's about this Deane affair? Has Miss Pretty been there—this morning—recently?"

"Not for some days," answered Simmons, quick to notice his brother's agitation. "No—we've heard nothing. What about Miss Pretty?"

John Hackdale was still staring at the portico under which the strangely assorted trio had disappeared. He nodded at it.

"Miss Pretty, a strange man, and that good-for-nothing Bartlett have just passed me and gone into the police station!" he said. "Something's up! But—"

"Bartlett?" interrupted Simmons, with a start. "Jim Bartlett. Ah!—somebody was saying last night—"

"Saying what?" snapped John. "What?"

"Oh, only that Bartlett hadn't been seen about lately," continued Simmons. "Bartlett, eh? And with Miss Pretty and a stranger? H'm!—did the stranger look like—say, a detective?"

John Hackdale made no reply. He was still staring at the portico, and Simmons was quick to see that he was upset and nervous. Suddenly he turned on Simmons.

"Look here, Sim!" he said, rapidly. "Shelmore is Miss Pretty's solicitor. Run and tell him what I've told you, and get him to come round to the police station: they'll be there with Mellapont. Shelmore'll find out what they're there for, and he'll tell you. Then, you can tell me—at dinner—time. Hurry up, Sim!"

Simmons nodded and went away towards Shelmore's office, thinking. What made John so palpably anxious to find out why Miss Pretty and Bartlett, accompanied by a strange man, had gone to the police? Why did John look frightened? What did John know about Bartlett—or, more to the point, did Bartlett know anything about John? Sly, crafty, plausible beggar, Bartlett, at any time, and damned sharp when he wasn't in rum, said Simmons to himself, as he climbed Shelmore's stair—if Bartlett had gone to Mellapont in company with Miss Pretty, then, by George! Bartlett knew something—and what might it be? In order to find that out, he told Shelmore of what had just been reported to him. To his surprise Shelmore remained fixed in his chair and showed no signs of getting out of it.

"No concern of ours, Hackdale," he said brusquely. "Have you got those deeds from Parmiter & Pulsford?"

Simmons was taken aback. Intensely inquisitive and curious himself, he found it impossible to understand anybody else being otherwise. But Shelmore was evidently unconcerned, and he had to produce his deeds and what was more, to pore over them for the rest of the morning—wondering, all the time, what was going on at the police station, and why his brother John had been so anxious to know.

If either John Hackdale or his younger brother had been able to see through brick walls into the superintendent's private room, they would have seen Mellapont at his desk listening in silence to the story which Bartlett, as spokesman, told in full, with due elaboration of his own part in it. Mellapont knew Bartlett—had known him as a broken man, a loafer, a drinker, a down-at-heels and out-at-elbow man, for two years, ever since he himself came to the town, and all the time Bartlett was talking he was wondering at this change in him—there he was, highly respectable, improved in looks, confident, self-assured, and revealing considerable powers—how, asked Mellapont to himself, had this come about, and (more important still) where had Bartlett got the funds from which he had evidently expended on his wardrobe? But he kept this to himself; all he asked of Bartlett when that worthy had made an end of his extraordinary statement was one personal question.

"Are you living in Portsmouth now?"

"Been living there for the last two or three weeks, Mr. Superintendent," replied Bartlett, promptly. "I came into a little money, sir—and left—er, the old surroundings."

There was a sort of suggestion in his tone that this was a new Bartlett, and not the old ne'er-do-well, and Mellapont nodded and glanced at the gold watch, which had been produced and now lay on his desk.

"I suppose there's no doubt whatever, Miss Pretty, that this is the watch that belonged to Mr. Deane?" he asked.

"None!" replied Miss Pretty.

"Wearing it when he came here?" suggested Mellapont.

"He was wearing it when he left Camborne!" said Miss Pretty. "The last time I saw it was at Bristol. Mr. Deane and I left Camborne together. We stayed a day or two at Exeter and then went on to Bristol. We stayed there three days, looking round; then I went to stay with a friend at Bath, and Mr. Deane went forward, alone, to the Midlands and the North. I last saw that watch at the hotel at Bristol—and he took it out at breakfast and corrected it to railway time. Of course, it's the watch!"

"You can identify the young woman who sold it to you?" asked Mellapont, turning to the jeweller. "To be sure!—well, I'll have to bring her and this man here. If you then will wait—"

He rose from his desk with the air of a man who faces a more than ordinarily important task—and, again bidding his visitors remain there until he came back, went out. The industrial strike in a far—away county which had deprived him of his regular forces was now over, and all his men were back, and the special constables relieved of their duties. Mellapont detected an old, experienced plain clothes man, one Nicholson, and giving him a brief outline of what he had just heard, set out for the Chancellor Hotel. He and Nicholson entered by the door at the back of the courtyard, and the first person they saw was Belling, talking just then to a tradesman at the entrance to his private parlour. He caught Mellapont's eye, understood the look in it, dismissed the tradesman and beckoned the two policeman into privacy.

"Here's a development at last, Belling," said Mellapont, when the door was closed. "Now listen! You remember that Deane had valuables on him when he was last seen here—diamond pin, diamond ring, gold watch? Of course!—well, the watch was sold to a Portsmouth jeweller, yesterday! By whom do you think?"

"Not—not by anybody here?" asked Belling, nervously.

"Here, right enough," answered Mellapont. "That chambermaid of yours, Mary Sanders!"

Belling stared and stared. "You don't say!" he exclaimed. "By—her?"

"Fact!" said Mellapont. "And she had with her, at the time, another servant of yours—Kight!"

Belling stared harder than ever.

"God bless me!" he murmured. "You don't mean it!"

"That, too, is a fact." replied Mellapont. "Now then, Belling, where are they? For—I want 'em!"

"The girl will be at her work—first floor," answered Belling; "Kight'll be asleep, I suppose, in his room. I can have him fetched down. She can be here at once. Shall I send for her?"

"Kight first," said Mellapont. "Get him here—then, so soon as he is here, fetch her in."

Belling went away troubled and perplexed, and the two policemen sat down and waited. Within ten minutes the landlord came back with Kight who was obviously half asleep, and had dressed hurriedly. Mellapont nodded to him.

"Morning, Kight," he said, affably. "I just wanted to have a word or two with you about that Deane affair. If you please, Mr. Belling," he went on, with a glance at the landlord. "Now!"

Belling took the hint and again left the room. But this time he was back again at once, ushering in the chambermaid. She entered unsuspectingly, but as soon as she caught sight of the night porter she turned pale and gasped, and Kight seeing her, just as suddenly swore under his breath.

"Just so!" said Mellapont. "But that'll do no good, Kight! Now then, we may be well out with it. Mary Sanders, you sold a gold watch for fifty pounds to a Portsmouth jeweller yesterday morning, and you, Kight, were with her—you waited outside the shop while she completed the transaction, and you went with her to the bank on which the jeweller had given her an open bearer cheque. Now, that watch has been identified as the watch that Mr. Deane, the murdered man, was wearing. What have you both got to say about it?"

He looked from one to the other, but his eyes rested finally on the chambermaid. She was red and white by turns now, and trembling all over. Her lips parted—but Kight got in a word before she could speak.

"Say nothing!" he growled. "Nothing! Keep your mouth shut. They'll get nothing out of me!"

"Very well," remarked Mellapont. "Then you'll both come with me to the police station. No!—you're not going out of the room to get other clothes, nor anything else! It's only a step down the street from your back entrance, and you'll come as you are—anything you want can be sent to you afterwards. Come on—now—no nonsense!"

Miss Pretty and her companions, waiting in the superintendent's room, at last heard the tread of feet, and presently saw the night porter, scowling and frightened, ushered in. At sight of the jeweller, Mary Sanders showed signs of collapsing. But she fumed on Kight.

"I told you how it would be!" she burst out. "I knew it would go wrong. Why not tell him and her—"

"Hold your tongue!" interrupted Kight angrily. "Let 'em prove anything they have against us!—that's their job. What do you charge us with?" he went on scowling at Mellapont. "Murder, I reckon! Likely thing, isn't it?"

"I shall charge you with being in unlawful possession of that article, my lad, to start with," replied Mellapont, pointing to the gold watch. "We'll see about the rest of it, later on."

"Going to lock us up, I suppose?" sneered Kight. "All right, mister!—but I reckon there's justice for us as for everybody!"

"You'll get plenty of justice, my lad, before you've done with it," retorted Mellapont. "So you'll neither of you think better of things and say a word or two? All right, then… "

When Kight and the chambermaid had been safely bestowed under lock and key, and Mellapont had given Bartlett, Miss Pretty, and the jeweller strict injunctions about appearing before the magistrates next morning, the last mentioned then went away. Bartlett and the jeweller had a short interview with Miss Pretty in her private sitting room at the hotel, and left it in high satisfaction with themselves; the jeweller, indeed, suggested to Bartlett that they should celebrate the morning's work in the bar parlour over a bottle of the best, but Bartlett firmly refused, and hurried him away to the station by a quiet by—lane. Bartlett, from Miss Pretty's window, had seen John Hackdale hanging about—in wait for him. But Bartlett had no wish to meet John Hackdale at present, and he avoided him and went off to Portsmouth. And John, anxious, perturbed, and wondering, went home to dinner. To him, eventually, came Simmons: he turned eagerly as Simmons walked in, and the younger brother could not fail to see the eagerness. But Simmons had heard nothing up to then, and by that time was as inquisitive about the whole thing as John was. The two walked back to the centre of the city together after dinner, and as they neared the City Hall, became aware of a crowd outside it. A labouring man of whom John asked information turned on him wonderingly.

"Ain't you heard, Mr. Hackdale?" he answered. "It's all over the town! They've collared Charlie Kight and Polly Sanders for the murder of that stranger gentleman! They're locked up in there—both!"

13

STILL OPEN

Simmons turned sharply on his brother as the labouring man let out his last words. He saw John start: he saw a curious look cross his face. It seemed to Simmons to be a compound of relief and perplexity—but as they moved away from the wood the perplexity appeared to gain the upper hand.

"Kight and Mary Sanders!" said John, in a hushed voice. "Night porter and chambermaid? How could they murder him?—they'd be in the hotel all night! And—he was murdered out of the hotel."

"How do you know that?" asked Simmons, with something very like a sneer. "Found in the sand pit, yes!—but the body might have been carried there. However, we shall hear more tomorrow—they'll be brought up before the magistrates in the morning."

"Tomorrow!" exclaimed John. He was impatient, being still uneasy and perturbed about the re-appearance of Bartlett. "Look here!" he went on. "You know all the police, Sim—couldn't you get hold of a bit of information this afternoon?"

"Don't know 'em as well as you do!" retorted Simmons. "You've been a special constable. Try Mellapont. But in my opinion they'll tell nothing—yet."

John Hackdale had no desire to try Mellapont—he had his own reasons for not showing any particular interest in the new development. But he spent an uneasy afternoon and unquiet night wondering what share Bartlett had in all this, and if Bartlett was going to let out that he'd received a hundred and fifty pounds from him to go away and keep his mouth shut. And at ten o'clock next morning he was at the magistrates' court, one of a crowd eager and anxious to hear the charges against Kight and the chambermaid.

There was something of a sensation and a disappointment in Court when the two prisoners were charged, not with the murder of James Deane, but with being in unlawful possession of certain property of his—to wit, a gold watch. But John Hackdale felt neither disappointment nor surprise: he had been reckoning up things and facts, and it seemed to him impossible that this capital charge could be brought against Kight and Mary Sanders. There were, however, two matters which did surprise him—the first, that Mrs. Champernowne was not on the bench of magistrates, though he knew her to be in town; the second, that Bartlett, though present in court, was not called upon to give any evidence. The evidence, indeed, was little more than formal—Hackdale got it into his head that Mellapont, for some purpose of his own, was keeping something back. All that Mellapont did was to outline the case against his prisoners in brief fashion; to call the jeweller to prove that they offered him the watch for purchase and that he bought it; and to put Miss Pretty into the witness box to swear that the watch was certainly that belonging to her late guardian. All this over, he asked for an adjournment for a week, remarking that a good deal of the late Mr. Deane's property was still missing, and that so far the accused persons had refused to make any statement.

But at this point the first sensation of the day came. Before the presiding magistrate could reply to Mellapont's application Kight suddenly turned to his companion and whispered to her. She nodded vigorously as if in emphatic approval of whatever he had said, and Kight looked down at the bench, pointing at the same time to the table at which several local solicitors were sitting.

"We want a lawyer!" he said boldly. "We want Mr. Shelmore!—to talk to him."

The magistrate looked at Mellapont, who was still on his legs. And Mellapont, after a questioning glance at the dock, nodded—sat down.

"W e had better adjourn for half-an-hour, to give Mr. Shelmore an opportunity of talking to the defendants," said the magistrate. He glanced at the solicitor's table. "That is," he added, "if Mr. Shelmore is disposed."

"We've plenty of money to pay Mr. Shelmore," said Kight, still bold and apparently unabashed. "We want him and no other."

Shelmore, who disliked criminal practice, and had only gone to the Court at the request of Miss Pretty, looked anything but pleased at his direct request, but he rose, went over to the dock, and held a whispered consultation with Kight, at the end of which he turned to the bench and asked to be allowed to see the prisoners in an adjacent writing room. Thither he presently retired with them and a couple of policemen: the magistrates left their chairs, and disappeared behind the curtains, and the crowded court, left to itself, began to speculate on what it was going to hear next. For it was very evident that Kight and Mary Sanders were going to tell—something.

Half-an-hour went by. Three men amongst the audience were debating and speculating in the secret chambers of their own minds on the probabilities of the forthcoming revelation. How would it affect himself and Mrs. Champernowne, wondered John Hackdale. Should he learn anything by which he might profit, wondered Simmons. Were the prisoners going to tell anything that would interfere with his plan of campaign, wondered Bartlett. All these turned furtive glances on Shelmore as at last he came back into Court—and learned nothing from what they saw: Shelmore was apparently unmoved.

The prisoners returned to the dock; the magistrates filed in again, and Shelmore rose to his feet at the solicitors' table and faced them.

"I have now had the opportunity of consulting with the two defendants," he said, in quiet level tones, "and I may as well tell your worships that on my advice they will withdraw their previous plea, and will now plead guilty to the charge of being in unlawful possession of the gold watch which, they fully admit, was the property of the late James Deane. Also they have authorised me to put before your worships a full and, as they allege, a completely truthful account of the way in which they became possessed of this watch, and of some other valuables, the present whereabouts of which they have informed me. In short, your worships, the defendants desire to make a clean breast of everything; they also desire to make reparation. The fifty pounds obtained by the sale of the watch is still untouched and will be given up: the other valuables will also be given up. I put all this before your worships, because as it will be necessary for you, the prisoners being willing to plead guilty, to commit them to the Quarter Sessions for sentence, I intend, in view of their wish to repair what harm thecy have done, to apply to you for bail."

Mellapont rose quickly from his seat.

"I shall oppose any application for bail, your worship ," he said. "There may be a graver charge arising out of this. I shall strongly oppose any such application!"

"I have no knowledge of what is in Superintendent Mellapont's mind," remarked Shelmore. "'I shall certainly make my application when I have finished I what I am going to say. Your lordships!—I propose, at the wish of both defendants, to tell you the full story as to their acquisition and possession of these valuables. They are both quite aware that they have done wrong in yielding to a sudden temptation, and they have nothing to offer in extenuation, though each has a right—which can be exercised afterwards—of bringing forward evidence as to previous good character. Now as to the factor—it will be within the recollection of your worships—it is indeed common knowledge—that very recently a Mr. James Deane, of Camborne, in Cornwall, came to stay at the Chancellor

Hotel in Southernstowe; that he left the hotel, mysteriously, about midnight, on the night of his arrival; and that his dead body was discovered, two days later, in a disused sand pit on the northern edge of the town. It has been believed up to now that Mr. Deane, at the time of his death, had a quantity of valuable jewellery and a large sum of money on him, and that he was murdered for it—that, in fact, when he went out of the hotel that night, he carried his money and his valuables with him. Now, in plain truth, he didn't—Mr. Deane's ready money, a very large sum, and his valuables are all in possession of the two defendants before you, and I am prepared, by their instructions, to hand them over to the police as soon as this court rises!"

Amid the murmur of irrepressible excitement caused by this announcement, Shelmore went on quietly.

"I am instructed to tell your worships precisely what happened!" he said. "About eleven o'clock on the night in question, Mary Sanders took to Mr. Deane's room a glass of hot milk. Mr. Deane was in his pyjamas and dressing gown, reading. Mary Sanders saw on his dressing table his gold watch and chain, his diamond pin and rings, some more money and a purse. Mr. Deane told her to bring him in some tea at seven o'clock next morning. She did so. On then entering his room she found he was not there. But on the dressing table still lay the valuables and money she had seen the night before. She had thought Mr. Deane had gone out of the room for awhile and went away. But later, when she found he had not returned, she thought he had gone for a walk before breakfast. Still later, when there was no sign of him, she removed the money, valuables and purse from the dressing table, and placed them under Mr. Deane's clothing in a drawer in the room, intending to tell him of what she had done when he returned. But Mr. Deane never did return. Eventually, news of the discovery of Mr. Deane's body reached the Chancellor. Mary Sanders heard of it, and of course she remembered what she had done with the valuables and money. And—she told Kight about that! Immediately afterwards Kight and Mary Sanders were questioned by Superintendent Mellapont, and they made out from what they then learned, and from the talk which went on—your lordships know how these things are talked about—that the police were firmly under the impression that Deane had his money in his pocket, his rings on his fingers, and his valuable diamond pin in his cravat when he went out of the hotel, and was murdered for the sake of them. And thereupon—I am not endeavouring to exculpate them, nor do they now wish to exculpate themselves—thereupon they yielded to temptation and decided to appropriate these properties. Mary Sanders took the various articles from the drawer in which she had hidden them, and handed them to Kight: Kight took them away and placed them in a secret receptacle of his own. As time went on, they felt themselves safe, and the day before yesterday, having a holiday together in Portsmouth, they decided to take the watch there and sell it—with the result that they are now… where they are. This is the plain truth about the whole matter as far as my clients are concerned. Superintendent Mellapont has thrown out some hint about a graver charge—he can only be referring to one thing, the murder of Mr. Deane. My clients, your worships, know nothing whatever about that. Both can easily prove that on the night on which that murder undoubtedly took place they were at the Chancellor Hotel, and never went outside its doors. As I have already said, I am instructed to plead guilty on their behalf to the present charge: I am also in a position to hand over to the police, at once, all the missing property other than the watch, which they already hold. The prisoners will have to be committed to Quarter Sessions for sentence, and I venture to suggest in view of their confession their willingness to make amends, and their undoubtedly previous good character, that it is not unwarrantable to ask your worships to grant bail."

"I oppose all questions of bail," said Mellapont firmly. "I ask your worships not to consider it at all at present, but instead to remand the accused in custody for a week from today."

Mellapont got his way. All the same, within an hour, Shelmore walked into the superintendent's private office at the police station with a brown paper parcel in his hand. Removing the paper he laid an old cigar box before Mellapont.

"According to Kight," he said, "all the stolen property is in there. He gave me full information as to where it was, and instructions to hand it over to you. See what's inside."

Mellapont, saying nothing, opened the box and removed some layers of paper which lay on the top This revealed the diamond pin, the two rings, some loose money, and an old fashioned purse. Within the purse was a quantity of bank-notes, which Mellapont immediately began to count.

"Two hundred and thirty-five pounds," he remarked. "A good deal to carry!"

"He was going on the continent," said Shelmore. "Well—that's all I can do!" He paused, looking enquiringly at Mellapont. "Do you seriously think there's any possibility of carrying any further charge against these two?" he asked.

"There are certain things to be considered," answered Mellapont. "To start with, just remember that Sanders told us lies when she was asked about this affair at first. She said that when she took the tea in that morning, the money and jewellery which she'd seen on the dressing table the night before were not there. Now she says—they were! That's not in her favour! Besides—there's a more serious thing than that."

"What?" asked Shelmore.

Mellapont gave him a keen, almost cynical look.

"How do I know that these two hadn't an accomplice?" he asked. "What about that idea. Eh?"

"You were—" began Shelmore, and stopped. "Don't quite understand," he went on. "You mean—in what respect?"

"How do I know that they hadn't an accomplice who followed Deane from the hotel, knowing he'd left all this lying about, and murdered him?" answered Mellapont. "It's possible."

"That would make it appear that the whole affair was a carefully arranged job," said Shelmore.

"Well, and why not?" asked Mellapont. "It's all very well, Mr. Shelmore, but I want to get a complete solution of this thing! I don't say Kight and Sanders murdered Deane, or that they conspired with some other person to murder him, but I do say that it's possible they did the last, and that it would be a very foolish thing to let 'em out on bail until we know more. This murder is a very mysterious one, and though I've worked hard at it, I've got no clue, no indicative, nothing—unless," he added, with a laugh which seemed to indicate doubt and scepticism, "unless something that I've got is a clue—which it probably isn't!"

"What's that?" asked Shelmore.

"Well, I'll show you," answered Mellapont "In confidence—between ourselves. I've never mentioned it to a soul, never shown it to anybody. It was this way—the day after the discovery of Deane's body, I went up to that sand pit alone. I had a very careful look round, to see if I could discover anything. Now, that sand pit, as you may be aware, having been a very long time disused, has become thickly overgrown with stiff wiry grass, on which it's scarcely possible to make any impression—that's why we failed to find any really important or useful trace of footprints. But amongst the bushes in the grass, close by where Deane's body was lying when discovered, I found—this!"

He had drawn a pocket—book from his tunic as he spoke, and now, from an inner compartment, he produced a small object which he balanced on his finger.

"See that?" he said. "Know what it is? It's the enamelled face of a cuff—link! It's been set on a base of gold and silver, or some other metal, worked loose, and then dropped in that sand pit. Now, it didn't come off the victim's cuff—links as his were plain gold. But—did it come off the murderer's?"

"If you could discover that—" said Shelmore.

"Aye, if!" answered Mellapont. "If—if! Well, who knows? But at present, Mr. Shelmore, as regards the actual murder, we're still where we were. This morning's proceedings don't help a bit! The question's still there—who killed James Deane... and why?"

John Hackdale had come to the same conclusion before he left the court, and his anxiety about Bartlett and his potentialities for harm deepened. He forced his way to Bartlett through the crowd as the Court cleared, and laid a hand on his arm. Bartlett scowled and shook himself free.

"You leave me alone, Hackdale," he whispered officiously. "Not at your beck and call, my lad!"

"You had money of me!" retorted Hackdale in a similar tone. "Money—"

"That I'd earned!" said Bartlett, maliciously. "Go and tell everybody why you gave it to me—if you dare!"

Then he moved forward in the crush of people, and Hackdale turned away baffled. He was unaware that Simmons was just behind him and had witnessed this encounter; unaware, too, that Simmons' sharp ears had overheard Bartlett's last peering defiance.

Chapter

14

WHICH GOLD MINE?

Bartlett had been quietly watching John Hackdale during the Court proceedings, and had observed the anxiety with which he followed every development. It seemed to him that Hackdale was relieved when it was proved that Kight and his fellow—defendant had become possessed of the watch: anxious and perturbed again when the explanation of their trip was given by Shelmore; still more perturbed, even to badly concealed agitation, when Shelmore said, in reference to Mellapont's scarcely veiled hint of a future charge, that it could easily be proved that the two prisoners never quitted the Chancellor Hotel on the night of the murder. Bartlett knew, or feared that he knew, what was passing in Hackdale's mind. If it was certain that Kight and Sanders, though guilty of the theft of Deane's money and valuables, were absolutely innocent of his murder, then the original question was still to be asked—who killed James Deane? Bartlett believed that John Hackdale either knew the answer to that question or had a strong suspicion as to what the answer might be: he was shielding somebody—himself or some other person; hence his anxiety. And Bartlett had also seen that anxiety deepen as he flung his defiant retort at him outside the Court—there was no doubt about it, he said to himself as he walked off. John Hackdale was frightened, frightened of him, frightened of what he could tell. Very well then, said Bartlett, with another sneer, the thing to do was obvious; he must consider how best to turn this fear to his own account, his own benefit.

He had meant to return to Portsmouth after the proceedings in the magistrates' court, but now, after some further thought, he turned away from the railway station, and making for the eastern outskirts of the city, sought a quiet tavern where he was known, and engaged a room for a day or two, telling its landlady that he had a little business in the neighbourhood and wanted peaceful and comfortable quarters. The landlady, struck by his altered and smart appearance, his evident handsome supply of ready money, and his generally changed manner, made him welcome, and at his suggestion cooked him a hot dinner, which she served to him in a private parlour. Bartlett, who had breakfasted very early at Portsmouth, did full justice to it, and took his time over it, and his allowance of rum when it was finished. And while he ate and drank and afterwards sipped his rum-punch and smoked his pipe, he emulated the habits of great generals, and considered and elaborated his future plan of campaign. Underneath all his thinking, speculating, contriving, designing, lay a basic question which he formulated as of vast importance. This question: "Which woman was he most likely to extract most money out of? Miss Pretty or Mrs. Champernowne? In other words, which policy would pay him best—to go for Miss Pretty's remaining rewards, or to blackmail Mrs. Champernowne?"

He thought out these things carefully, slowly. First, as regards Miss Pretty. He had already got the reward of a thousand pounds which she had offered for information about the jewellery: Miss Pretty had given him a cheque for the full amount as soon as she, he, and the jeweller had seen Mellapont, the day before, and Bartlett had returned to Portsmouth with it and opened a banking account, and had left the bank feeling several inches taller than when he entered. Yes—that had come easily enough—and all by a stroke of sheer luck. Miss Pretty had parted with her money readily—she was a young woman of her word. But... would it be as easy to get more money out of her? She had offered a similar reward to anybody who could prove that he or she had seen Deane on the night of the murder—well, to be sure, he, Bartlett, had seen him and spoken to him— another rare piece of luck for him, that; the original piece of luck—but... how could he prove it? That was impossible—impossible, at any rate, to prove it to Miss Pretty. In spite of the readiness with which she had given him her cheque for the first reward, Bartlett had seen several little things in Miss Pretty which convinced him that she was a smart and keen young woman of business, who would want much more than his mere uncorroborated assertion that he had seen and had speech with Deane. True, he could bring proof in this way: he could say "I met Deane—he asked me the whereabouts of Mrs. Champernowne's residence. Ashenhurst House, I told him; he went that way; later on I told John Hackdale of this occurrence; Hackdale gave me a considerable sum of money, which I believe he got from Mrs. Champernowne, to go to America so that no one could question me, and promised a similar sum on my reaching America—that's corroborative evidence of the truth of my assertion." But that would cut into another matter—and he dismissed it. He dismissed also the idea of going in for the third and most considerable a—reward, the one of three thousand pounds for definite information that would lead to the arrest and conviction of Deane's actual murderer. Bartlett, whatever suspicion he might have about some doubtful business between Deane and Mrs. Champernowne and Mrs. Champernowne and Hackdale, hadn't the ghost of a notion as to who killed James Deane, and saw no possibility of ever getting at one: it was a mystery which, in his opinion, would forever remain a mystery. No—he saw no chance of the third reward, nor of the second; Miss Pretty as a gold mine, a treasure house, a milch cow, was, accordingly, exhausted, worked out, dried up. Well… anyway, he had got a thousand of the best out of her.

And… there was Mrs. Champernowne. Mrs. Champernowne was a rich, a very rich woman. She rolled in money—so those people said who were in a position to know. And she was a person of very great importance—a big figure, socially, publicly, politically; big in divers ways. She was Mayor of Southernstowe. She was a governor of the Hospital of St. Peter and St. Paul. She was chairman of the Trustees of Auberon's Charity. She was president of the Southernstowe Women's Conservative Association. Heaven knew what she wasn't in that sort of thing, mused Bartlett. And she was going to marry Sir Reville Childerstone, of Childerstone Park, and blossom out as My Lady. That was a big, a very big thing: Sir Reville was none of your modern mushroom men, not he—he was the fifteenth baronet, and long before his ancestors attained the dignity of the Bloody Hand, they had been settled at Childerstone for centuries. Clearly, Mrs. Champernowne—Lady Childerstone that was to be—was surely the very person to pay a good price for keeping her name out of—should he say, scandal?

Bartlett kept very quiet all that afternoon, and the landlady of the quiet inn, who had known him in the old days as a man greatly given to liquor, was surprised to find that he had become quite abstemious, and had taken to drinking a dish of tea at five o'clock. He went out for a little stroll in the neighbouring lanes thereafter, and, on returning, asked for pen, ink, and paper. A good clerk in his time, Bartlett prided himself on writing a beautiful hand, and he took particular pains in inditing the following epistle:

"The Waggoner's Rest,

"Wednesday evening.

"Sir,

"It would probably be to the best interest of everybody concerned if you would call upon me in my private apartment at the above mentioned house at any hour of tonight which is most convenient to yourself.

"Your obedient servant,

"James Bartlett."

Addressing this precise and formal communication to Mr. John Hackdale, 23 St. Sigfrid's Square, Bartlett handed it over, with half-a-crown, to the landlady's boy for immediate delivery, and then sat down to await the result. But he was sure that Hackdale would come, and at seven o'clock he came. It would have been well for Hackdale if he had been able to confront Bartlett with even an assumption of indifference, if not of determination. But Bartlett was quick to note the old air of anxiety. Hackdale looked at him, as soon as he entered the room, as a nervous man might look at a strange animal which may or may not suddenly spring on him. He replied to Bartlett's polite greeting with a mere nod, and taking the chair which he indicated, spoke—almost sullenly.

"What do you want?" he demanded. "I've come, do you see."

"Business, Mr. Hackdale, business!" answered Bartlett. "The old business! As I said in my letter—for the best interest of everybody concerned. I've something to tell, and I think you know of the most likely buyer. But—if you don't, you know, I'm aware of another!"

"You don't stand by your bargain," said Hackdale.

"Depends on the bargaining," retorted Bartlett. "If you find you've been cheated—"

"Cheated?" exclaimed Hackdale. "Do you mean—"

"What do you call it but cheating to give a man two pence when he deserves two shillings?" asked Bartlett. "Metaphor, of course, but you know what I mean, as well as I do."

Hackdale looked round at the door.

"Safe as safe can be," said Bartlett, reassuringly. "Double door there, as you see, and nothing but a long and empty garage beyond. Say what you please."

But Hackdale lowered the tone of his voice to a whisper.

"I paid you a hundred and fifty pounds on strict conditions that you set off that very night to Southampton, to sail next day for America," he said, "and you were to have the same amount cabled to you as soon as you announced your arrival in New York. But you never went to New York—you took my money—"

"Not yours!" interrupted Bartlett.

"Anyway, you didn't keep your promise!" concluded Hackdale.

"Promises are like pie crust, as the old saying is," remarked Bartlett. "Made to be broken."

"Not by honest and honourable men," said Hackdale.

"I think we'd better leave honour and honesty clean out," announced Bartlett drily. "They seem—a bit out of place. But—business! Of course I didn't go to New York! Meant to? But you see I hadn't seen Miss Pretty's offer of a reward then. I did see it, however, very soon after I'd seen you—while I was packing my duds together. And—I changed my mind. You see, all I was to get out of—your client—was three hundred pounds. But Miss Pretty offered much more."

Hackdale was looking Bartlett carefully over, noting his good clothes, clean linen, his new boots, his general respectability.

"You seem to have handled some of Miss Pretty's money," he said, bitterly. "You're in pretty good feather!"

"Wrong, my son!" retorted Bartlett. "This purple and fine linen—metaphor again—came out of your money—or, I should say, your client's money. And—I want to know," he went on, suddenly assuming a determined air, "I want to know if your client is going to be reasonable; if she's going to pay me a proper sum for my silence? A hundred and fifty is a flea bite! Three hundred is—nothing. Miss Pretty will stump up three thousand—what's she prepared to run to? When I use the feminine indicative, Hackdale, I mean a certain particular lady. You know who!"

"And supposing I tell you that she won't stump up one penny more?" answered Hackdale. "What then?"

70

"Then, of course, I put on my hat, walk along to Superintendent Mellapont, and tell all I know—incidentally, I call on Miss Pretty, at the Chancellor Hotel, and, in telling her of what I've done, lay claim to the three thousand pounds," said Bartlett. "That's the procedure, my lad! But," he went on, eyeing Hackdale closely and slyly, "it won't come to that—it won't come to that!"

"Why not?" demanded Hackdale.

"Because," replied Bartlett, bending forward from his elbow chair, and laying his hand on Hackdale's knee, "because a lady of great social and public importance, a lady, moreover, who is about to become the wife of a baronet, cannot afford to have ugly rumours circulating about her, nor have the police enquiring into nasty episodes! And I— I am the man who can start the rumours and investigate the enquiries! Hackdale—I'm like the big dam across some enormous reservoir—again I speak in metaphor. Yes, a dam! a good image. Break me down!—and out rushes the destroying flood! Comprehend?"

"What is your game, Bartlett?" asked Hackdale, "Do you seriously think that a word from you would—would—"

"You're afraid to say it!" sneered Bartlett. "My son!—you don't know what I know! You don't know how clever I am either. They didn't mention my name today at the magistrates' court, but it was I, yours truly, who tracked the gold watch, and gave Master Charles Kight and Miss Mary Sanders in charge! And I know a lot more than you—and your client—are aware of, and I say to you—if you're sensible, buy Jim Bartlett's silence once and for ever and be safe!"

"How do I—we—know that what you know isn't known to others?" asked Hackdale.

"Then you're off it, my son!" said Bartlett confidently. "I do know this, for an absolute fact. Nobody in this world knows what I know about this matter—nobody! I'm the sole repository. Make a golden key, Hackdale, insert and turn it in the safe of my breast, and the secret's locked up for ever and ever!"

"How much do you want?" questioned Hackdale. "A figure."

But Bartlett waved his hand.

"Too precious, my lad," he said carelessly. "That's to be discussed—with your principal."

"My principal!" exclaimed Hackdale. "Mrs.—"

"H'sh!—no need to mention names," said Bartlett. "Your principal—this lady. I suggest that you take me to see her. Why not? I'm respectable—my manners are good— my speech excellent—my address all that it should be. I moved in very good circles once, Hackdale—I was very nearly being a gentleman!"

Hackdale was stroking his chin, thinking, wondering. Bartlett was a puzzle; he was beyond him. But he suddenly remembered Mrs. Champernowne could be hard as marble and tough as steel on occasion—why not turn Bartlett over to her? Before he could speak, Bartlett leaned nearer, confronting him with a cynical smile.

"And why be backward in presenting me in person to—this good lady?" he asked. "Why should you shield her, my lad? Come!—Why don't you look after your own interests a bit? You're in possession of a secret—my secret, if you like, or, rather, some of it. You know—what I've told you! Why don't you turn that to advantage? But… perhaps you've done that already—eh?"

Hackdale flickered a little under Bartlett's mocking eyes. He knew, well enough, that his real anxiety was not for Mrs. Champernowne at all, but for himself. He had not the remotest idea of what her secret was, or why she was mortally afraid of having her name mentioned in connection with the Deane affair—all he knew in that relation was that there was a secret and that she was afraid. That only concerned him as it affected, or might affect himself. But it was in his mind that if Mrs. Champernowne were hit, he might be hit, too. All the recent arrangements might come to an end; his new post might never materialise; everything might be wrong. He had seen and heard enough to know that Mrs. Champernowne had the strongest and gravest reasons for not wishing it to be known that she knew anything of Deane; it was in his own interest to further Mrs. Champernowne's decision. Either as Mrs. Champernowne or as Lady Childerstone, she could be of immense use to him and his career, and she must be protected, at any cost. Bartlett was evidently an integral part of the cost—and perhaps she could tackle him better than he, Hackdale, could. He rose from his chair, abruptly. "Very well, then," he said. "Come along now!"

"At your service, sir," answered Bartlett. "As soon as I've put on my coat and hat. Will you have a drink before we go, Mr. Hackdale?"

"No thank you," replied Hackdale. "Don't let me stop you, though."

"Never drink when I'm doing business, sir!" answered Bartlett. "Not now, at any rate. Stopped all that! When a man begins making money—"

He laughed at his own wit, and led the way out. But outside the tavern John Hackdale took the lead, going in front. In silence he led Bartlett across the north east edge of the city and straight to Ashenhurst House. When he knocked at the door, Jane Pratt opened it.

15 ## THE UNCURTAINED WINDOW

The parlourmaid received Hackdale with her usual demure and quiet smile. But she looked questioningly at Bartlett, and his guide hastened to explain matters.

"Mrs. Champernowne in, Jennie?" he asked. "Just so!—Well, this gentleman and I have some business with her. But—mine first. Can you put him in the little morning room while I see Mrs. Champernowne?"

As if sure of his answer, Hackdale strode into the hall, motioning his companion to follow. Jane Pratt opened the door of a small room close by, switched on the electric light, and stood aside for Bartlett to enter. But Hackdale remained at the door, waiting while the girl went down the hall and entered another room. He knew that Mrs. Champernowne would see him at once—and within the moment he had obeyed Jane Pratt's beckoning hand and gone forward.

Mrs. Champernowne, alone, was in her drawing room, a big, brilliantly lighted room, overlooking the lawn. She sat at an escritoire, placed in the recess of the wide window, evidently writing letters. Hackdale observed as he walked across the room to her side that neither blinds nor curtains were drawn across the window, and that shafts of light from the electric bulbs fell across the green sward and on the ornamental shrubberies outside. But all this was in a glance, his eyes fastened on Mrs. Champernowne, and in hers he saw new anxiety.

"Well," she said, pointing to a chair close to her own. "Well?"

Hackdale sat down and leaned towards her. "Sorry, Mrs. Champernowne," he answered in a low voice, "but I had to come to you, and at once—thought it best. In fact, the only thing to do. It's the old trouble, Mrs. Champernowne! That man I told you about. He's—back!"

Mrs. Champernowne's fingers came together in a startled movement, and her face paled. She looked at Hackdale with plain indications of fear.

"You said you'd—got rid of him!" she murmured. "For—good!"

"I thought I had," said Hackdale ruefully. "I did my best. I paid him that money—a hundred and fifty!—and promised him the same amount by cable, as soon as I heard that he'd landed at New York. But—he never went! I don't know what he did—all I know is that he left the town that night, and went somewhere. It must have been somewhere close by, because he's been keeping an eye on things. It was he who found out about the watch, and gave information that led to the arrest of those two people at the Chancellor. Of course you've heard of all that took place at the city court this morning?—though you weren't in the place."

"Yes," answered Mrs. Champernowne. She remained silent for a moment or two, watching Hackdale, and turning over the rings on her plump fingers. "So it was he who ferretted that out?" she said at last. "The same man?"

"Same man!" asserted Hackdale. "A dangerous, sly, crafty man! He's got the thousand pounds reward that Miss Pretty offered to whoever found out anything about the missing valuables. The thing about it is, I don't know how much he knows about—about what he hinted at, at first. You know what I mean. But—I'm afraid he knows more than he's told—up to now. The question is—what can he tell?"

"Haven't you any idea—any theory?" asked Mrs. Champernowne, anxiously.

"Well," replied Hackdale, slowly, and sinking his voice still lower. "I have: I told you at first that this man told me that Deane stopped him that night near North Bar, and, mentioning your name, asked to be directed to your home. He told Deane where the house was, and saw him go in that direction, that's all he admitted to me, and, of course, I bribed him to keep his tongue still about even that much. But, it's my opinion, Mrs. Champernowne, that he followed Deane, and saw Deane with you, in your own grounds!"

He watched Mrs. Champernowne carefully as he spoke the concluding sentence, and he saw that her anxiety increased. And he began to wonder. Was it possible...

"The thing is," said Mrs. Champernowne, suddenly, "the thing is—has he ever told anybody but you what he told you? Anybody?"

"On that point, I'm certain!" answered Hackdale. "I feel absolutely certain that he hasn't told a soul! He's too late! He knows that he can get more out of you than he could get out of anybody else—that is, if it's really necessary that the fact that Deane came to see you that night and did see you, must be kept... secret. Is it, Mrs. Champernowne?"

Mrs. Champernowne gave him a strange but steady look.

"It is!" she answered. "Dead secret!"

"Then this man will have to be squared," said Hackdale. "That's flat. There's no use in arguing about it—he's got the whip hand."

"But—where will it end?" asked Mrs. Champernowne. "Give him more now—and he'll turn up again! It will be a perpetual blackmail. If he could be silenced, once for all... "

"There may be a way," remarked Hackdale "I've been thinking things over as I came here But first let me ask you this—you know me, Mrs. Champernowne, and that I've done my best for you in this matter. Now, is it utterly impossible for you to—well, to go to the police, to Superintendent Mellapont, tell all you know about it, and have the thing completely cleared up? Cleared up for good!—So that you could snap your fingers at this fellow? Think, Mrs. Champernowne!"

Mrs. Champernowne became silent. Whether she was thinking or not, Hackdale could not tell. She began drawing her fingers backwards and forwards over the blotting pad in front of her; she kept glancing from them to Hackdale, from Hackdale to her fingers. Her eyes grew sombre, strange. And suddenly she spoke.

"Absolutely impossible!" she said, in a hard, strained voice. "The man must be bought! Once for all. But I wish I were sure, were certain—"

"Sure certain of what, Mrs. Champernowne?" asked Hackdale, as she paused.

"Certain—beyond doubt—that nobody else knows that this man knows," she answered. "If I could be sure of that... "

"I think you may be perfectly sure of it, and for a very simple reason," remarked Hackdale. "I am!"

"What reason?—and why are you here?"

"Why, this reason," replied Hackdale, with a confident laugh. "If there was anybody—anybody!—man or woman—in Southernstowe who knew what he knows, he or she would have been after Miss Pretty's reward long since! No, Mrs. Champernowne, he's the sole repository—and the sole danger!"

"Then he must be bought," she repeated firmly. "But—how to ensure his future silence? You hinted at some notion of yours, what is it?"

"I shouldn't recommend giving him a big lump sum of money," said Hackdale. "He might go through it and then demand more. My notion is—well, something like a pension, an annuity—so much a year, you know."

"For life?" asked Mrs. Champernowne.

Hackdale gave her a significant look.

"While he lives he'll be able to tell, at any time, what he might tell now!" he said. "Yes!—it would have to be for life."

"Who is the man?" demanded Mrs. Champernowne abruptly.

"James Bartlett!" answered Hackdale. "James Bartlett."

Mrs. Champernowne let out a little cry of dismay.

"Bartlett!" she exclaimed. "He drinks. A man who drinks—talks!"

But Hackdale shook his head.

"Used to," he said. "But he seems to have reformed and become quite steady—a bit too steady I think, for my liking. I think money reformed him. In my opinion, he's transferred his affections from his bottle to his bank balance! He seems unusually keen on adding to that, anyway. No—if he's squared, in the way I suggest, Mrs. Champernowne, he'll not talk. I don't know any man in Southernstowe who's more keenly alive to his own interests than he is—now."

"Well," said Mrs. Champernowne. "This plan of yours, then. Will you see him about it?"

Hackdale nodded at the door by which he had entered.

"He's here, Mrs. Champernowne," he answered. "I thought it, knew it, to be best to bring him. You see him!—put on your hardest, most businesslike air—let him see that he's dealing with you at your keenest—be firm with him. Far better for him to deal with you, as principal, than with me as go-between! Shall I bring him in, Mrs. Champernowne?"

He rose in accordance with her nod, and, leaving the room, went along the hall to fetch Bartlett. As far as he observed, the hall was empty. But it was not. In the shadows of its further extremity Jane Pratt, watchful and suspicious of the doings of Simmons' brother, was lurking and keeping her eyes and ears open. She saw Hackdale fetch Bartlett from the little morning room; saw the exchange of whispers between them as they walked up the hall; saw them disappear into the drawing room. The door closed. And Jane Pratt, suddenly remembering that her mistress had a strange, curious objection to drawn blinds and curtains, stole out of her shadows, slipped from the house by a side door, and went round to a shrubbery, from amongst the laurels and lilacs of which she, herself safely hidden, could see right into the drawing room window.

Bartlett followed Hackdale into Mrs. Champernowne's presence with a good deal of curiosity. He remembered that he had once met her under very different circumstances. The meeting place was the city police court, and while Mrs. Champernowne sat on the bench, he stood in the dock. Mrs. Champernowne, as presiding magistrate, had not only fined him, but lectured him—severely: she had made him feel very small indeed. But now things were changed: Bartlett was disposed to consider himself as judge and Mrs. Champernowne as culprit. He held his head high, and assumed his best and grandest manner, remembering, as he had already said to Hackdale, that once upon a time he had been very nearly a gentleman.

But Bartlett found himself considerably taken aback. Mrs. Champernowne, seated at her escritoire, was not one whit less formidable than Mrs. Champernowne, Mayor of Southernstowe in the big magisterial chair. Handsome and taking as her well-preserved face was, she could make it uncommonly stern and even forbidding, and she looked at Bartlett as Hackdale brought him forward much as she might have looked at a newly captured burglar hailed to the seat of justice. And while she motioned Hackdale to seat himself, she left Bartlett standing, and, as he stood, looked him over from head to foot in a fashion which made him feel at a decided disadvantage. It was not at his raiment she was looking—Bartlett was too certain of his respectable and even fashionable appearance to be uneasy on that point—it was as if she was examining his very soul: looking inside him as it were. He suddenly noticed that Mrs. Champernowne was neither as soft as butter nor as pliable as thin metal, and his self-assurance began to melt.

"Well, Bartlett!" began Mrs. Champernowne, in a sharp, business-like tone, "it seems that we are to have some dealings together, but I don't care to have any transactions with men who are not steady. It's not so very long since you were brought before me for drunkenness: I fined you for it. How do I know that you've altered your habit?"

Bartlett spread out his hands with a look of injured innocence.

"Do I look like a man of—of such habits as you refer to, Mrs. Champernowne?" he asked aggrievedly. "That—that was some time ago, ma'am. I may say I've adopted other habits—and a different course of life. I'm going in for respectability, Mrs. Champernowne—eminent respectability! Of course, ma'am, it's merely to return to what I used to be—there are plenty of people in this neighbourhood, Mrs. Champernowne, who can remember me as a highly respectable person!"

"Glad to hear you've reformed, Bartlett," said Mrs. Champernowne. "But I'm afraid that if you lead a leisured life on easily gained money you may fall into pleasure loving ways and get amongst convivial companions, and go back to your old excesses. And when wine's in, truth's out!—I dare—say you know what I mean."

"Oh, I quite take your meaning, Mrs. Champernowne," responded Bartlett, "and I'm not offended in the least, ma'am. But I assure you, Mrs. Champernowne, that my ambition is otherwise—quite otherwise! For one thing, ma'am, I've no intention whatever of remaining in this neighbourhood, and so I shall have no temptation to rejoin the convivial companions of whom you speak. Clean cut, Mrs. Champernowne, clean cut!—that's what I intend to make."

Mrs. Champernowne exchanged glances with Hackdale. Hackdale took hers for an invitation to join in.

"You were going to make a clean cut a little while ago, Bartlett," he said. "You were going to America. You didn't!"

Bartlett looked from one to the other of his inquisitors with a smile that was half a grimace and half an appeal.

"Why, now, Mr. Hackdale!" he exclaimed almost pathetically. "Now, sir—and now, Mrs. Champernowne—is it to be expected of a man to withdraw from the chance of making a bit of money? There was that handsome reward offered—"

"We don't want to hear anything whatever about any reward or anything else, my man!" interrupted Mrs. Champernowne sharply. "We don't want any reference, explanation, or anything, verbal about anything!—there's a tacit understanding already between the three of us. And I, too, believe that you'll live a sober and steady life, and not let your tongue wag!"

Bartlett's self assurance came back to him at this, and his tone grew in confidence. "It's to my interest—if we come to terms—to be both stead and sober, Mrs. Champernowne," he answered. "I should think you see that yourself."

"I think we can provide you with an incentive to be sober, steady, respectable in life and cautious and reserved in speech," remarked Mrs. Champernowne, drily. "My terms will be conditional oh your being all that, Bartlett! I'm not going to have terms dictated to me, my man! But—what are your ideas about terms? Out with them!"

Bartlett hesitated a moment. Then, growing bold, he spoke.

"Well, nothing less than Miss Pretty offered—for information," he said. "Miss Pretty mentioned three thousand."

"Three thousand fiddlesticks!" interrupted Mrs. Champernowne. "You're not going to get three thousand anything out of me, my good fellow!—not you! What you'll get is a regular allowance—which you'll forfeit if I have reason to complain of your conduct—in fact, it'll only be paid if I find that you're keeping sober and steady, and holding your tongue. Do you understand that?—an allowance!"

"For life?" asked Bartlett, sharply.

"For life—yes," answered Mrs. Champernowne.

"Paid weekly?" demanded Bartlett.

"Every Friday," said Mrs. Champernowne. "Mr. Hackdale will pay it."

"Well," said Bartlett. "But—how much?"

"Four pounds," replied Mrs. Champernowne.

"Five, I think, ma'am," Bartlett suggested. "Five! Can't be done for less—and, in addition to that, I must have at any rate the thousand which I could get by going straight to Miss Pretty and telling her that—"

Mrs. Champernowne stopped him with a look and a word. They began to bargain. Eventually Mrs. Champernowne gave in to Bartlett's terms—a thousand pounds cash down through a cheque made out to John Hackdale, and five pounds a for life to be paid by Hackdale every Friday. So there was an end.

The parlourmaid, hearing nothing, saw much. She saw Mrs. Champernowne eventually produce her cheque book, write a cheque, and hand it to Hackdale, then Hackdale and Bartlett left the drawing room. Jane Pratt heard them let themselves out of the front door and go down the drive and away. And she herself, marvelling and suspicious, was returning to the house, when from the trees in the orchard she heard a low and peculiar whistle. She turned from the house at that and made for deeper shadows.

DISCOVERIES AND AMBITIONS

THE parlourmaid cautiously slipped away from the vicinity of the house, and, keeping in the shadows of the trees that separated the garden from the orchard, stole through a gap in the hedge and turned, as if well accustomed to this procedure, to the right, and amongst a cluster of laurel bushes. In the darkness an arm stole round her waist, and a pair of ready lips sought hers. For a few minutes she and the owner of the arm indulged a mutual inclination for love making, in silence. But suddenly she disengaged herself from her unseen lover and began to whisper.

"How did you know I was there, Sim?" she asked.

"Saw you against that lighted window," answered Simmons readily. "Knew you in less than a glimpse!—isn't another girl in the town with a figure like yours, Jennie! But—what were you doing there?"

"Come further away from the house," said the parlourmaid. "Come down the orchard—to the bottom. I've got some news for you—there's something queer happened in there, just now."

She drew Simmons away through the trees until they came to the edge of the sand pit in which Deane's dead body had been found. Simmons remembered that on their first walk together they had come round by that sand pit, and Jane Pratt had been frightened. But she showed no fright on this occasion; all recollections of the place and its associations had vanished before the curiosity recently aroused in her.

"You want to know what I was doing at that window?" she whispered, as she and Simmons halted in the shadow of a clump of beeches. "I'll tell you! I was watching!"

"Who?" demanded Simmons.

"Well, you'd never guess," she replied. "I'll tell you all about it. Getting on to perhaps an hour ago there was a ring at the front door. Of course, I went. There was your brother!"

"John?" exclaimed Simmons.

"John, of course—you have no other that I know of. John! But—he'd somebody with him. Who do you think?"

"Haven't a notion! Who, then?"

"That Bartlett man!—dressed like a gentleman!"

"What, Jim Bartlett! With John? Why... " Then he paused, thinking. He had seen Bartlett in court, and in the street, and had observed the striking change in his appearance—it was clear enough that Bartlett had somehow or other come into funds. But—with John?—at Mrs. Champernowne's?—

"Well," he asked sharply, "what happened?"

"Your brother said they wanted to see the mistress. He wanted to see her first. Bartlett waited while he went in to see her. And I hid myself behind the curtain at the end of the front hall and watched. Your brother was in the drawing room with the mistress some time; then he went and fetched Bartlett. And so I slipped out and went round to the window—the mistress has a queer fad about blinds and curtains; she won't have 'em drawn so I knew I could see into the room."

"What did you see?" asked Simmons. He was already sure that some secret lay behind all this—this bringing together of Mrs. Champernowne, John Hackdale, and James Bartlett meant something. "If you could only have heard, now!" he added regretfully. "Heard!"

"I. couldn't hear anything, of course," replied Jane Pratt. "But I could see easily enough from where I was. Mrs. Champernowne talked for a while to Bartlett: your brother talked a bit, too—they all talked, but she did most of it. And in end she got out her cheque book."

"Ah!" exclaimed Simmons. "She did, eh?"

"And wrote out a cheque," continued Jane Pratt. "When she'd written it she handed it to your brother—"

"Not to Bartett?" interrupted Simmons quickly.

"No—to John Hackdale," said the parlourmaid. "I noticed that particularly. And then they went away—straight off! They'd just gone down the drive, and I was going back to the house when I heard you whistle."

Simmons, in the darkness, was rubbing the tip of his nose with the fingers of his left hand: a trick that he had when he was full of thought. His right arm was round the parlourmaid's slender waist, and he gave her a sudden squeeze.

"Jennie!" he said, confidentially. "You're a damned smart girl, and you and me'll pull something big off out of this—you see if we don't! But look here!—while I think of it. Where did the missus write that cheque?"

"At her writing desk—near the drawing room window," replied Jane Pratt.

"There'll be a blotting pad, then," said Simmons. "You get hold of the top sheet of it— take it off and keep it for me. Eh?"

"That's easy enough," answered the parlourmaid. "I often take off the top piece—I can do that tonight. But I say—what do you think it all meant?"

"God knows!" declared Simmons with cheerful irreverence. "But I'll jolly well find out. It's all got to do with this, of course. Any hurry to get in?"

"No!" replied the parlourmaid. "Why?"

"Can you ask?" said Simmons, amorously. "Come on!—hang all that, now. Let's have a nice half hour to ourselves."

The demure parlourmaid had no objection. She retired with Simmons to a still quieter corner of the wilderness, and eventually went back to the house well satisfied with the atmosphere of love, intrigue, mystery, and spy business into which her swain was cleverly inducting her. She had had young men before—but they were ordinary and dull in comparison with Simmons. Simmons, in Miss Pratt's opinion, had a brain: a young man who possessed a brain was much more interesting—and amusing—and generally diverting—than the young men who—apparently—had none. She found a good deal of pleasurable excitement in playing up to Simmons, and when they next met she was ready with the purloined sheet of blotting paper. This was on Miss Pratt's weekly afternoon out, which was also Simmons'—they met in a quiet spot on the outskirts of the town, and there being nobody whatever about when she handed over the desired object, Simmons immediately produced a small hand mirror from his pocket.

"Whatever's that for?" demanded the parlourmaid.

"Watch, and you'll learn something, Jennie," replied Simmons. "It's a trick well worth knowing if you want to get at other people's secrets. Now, see, there's not much on this blotting paper. And there, there, Jennie, is the impression of the cheque you talked about. Now, then, see, I hold the mirror with one hand; I put the blotting paper before it with the other. Now I look into the mirror. What do I see—good heavens!"

Simmons let out this exclamation through genuine astonishment. He saw by means of the mirror that Mrs. Champernowne had made out a cheque in favour of John Hackdale for one thousand pounds. Why? Was it for John himself?—Or was it for Bartlett?—Or was it for both? And was it— hush money?

The more Simmons thought things over, the more he was convinced that he was on the right track, The James Deane who had been murdered at, Southernstowe was the same man as the James Arradeane who had made a mysterious disappearance from Normansholt, some twenty years before; Mrs. Champernowne of Southernstowe was the same woman as Mrs. Arradeane of Normansholt. Everything seemed to indicate that Mrs. Champernowne or Mr. Alfred had shot Deane to keep his tongue quiet for ever. Now then—were John Hackdale and Bartlett accessories after the fact?—accessories in this way, that they had become possessed of knowledge about the murder and were keeping silence about it for the sake of the money they were undoubtedly getting from Mrs. Champernowne. It appeared to Simmons that the evidence against his brother was strong—strong enough already, he considered, to put John in the dock. This thing, this murder, happens, he mused; next day John Hackdale gets from Mrs. Champernowne an appointment which he certainly never dreamed of getting twenty-four hours previously —and now he handles a cheque for a thousand pounds. Clearly, John knew a lot—was probably being well paid, squared, bribed, call it what you like, to cancel a lot. But what about Bartlett? Where did he come in? Why was he present at Mrs. Champernowne's, with John, when the cheque was drawn?

Bartlett was the puzzle—to Simmons. He tried to get hold of Bartlett, hoping by means of rum and conviviality to pump him. But Bartlett was not to be found in Southernstowe; he had, as a matter of fact, returned to his quarters at Portsmouth. Then Simmons vainly and unobtrusively tried to suck the brains of two or three of the policemen who did clerical work at the police station. He got nothing out of any of them—either they knew nothing whatever about Bartlett, or pretended that they didn't. And then Simmons remembered that John had drawn his attention to the fact that there, in the open street, heading for the City Hall and—presumably—the police, were Bartlett, a stranger, and— Miss Pretty. So—Miss Pretty must know something about Bartlett. And Miss Pretty must be cajoled, or persuaded, or made, to tell him, Simmons Hackdale, what that something was.

He went to call again on Miss Pretty—after long and careful consideration of the best way to get round her. Miss Pretty, who was somewhat bored of an evening, despite the polite attentions of Shelmore and his aunt, and those of sundry towns folk who were anxious to do something for her, received him readily. In spite of his red hair, sharp nose, and close set eyes, she thought Simmons interesting, and she was sure he was no fool— moreover, she was not averse to male admiration, and she had seen from the first that Simmons, youthful as he was, had a keen eye for a pretty girl. When, therefore, he entered on this occasion, she had a smile for him.

"Found anything out?" she asked, when they were alone, and facing each other across the hearthrug.

Simmons smoothed the nap of the rakish hat which he nursed on his knee, and regarded Miss Pretty with sidelong glances.

"In cases like this, Miss Pretty," he observed, "there's a great deal of mystery! And one's got to be cautious—even with principals. I might spoil everything by telling you— even you!—too much, too soon. And I'm a bit handicapped—through not knowing all I might know. I daresay, now, you could tell me something that would be very helpful to me?"

"What?" asked Miss Pretty.

Simmons suddenly made up his mind to be bold.

"What had that man James Bartlett to do with the watch business?" he asked. "He wasn't called when Kight and Sanders were before the magistrates, but I'm sure he'd something to do with the affair, because I saw him with you and the jeweller to whom the watch was sold."

"I don't know that there's any secret about it," replied Miss Pretty, unconcernedly. "The police didn't call Bartlett because it wasn't necessary. But he was the man who gave information about the night porter and the chambermaid. He saw them go to the jeweller's shop, found out what they were after, and told me."

"So—you paid him that reward you offered?" asked Simmons.

"Certainly! He'd earned it," answered Miss Pretty.

"And I daresay he'd like to earn the other rewards—especially the third one!" remarked Simmons. "He'd do with them!"

"I daresay," assented Miss Pretty. "But he doesn't know anything else—or I'm jolly well certain he'd have been after more money from me before now! No—Bartlett knows nothing more. I should know if he did!"

"You're very anxious to have this mystery cleared up, Miss Pretty?" suggested Simmons. "You feel that it's up to you to be—revenged, eh?"

"I don't think it's either a desire to be revenged, or a feeling of vindictiveness," replied Miss Pretty. "What I feel is just this—I think it's an abominable thing that a quiet, harmless, elderly man like my guardian should come into this town and be murdered in cold blood!—as I'm now sure he was. And I'm going to leave no stone unturned until I bring murderer to justice!"

"They say that murder will out," murmured Simmons "But I don't know! We hear—we lawyers—of some strange, unsolved mysteries. Miss Pretty. However, I'm doing my best to solve this. Make no pretence, Miss Pretty—the money you've offered as a reward would be highly useful to me. I'm the poor young man who's got to make his way in the world, and, of course, I've got ambitions. I want to get on and to do well, so that I can have a home of my own and marry and—"

"Are you engaged to be married?" enquired Miss Pretty, naively.

"Oh, dear me, no, Miss Pretty!" answered Simmons, affecting great innocence. "I—I haven't even got a young lady!—I'm talking of—of the future. Dreams, you know. Miss Pretty. May I ask if—if you're engaged?"

"You may," replied Miss Pretty. "I'm not!"

"I'm surprised!" said Simmons, with a look of respectful admiration. "I should have thought you would have been."

"I only left school a year ago," remarked Miss Pretty. She was taking quiet glances at Simmons, and she said to herself that despite his fiery hair and ferret eyes he was decidedly clever looking. "I haven't had much chance," she added. "I had to give a lot of time to business."

"You're certainly a business woman," said Simmons. "Clever!"

"I come of business people," answered Miss Pretty. "I know all about business—my business—and money matters, too. Don't you go thinking me a fool about money, either!—If I've offered all this money for information about my guardian's murder, it's just because I feel it due to him to clear it up, and because—well, I can afford it. Now that he's dead, the business that was his and mine becomes mine entirely."

"Is that so?" said Simmons, respectfully. He immediately began to wonder which path it would be best to take—that which led towards Miss Pretty's tin mine and money bags, or that which pointed—indefinitely, yet—to a point from which he could blackmail Mrs. Champernowne. "Dear me. Well! I'm doing my best, Miss Pretty." He rose to go and Miss Pretty offered him her hand. "I—I'm afraid it's very lonely for you here," he said in his suavest tones. "I—I was going to suggest a little—er—diversion for you, if you'd allow me."

He was still holding the hand which Miss Pretty had given him, and looking down at her with a glance in which admiration and almost humble reverence were skilfully mingled. Miss Pretty thought him very remarkable for a mere boy, but she had no objection to his admiration or his reverence.

"Yes?" she said enquiringly.

"This is, a very beautiful neighbourhood," said Simmons. "You've no idea, if you haven't been much outside the city. There are some lovely spots—delightful! Artists—they come here in scores, summer, autumn, too, some of them. Danesley Dingle now, ah, that's a most beautiful bit! If you'd care to see it. Miss Pretty, or any other part of the district, I should be—"

He paused, looking at her, and Miss Pretty, becoming wholly feminine, dropped her eyelids—and lifted them, a moment later, very demurely.

"You can take me there, if you like," she said. "Of course, I'd like anything of that sort."

"Sunday afternoon, now," suggested Simmons, boldly. "If you would meet me at, the end of High Street? Then we go across the fields and through the woods—a delightful piece of country. At—shall we say three o'clock?"

He went away presently with Miss Pretty's promise to meet him, and certain new and ambitious ideas in his scheming brain. Why should he not aim at higher flights than he had as yet dared to think of? Here was a girl as pretty as her name, well endowed with this world's goods, and obviously impressed by his cleverness and shrewdness. Why not—as he phrased it—put in for her? Again he asked himself—Why not?

Chapter

17

THE WOOD AND THE ORCHARD

Miss Pretty, left to meditate in her private sitting room at the Chancellor, was conscious that this last interview with Simmons had been rather pleasant. She thought that for a youth of his age Simmons had a way with him which induced liking. She had felt quite a thrill when he held her hand: the suggestion of a walk with him in romantic regions had appealed to something in her—unmistakably: already she was looking forward to Sunday. Business like young woman as she believed herself to be, she was also disposed to sentiment, and by no means disinclined for love making. She stood for some time by the mantelpiece, mechanically fingering its ornaments and staring abstractedly at each in turn; in reality she was thinking about Simmons, and wondering if he might not be what she thought of as a nice boy. She continued to think—and by the time she went to bed she had decided that Simmons had a brainy forehead, the, his hair was in reality an unusual and attractive auburn, and that his eyes, even though set rather close, were of a pleasing steel-blue colour.

"And certainly he's clever, and speaks well, and dresses well," mused Miss Pretty. "And he has ambition and says he means to win high. Quite a nice fellow, really!—much nicer than that stiff and proper Shelmore. And if—"

But there Miss Pretty's thoughts were hurried into the most secret recesses of her mind and became dream like and vague. She was still feeling pleasantly dreamy and sentimental when Sunday came round—but she was sufficiently practical to take unusual pains with her toilet, and to set forth for the trysting place arrayed in a fashion that made the chambermaid stare and wonder. Somehow—this being the very first time in her life that Miss Pretty had ever had an appointment with a young man—she felt instinctively that it was up to her to look at her best. She was already aware that Simmons admired her and she had no objection to his admiration reaching still greater heights.

Simmons, on his part, had also taken great pains in the adorning of himself. Even if he had red hair, a longish nose, and small, sharp eyes, he possessed a graceful figure and a taking address, and ever since he had blossomed into young, very young manhood, he had been most punctilious in arraying the one and cultivating the other. He saved every shilling he could lay hold of toward the cost of his wardrobe, and the tailor in the High Street had no more exacting or particular customer. Simmons, indeed, as regards his outward showing, was a veritable mirror of fashion, and looked all the more distinguished because his taste in clothes was of a quiet and unpretentious sort. He knew a cloth and its possibilities as soon as he saw it: he knew that severity in tone is the proper complement to perfection of cut; there was not a trick of the tailoring trade that he was not up to, and a Savile Row artist need not have been ashamed to take a hint from him. Now Miss Pretty, who in some ways was a bit of a feather brain, had a decided weakness for appearances, and loved to see well dressed men, and when she met Simmons at the appointed place, and noted the perfection of his raiment, from his well chosen hat to his smart socks and shoes, the soft feeling which had been coming over her for two days and nights deepened into absolute surrender to something or other—she didn't know what—and when she gave Simmons her daintily gloved hand it was with shy eyes and a blush that made him several inches taller—figuratively.

But Simmons was too sharp to show any sign of his satisfaction. He was polite, attentive, respectful, informing—a model of good manners: Miss Pretty thought him delightfully simple and unaffected. But all unknown to her, Simmons was being sly and crafty enough. He knew every inch of the surroundings of Southernstowe and where

Sunday strollers were likely to be and not to be, and he took Miss Pretty by lonely and deserted paths, and through still leafy lanes and quiet coppices, and so managed things that they walked in satisfactory solitude from the edge of the town to Danesley Dingle. It was solitary enough there, but after Simmons had discharged his duties as guide and shown his companion the ancient earthworks, tumuli and archaeological features of the spot, he purposely led her into still more solitary recesses of the neighbouring woods. And then, in a quiet alcove amongst the pines, he suggested that they should rest on a conveniently fallen tree. Miss Pretty was by no means averse; she had been wondering, secretly, for half—an—hour, if Simmons was going to make love to her. She sat down and began to draw patterns in the sandy soil with the tip of her slender umbrella: Simmons seated himself at her side: silence fell on the solitude... and on them. But suddenly Simmons spoke—his voice as sugary as it was soft.

"Fancy being here with you!" said Simmons.

Miss Pretty gave him a side glance and found his penetrating eyes fixed on her—she thought, on a certain dimple in her cheek.

"Why?" she asked, demurely.

"Couldn't have believed it possible!" declared Simmons. "Any more," he added boldly, "any more than I could have believed that—that you hadn't already got a sweetheart! That's—incredible!"

"Why incredible?" asked Miss Pretty, laughing softly.

"Why? Marvellous!" exclaimed Simmons. "Extraordinary! Do you know what I said to myself that first time you walked into Shelmore's?"

"No!" murmured Miss Pretty.

Simmons edged himself nearer to her and sank his voice to a whisper that suggested conviction as well as confidence.

"I said to myself, 'By George,' I said, 'that's the prettiest girl I ever saw,' I said. I did—and I meant it, too. Fact!"

"Nonsense!" said Miss Pretty.

"Is it!" protested Simmons. "Not much! No!—do you think I'm blind? Besides, every time I've seen you I've thought the same. With a difference.'"

"What difference?" asked Miss Pretty.

"Just this!" declared Simmons. "Every time I've seen you, I've thought you prettier and prettier! But then, what wonder? I never saw a girl with such eyes, or such hair—or such a pretty mouth! I say: don't be cross!—Shouldn't I like to kiss you! By George! Shouldn't I!"

Miss Pretty looked down and blushed. But Simmons saw a slight curve show itself at the corner of her lips next to him. It spread—and he slipped his arm round her slender waist.

"What do you say?" he whispered. "Come!—why not?"

Miss Pretty made another pattern with her umbrella and regarded it steadily.

"Never have been!" she faltered.

"No reason why you shouldn't be!" protested Simmons, and drew her closer. "Come along!—We're all alone!"

Miss Pretty glanced around her. Certainly the place seemed secret enough. And Simmons' arm was appealing.

"Won't you let me?" he whispered. "Come, now."

Miss Pretty again glanced round—shyly anxious.

"Sure there's nobody about?" she asked. "Shouldn't like anybody to—"

"Not a soul!" declared Simmons. "Quiet as the grave here... nobody... "

Miss Pretty released her hold on the umbrella. It slid to the ground as she half turned to her suppliant. "Don't mind, then!" she whispered. "But —oh, what a bold boy you are! Really—"

Simmons lost no time. His ready Ups sought Miss Pretty's. He kissed her once, twice, thrice—and yet again. Miss Pretty, made no protest against repetition. In plain truth, as soon as she had tasted the hitherto unknown fruit, she was not only willing but quietly eager to eat her fill of it. She suddenly became demurely complaisant—and within a few minutes Simmons had drawn her on to his knee, settled head on his shoulder, and was taking toll of her lips in the same lavish spirit as that in which she was willing to pay it. Miss Pretty closed her eyes...

Possibly if she had kept them open, she would not have seen anything but the leafy boughs and kindly shrubs under which she and Simmons were hidden. Just then she was giving herself up to the excitement and novelty of an actual encounter with a lover, and would probably have seen nothing if she had owned six pairs of eyes. Nor did Simmons see anything; he had realised in a second that Miss Pretty, however inexperienced she had been, was, in his own parlance, about as spoony as ever they make 'em, and, the ice being broken, was more than willing to meet him half way, and to give as good as she got, and he was absorbed in taking full advantage of his opportunities. Moreover, he knew that wood and that particular part of it: it was a solitude: he had brought Miss Pretty there on purpose, knowing its solitariness: accordingly, he felt absolutely safe from any observation.

But, as a matter of fact, Simmons and Miss Pretty were observed. Beyond the further edge of the wood, set between it and the brow of the neighbouring hill, lay a moorland farm, a small place from which a working farmer, one, Trevice, fed a few sheep and cattle. Trevice made little of a living out of it, and his grown-up daughters were obliged to go into domestic service. One of them, Kitty, was housemaid at Mrs. Champernowne's. Now Kitty had every other Sunday afternoon out: it was her afternoon out this Sunday. She set off to spend it with her father and mother at the farm, and knowing the district, she took a short cut through the wood which was just then sheltering Mr. Simmons Hackdale and Miss Cynthia Pretty. In the deepest part, Catherine heard a girl laughing in subdued tones; with all the craft of a young woman, born and bred to woodland life, she slipped through the bushes in the direction of the sound. And although they never saw her, and hadn't the slightest idea that she was within a dozen yards of them, Catherine saw Simmons and the young lady who was staying at the Chancellor, and watched them... and eventually stole away as quietly as she had stolen near, and went off— meditating.

And in the end Simmons and Miss Pretty left the wood behind them, and in the autumn dusk went homeward towards Southernstowe by the quiet lanes and paths along which they had first set out. Each was highly satisfied with the other, and when they parted, on the edge of the city, it was with a mutual pledge to meet again OB the following evening. Miss Pretty went to the Chancellor, and Simmons, feeling that he had done a splendid afternoon's work and convinced that Miss Pretty was going to be his girl, and perhaps something still more important, proceeded to his favourite house of call and treated himself to a drink. Half way through it, he suddenly remembered Jane Pratt—and he let out a sharp whistle.

Lately, on Sunday evenings, he had attended Jane Pratt to church, and had afterwards taken her for a quiet walk. He looked at his watch—too late. But he could meet her as she came out of church. There was plenty of time for that, however, so he had another drink, and a quiet smoke, and he thought a good deal, planning and scheming. Miss Pretty and her fortune loomed large in all his pictures: it seemed to him that he would make an excellent manager of both.

At last he went round to the church which Miss Pratt patronised. She did not emerge with the rest of the congregation, nor at all, so Simmons, after assuring himself that she hadn't been to her devotions, went off to Ashenhurst House. There existed a code of signals between Jane Pratt and himself: one of them brought her out to him in the shrubberies. Together, in the darkness, they paced into the orchard.

"You didn't come to church, Jennie!" whispered Simmons. "Why?"

"Couldn't, boy!" replied the parlourmaid. "The missus has some people there, and she asked me to stay in for once. Can't stop long with you— I've got to lay the table for supper."

"Well, give me a kiss, anyway," suggested Simmons. "Time for that, old woman!"

Miss Pratt, like Miss Pretty, had no objection to being either kissed or embraced, and she rewarded Simmons generously for his devotion.

"Then you haven't been out at all to-day?" asked Simmons, these incidents over. "Not even this afternoon?"

"No!" replied Miss Pratt. "Stopped in all the afternoon. Meant to meet you tonight— only these people turned up. What've you been doing all the afternoon?"

"Oh, usual Sunday business!" answered Simmons, lightly. "Bit of sleep, bit of reading, bit of smoking—dull work. All alone of a Sunday, you know—John spends all his Sundays at Selbeach, by the sad sea waves. Now if I'd only had you with me in our sitting room, Jennie, eh?—nice warm fire, and a nice comfortable sofa before it—eh? There— what the deuce is that?" This exclamation was evoked by Simmons striking the toe of his elegant shoe against some solid, unusually hard object which lay in the grass at his feet: there was something in the feel of it which made him stoop and grope for it. Another exclamation, half stilled, came from his lips, and to the parlourmaid's astonishment, he suddenly produced and switched on a small electric torch. And, as its light flared across the square foot of ground on which he turned it he let out another and more earnest and startled exclamation.

"Good God!—what's this? A revolver!" He stood up—stared at his companion— looked down again—stooped once more, picked up the revolver from the thick grass in which it lay, and turned the full flare of his torch on it.

Miss Pratt uttered a little cry and shrank away from it. "Sim—be careful! Oh! I say— do you think that's—the—you know!"

"I know!"—muttered Simmons. He was turning the revolver over, eyeing it keenly, and he let out another exclamation—as if to himself.

"Heavens above!" he said. "Who'd have thought... " He stopped there, and looked at the parlourmaid as if something had suddenly bereft him of his ready wit.

"Jennie!" he went on hoarsely. "Jennie!—you see this? Not a word, Jennie!—Not a word! I—"

Somewhere in the house a bell rang sharply. Miss Pratt started.

"I must go, Sim," she whispered. "That thing?—you'll take care! It—it may be loaded. Oh, do take care!"

"I'll take care!" answered Simmons, in a queer, grim voice. "Yes—go!—the bell! And—not a word. Jennie—not a word."

The parlourmaid hurried away, and Simmons left alone, put the revolver in his pocket, and moved off from the spot where he had found it. But suddenly pausing, he turned back and carefully paced the distance from that spot to the bottom of the orchard, where a low hedge divided it from the and pit in which Deane's dead body had beer found. Fifteen

86

yards—well, anybody standing behind that hedge could easily have flung the revolver that distance into the orchard. And… somebody had flung it.

He passed through a gap into the sand pit, crossed its deserted and melancholy expanse, and entered a by-lane which led to the square in which he lived. He went along with hunched shoulders, bowed head, and hands in the pockets of his trousers, absorbed. The afternoon's amorous adventure with Miss Pretty had vanished clean away from his thoughts: he could think of nothing but his discovery. He had said nothing to Jane Pratt— no, no, he repeated to himself, he had said nothing, not one word to her! But… he had recognised the revolver. It belonged to John Hackdale, his brother. There were John's initials on it. Oh, yes!—it was John's right enough! And—what next?

He got home at last. In the parlour sacred to himself and John, supper was laid for the two. But Simmons knew all his brother's Sunday movements: John invariably spent Sunday with friends at Selbeach, a seaside place seven miles off, and always came home by a certain train: he would not be home for a good half—hour. And Simmons carried the revolver into his own bedroom, locked the door, and carefully examined it. One chamber had been discharged. He put the revolver away—in secret.

18

GREEN EYES

But when Simmons had hidden the revolver in a place where there was no chance of anyone finding it save by a search such as was not likely to be made, he proceeded to another stage in the path to uncertainty. He had no doubt whatever that the revolver was his brother's: Simmons knew all about it, how and why John 'had got it, and where John kept it. There was no secret about that; the revolver's usual resting place was in a certain drawer in John's bedroom—a drawer in which lay a miscellaneous collection of odds and ends and was always unlocked. He repaired to that drawer—to make sure. There was no revolver there: he had never thought there would be. He had the revolver; that revolver; the revolver with the initials J.H. scratched on the metal. So that was—that! When the whole thing was summarised it came to this—he, Simmons, had found a revolver in Mrs. Champernowne's orchard, close to the place whereat James Deane's body had been found, shot through the head, and the revolver was undoubtedly the property of his brother, John Hackdale. That was certain—certain as that he was Simmons, and that that was cold beef, there on the supper table. All right !—but what next? His ideas were still a little confused, but he had no doubt about one thing. He was going to turn this, and everything else connected with it, to his own advantage. All his life he had been sedulously sucking into his mental system the lesson which his elder brother had taught him from childhood—"Look to yourself! Self first!—and damn the rest!"—that was Simmons' creed, and he was a veritable bigot in his belief in it. He was not greatly concerned as to whether his brother actually shot Deane, or whether Mrs. Champernowne did, or whether Mr. Alfred did, but he was sure that one or other of 'em did, and that he had the means of proving their guilt—probably all three were guilty, as principals or accessories. Never mind that—it was an insignificant detail; for all he cared they could have shot Deane every day in the week if they liked. His care was for what he could make out of his knowledge. Mrs. Champernowne must pay—she was the person with the purse. Oh yes !—at last he had got her, and John, and all the lot in a string, and he would pull the string !—tightening and tightening it until they crawled to his feet, if need be. There was only one person to be considered—himself. He would cheerfully throw Mrs. Champernowne and her brother to the police if need be—cheerfully. And John, too—for it was self first, self all the time. But Simmons knew there would be no throwing anybody to the police—Mrs. Champernowne would pay. And all that was necessary now was, to walk warily, make sure of one or two little points; and then choose the exact, the psychological moment for a swift, determined, ruthless stroke.

His brother came in. Simmons behaved as if nothing had happened. He ate his supper, chatted, sat up a while smoking cigarettes while John-smoked his pipe, and eventually went to bed congratulating himself on his luck. What with his undoubted success with Miss Pretty and his discovery in the orchard he had had a good day, a splendid day. He slept soundly.

But if Simmons had only known what was going on in a certain bedroom in the domestic quarter at Ashenhurst House he would have had nightmare, and cold sweats, and shivers that would have shaken him from top to toe, and left him reduced to the condition of a jelly-fish stranded on a rapidly drying beach. All unknown to Simmons his scheme was being undermined, his web torn to fragments, his ground cut away from beneath his feet.

Kitty Trevice returned to Mrs. Champernowne's from her afternoon out at ten o'clock in the evening and found Jane Pratt and the other servants at supper; later, she and Jane retired to the apartment which they shared together. Kitty and Jane, because of long association, were close friends, with no secrets about their love affairs, and Kitty was well aware that Simmons was Jane's late flame and one to whom she was not disinclined to stick: she knew, in fact, that the parlourmaid was quite willing to become Mrs. Simmons Hackdale. And in the process of unrobing for the night she suddenly turned on her friend with a look that implied more things than one.

"Jennie," she whispered. "I've got something to tell you! And you take it in the right way, my dear, and be thankful you've been warned in time!"

"Warned!" exclaimed Miss Pratt, turning a suddenly suspicious face on Kitty. "What about?—who against? What've you been hearing?"

"Hearing, nothing—seeing, a lot!" said Kitty. "Look here—don't you have anything more to do with that Simmons Hackdale! He's having you for the mug!"

Miss Pratt dropped the garment which she was about to array herself in, and turned on her friend with a gasp.

"What—whatever do you mean. Kitty Trevice?" she said. "Somebody's been—"

"Nobody's been doing anything in the way of telling me anything," affirmed the housemaid. "I'm talking about what I know myself, so there! Simmons Hackdale is treating you shameful!—he's deceiving you. He's walking you out, and making love, and all that sort o' thing—yes, and all the time he's carrying on with that young lady at the Chancellor—if she is a lady! Which," concluded Kitty, with a toss of her head, "there might be two opinions about."

"What do you mean?" repeated Miss Pratt, faintly.

"I'll tell you," said Kitty. "When I was going home this afternoon, I went through Danesley Old Wood—you know how lonely it is there. Well, though they never saw me, I saw this Miss Pretty and your Sim there—in a nice, quiet corner—oh, yes!"

"You didn't!" exclaimed Miss Pratt. "He told me he was at home this afternoon!"

"Then he told you a great big story!" declared Kitty. "Lor' bless you!—I was close to 'em. They'd ha' been mad enough—she would, anyway, I'll bet!—if they'd known how close!"

"What—what were they doing?" asked Miss Pratt, in still fainter accents.

"Doing? Kissing and cuddling, like good 'uns—or bad 'uns," answered Kitty. "I can tell you I saw plenty! If that's how young ladies behave with young men, well—all I can say is that I'm thankful I know how to behave myself better! Anyway, I'm telling you the truth, Jennie, and if I were you, next time Sim Hackdale comes whistling round our orchard, I should either let him whistle or send him off with a flea in his ear—a good-for-nothing young scamp!"

Miss Pratt made no reply. She got into bed. Within five minutes she heard Kitty Trevice breathing the faint and regular suspirations of healthy sleep. But Miss Pratt did not sleep. She knew Kitty; Kitty was a truthful wench. Therefore Sim was a wicked liar. Yet—she had taken a great fancy to Sim. He had made love to her as she had never been made love to before: boy though he was, she knew him to be an adept at love making. She had liked him to kiss her at their secret meetings in the orchard and the adjacent lanes—and now she was told, on positive evidence, that he was expending his kisses and embraces on another girl. She had seen the other girl—and her fine clothes—and pretty face—and all the rest of it. Jealousy, fierce, unreasoning, clamorous, sprang up in Miss Pratt's bosom. The longer she lay awake, the fiercer it grew. It was with her when at last slept; it was there when she awoke, tired and heavy—eyed in the morning; it gnawed at her all day. And now and then Kitty Trevice helped to feed its fires.

After Mrs. Champernowne and Mr. Alfred had dined that Monday evening, Jane Pratt asked and received permission to go out. She made a very careful toilet, and under cover of the dark departed townwards. She walked straight to the back entrance of the Chancellor Hotel, and going to the kitchen door asked for Gracie White. Gracie White was another friend of hers, who for some time had been second chambermaid at the Chancellor, and had succeeded the erring Mary Sanders as first chambermaid: Miss Pratt thought it more than possible that Gracie could tell her something she wanted to know. And when Gracie appeared she drew her away into a quiet corner of the courtyard.

"Gracie!" she said. "You know that young lady that's stopping here—the one who's something to do with the gentleman that was murdered?"

"Of course I do." answered Gracie. "Miss Pretty. She's on my floor—got a private sitting room and a bedroom there."

"I want to know something—between you and me," murmured Miss Pratt. "You know Simmons Hackdale?—does he ever come here to see her?"

"Oh, yes!" exclaimed Gracie. "He's been here several times, of an evening. He's with her now."

"Now?" said Miss Pratt. "Now?"

"Yes," answered Gracie. "She went out just after dinner and was out for an hour or so. He came back with her. They're in her sitting room. They've been there—oh, some time."

"By themselves?" suggested Miss Pratt.

"Of course," assented Gracie. "It's a private room. What do you want to know for, Jennie?"

But Miss Pratt shook her head.

"Never mind, now," she answered. "I'll tell you—some other time."

Then she bade her friend good-bye and went away. She walked very slowly along the street outside, her head downcast, her eyes fixed on the pavement, as if she were thinking. She was thinking—and as a result of her cogitations she suddenly looked up, smartened her pace, quitted the centre of the city, and marching straight to Shelmore's private house on the outskirts, rang the front door bell, and asked if Miss Pratt could see Mr. Shelmore at once on private and highly important business.

Shelmore, who at that moment was playing chess with his maiden aunt. Miss Chauncey, looked up in wonder at the maid who delivered Jane's message.

"Miss Pratt?" he exclaimed. "Who on earth is Miss Pratt?"

"Mrs. Champernowne's parlourmaid, sir," answered the girl.

Shelmore glanced at his aunt, at the chess board, at the clock on the mantelpiece; finally at the maid.

"Take her into the study," he said.

He went off to the study presently, to find Jane Pratt very rigid and pale on the edge of a straight-backed chair. She rose at his entrance and made him a polite bow; Shelmore saw at once that here was a young woman who was obviously agitated, but who was also resolute and determined—about something. He motioned her to an easy chair by his desk.

"Sit down," he said, kindly. "You want to see me—professionally?"

Jane Pratt took the chair he pointed out and nodded her head—on which was her best smart hat.

"Yes, Mr. Shelmore, sir, I do," she answered, a little tremulously, but with a gleam in her eyes which showed her hearer that whatever it was she had come to tell she was going to tell it. "I do, indeed! I know something!—and I will not keep it back any longer. You're a lawyer, and you'll know what to do, Mr. Shelmore!—Do you know that your clerk, Simmons Hackdale, is playing a rare game?"

"What game?" asked Shelmore.

"A bad, wicked, deceitful game!" declared Jane Pratt, with emphasis. "And he's tried to drag me into it!—he's a tongue that would get round anybody, I think. But I've found him out, and I won't have anything more to do with him or it—I won't!"

Shelmore glanced at the door. It was tightly shut, and lie drew his own chair a little nearer to his visitor's.

"Tell me all about it," he said, invitingly. "Take your time."

Jane Pratt took her time. Before she had been talking many minutes, Shelmore picked up pencil and paper and began to make notes. And when his visitor had come to the end of her statement he found himself confronting certain points which were not only interesting but serious. He glanced them over again in silence.

1. On the night of the murder of James Deane, Jane Pratt saw Mrs. Champernowne in company with a strange man in the grounds of Ashenhurst House.

2. Jane Pratt told Simmons Hackdale of this in strict confidence.

3. From various things said and done since then, Jane Pratt formed the opinion that Simmons Hackdale was endeavouring to trace the murderer of James Deane—and knew more than he had told her.

4. On a recent evening John Hackdale and James Bartlett called on Mrs. Champernowne. John Hackdale saw her alone; then fetched in Bartlett. Jane Pratt watched through drawing room window, and saw Mrs. Champernowne write a cheque and hand it to John Hackdale, in James Bartlett's presence.

5. Jane Pratt told Simmons Hackdale of this, and at his suggestion appropriated the sheet of blotting paper on which Mrs. Champernowne had dried the cheque. Simmons, by means of a hand mirror, showed her that the cheque was made out for one thousand pounds.

6. On the previous evening, she and Simmons being in the orchard of Mrs. Champernowne's house, Simmons picked up a revolver which had been lying amongst the long grass. He carried it away with him.

Shelmore read his notes twice through. Then he gave Jane Pratt a steady, searching look.

"I gather from what you say that you and Simmons have been—sweethearts, eh?" he asked.

"He forced his attentions on me!" answered Jane Pratt. "I didn't go after him!"

"But—you've evidently been keeping company," said Shelmore. "Pretty closely, I think! Now—what's happened to make you come and tell me all this?"

Jane Pratt hesitated, studying the pattern of the carpet.

"You can say anything you like to a solicitor, you know," suggested Shelmore. "Come, now—you've had some reason for—is it jealousy? There's some other girl?"

Jane Pratt's anger flared up.

"Girl?" she exclaimed. "It's that fine young madam at the Chancellor! He's carrying on with her! He was with her—kissing her—and all that—in Danesley Old Wood yesterday afternoon, and—and then he'd been promising to marry me, as soon is ever he got this reward."

Shelmore preserved an unmoved countenance—even at the mention of Miss Pretty. "I see," he said. "Evidently playing a double game. Very wicked of him! But now, is there any other reason for your coming to me?

"Well!" answered Jane Pratt, after a pause during which her temper appeared to cool down a little. "There is that revolver business. That frightened me—seemed to—to—"

"To bring the murder rather too close, eh?" suggested Shelmore.

"Yes," assented his visitor. "When it comes to revolvers, I don't want to have anything more to do with it. Nor with Sim Hackdale! He's bad—he can't open his lips without lying! And I've told you all about it, Mr. Shelmore."

"Very well." said Shelmore. "Now then, listen to me. Don't mention one word of all this until you see me again—I'll attend to it. Keep it as close as—"

"There's nobody can be closer than I can if I like, Mr. Shelmore," interrupted Jane Pratt.

"Then—be close," repeated Shelmore. "Keep absolute silence—and wait!"

He saw her out of his front door, and watched her go away. And though he went back to the chess board. Miss Chauncey soon perceived that his thoughts were not with it or her.

THE MAN WHO GOT OUT

While Simmons Hackdale slept soundly and Jane Pratt cried herself to sleep as a result of her fit of mingled jealousy, anger, and revenge, Shelmore lay awake, sorely perplexed by what he had heard from the parlourmaid. He was not altogether surprised at her news about Simmons: for some time he had realised that his clerk was a crafty and astute young person, of great natural ability, who would, probably, and sooner or later, arrive at a turning point in life and be obliged to decide whether he would abide by a straight road or deviate into a crooked one. Nor was he surprised by what he had heard of Miss Cynthia Pretty. He and his aunt had shown considerable hospitality to that young lady and had consequently seen a great deal of her, and Shelmore had come to the conclusion that she was not only resolved on having her own way about anything and everything, but was also a flirt who might easily develop into a female rake. In a strictly professional way, he had advised Miss Pretty to go home to Camborne and leave matters to him; Miss Pretty had made a mouth and intimated that she was quite well where she was, for a time, and had let him see plainly that she loved liberty, and knew that nobody could prevent her from exercising it. No!—there was nothing in all that to surprise him; he was conscious of the fact that Miss Pretty had tried to flirt with him and that he had remained severely cold: no wonder, then, that she had turned to his clerk, who, as he well knew, would be as plausible as he was crafty, and as ingratiating as he was sly. He was not sure that Sim Hackdale and Cynthia Pretty would not make a well-matched, materialistic young couple.

No again!—those were not the perplexing things. What did perplex him was the question—what was it all leading to? Deane asking information of Belling as to who and what Mrs. Champernowne was—Mrs. Champernowne being seen in her own grounds on the night of the murder with a stranger who was almost certainly Deane—Deane's dead and murdered body being found just behind Mrs. Champernowne's grounds—Mrs. Champernowne giving a cheque to John Hackdale in James Bartlett's presence—the finding of the revolver in Mrs. Champernowne's orchard—what, brought into co-relation, did all these things mean; what did they suggest? Shelmore fell asleep over these questions; they were with him when he awoke next morning. "Mellapont!" he muttered, as he rose. "Mellapont! I must see him at once."

He took the police station on his way to the office, judging it best to see the superintendent before he saw Simmons. Closeted with Mellapont, and armed with the notes he had taken, he disclosed everything that Jane Pratt had told him the night before. Mellapont's obvious amazement increased as the story went on.

"Do you think that's all true?" he asked, as Shelmore made an end. "That the girl wasn't—well, exaggerating if not inventing? She admitted that she came to you out of jealousy. Now a jealous woman—eh?"

"I've no hesitation in saying that I consider her an absolutely credible witness," said Shelmore. "I don't think she was either inventing or exaggerating. I think that the finding of the revolver last night made her reflect more seriously—in addition to her jealousy about my clerk, she got the feeling that things were getting—well, a bit too hot."

"You've thought a good deal about it since last night, no doubt?" suggested Mellapont. "Weighed it up, of course?"

"I've thought about nothing else," replied Shelmore, grimly.

"Well?—what do you make of it?" asked Mellapont.

Shelmore shook his head. But the gesture denoted not so much perplexity as a certain regret that the necessity for coming to a conclusion should have arisen.

"I don't think there can be any doubt that in some way or another, Mrs. Champernowne has been and is mixed up in the affair," he answered. "If you remember, Mellapont, when you and I first made enquiries at the Chancellor, Belling told us that when Deane returned from the picture house that night—the night of his arrival here, and, as far as we know of his murder—"

"From the medical evidence, it was the night of his murder," interrupted Mellapont. "The medical men agreed that he'd been dead forty—eight hours or thereabouts when John Hackdale found the body that Wednesday evening."

"Very well—on the night of his murder, then," continued Shelmore. "You remember, anyway, that Belling told us that on his return from the picture house, Deane asked him questions about Mrs. Champernowne. How do we know that he hadn't recognised Mrs. Champernowne as somebody he knew?"

"But he asked Belling—to begin with—who she was?" said Mellapont. "He didn't know who she was until Belling told him. I remember that—distinctly."

"That may have been a blind," remarked Shelmore. "He may have known well enough who she was, and yet have wanted, for reasons of his own, not to let it be known that he knew. What he probably wanted was information about her status in Southernstowe. What more likely than that he should preface his questioning of Belling by asking who the lady was who seemed to be a person of some consequence? I think Deane knew Mrs. Champernowne. And I think it was Deane who was with Mrs. Champernowne in her grounds that night."

"If we only knew that for certain," said Mellapont. "If!"

"It seems to me to fit in," said Shelmore. "Anyway, we do know that Deane, evidently acting on some sudden impulse, left the Chancellor and went out. It must have been Deane that this girl saw! But after that—ah! There are missing links, of course—always are! Can they be supplied?"

"That episode can—and will have to—be gone into," remarked Mellapont. "For instance, if it comes to further questioning the girl, I should ask her more about her mistress's movements that night, after she'd been seen with this man in the grounds—did she go into the house soon after Jane Pratt saw her with him, or did she stay out any time longer? Important, that! But what I'm most curious about, Shelmore, is the Hackdale—Bartlett cheque incident. Hackdale and Bartlett have an interview with Mrs. Champernowne. She's seen to write out a cheque and hand it to Hackdale. Now if Hackdale had been alone, I shouldn't have thought much of it. But Bartlett was with him. Presumably, the cheque was for the two of them. Why? Bartlett is a sly fellow—unprincipled! And this puts me in mind of something—up to very recently Bartlett was in very low water, very low water indeed. He was hanging about the city—why, as a matter of fact, he was glad to go errands, or hold a horse! He was thankful for a shilling. He disappeared suddenly—and then all of a sudden, he turns up with information about that watch and he's well dressed, smart, was very smart, as you may have observed: good clothes, linen, boots, hat. Where did he get his money? Strikes me, Shelmore, Bartlett probably knows a damned lot."

"Do you know where he is—now?" asked Shelmore.

"I do, fortunately," answered Mellapont. "He's living in Portsmouth, and I have his address. I told him he'd have to be in attendance when Kight and Sanders are brought up again, and he told me where he was staying, quite willingly. I shall be on to Bartlett, he knows something! But now—this clerk of yours, young Sim? What's he after?"

94

"The reward which Miss Pretty so foolishly offered," replied Shelmore. "He's greedy about money! That's his notion—the reward!"

"Aye!" said Mellapont. "But—are you sure! Looks to me as if the young ferret was quietly gathering all the information he could for—another purpose."

"What?" asked Shelmore.

Mellapont gave his caller a knowing look.

"Mrs. Champernowne's a very wealthy woman, Shelmore," he said. "She's wealthier than Miss Pretty, I guess! There's such a thing as—blackmail!"

Shelmore started. He had not thought of that. "Maybe," he said. "He's—unprincipled."

"You haven't said anything to him since seeing Jane Pratt?" asked Mellapont. "You haven't?—that's good. Look here, let's meet craft with craft. Do you think you could get Master Simmons clean out of the town, at once, within an hour or two, for a couple of days?"

"Why?" asked Shelmore, in surprise.

"So as to prevent him from communicating with anybody, Jane Pratt and Miss Pretty in particular, while I get to work," answered Mellapont. "Advisable, I assure you!"

"I could," said Shelmore, after a moment's reflection. "Yes—I can send him away at once, to London, on business that'll keep him there a day or two—three, if you like."

"Two will do," said Mellapont. "Get him off at once until day after tomorrow. In the meantime—" he gave his caller a significant glance, "-in the meantime, I'll make some enquiries that'll help me to be better fitted to encounter him than we are now! You'll be careful, of course, not to let him know that you've heard anything?"

"Oh, of course!" said Shelmore. "I've an excellent excuse for sending him away— excellent! He'll think it's all in the way of business."

He rose to go, and Mellapont rose, too. But ere they reached the door, the superintendent suddenly pointed to the chair which Shelmore had left.

"Just sit down again for five minutes, Shelmore," he said. "I've an idea! I won't keep you longer—less, perhaps."

He left the room, and within the five minutes was back again, looking unusually grave.

"I say," he said, in a low voice, coming up to Shelmore's side. "I've just found out something that's a bit—well, both serious and significant. You know that anybody who wants to keep fire-arms nowadays have not only to take out a license but to get police permission?"

"Of course!" replied Shelmore.

"Well, I've just looked over our register," continued Mellapont. "I find that Mrs. Champernowne has a revolver. So has John Hackdale."

Shelmore reflected a moment in silence.

"Yes," he said at last, "but if—if either she or he did—what we know was done, it's not at all likely that the revolver used in doing it would be thrown away in that orchard! Is it, now?"

"Quite true, it isn't!—You're right there," agreed Mellapont. "However, get that clerk of yours out of the way while I make some enquiries. You don't know what he'll be getting his nose into if he stops about here—I don't want him in the town just now."

Shelmore went away to his office. He was not exactly clear in his own mind as to why Mellapont wanted to clear Simmons out of Southernstowe for forty-eight hours, but the proposal fitted in with his own inclinations; somehow or other, he scarcely knew why, he had just then no great liking for his clerk's company. And as soon as he had gone through his letters he turned on Simmons, intent on getting him off at once.

"Hackdale!—you can leave all that for me to attend to; that, and everything else," he said. "There's something I want you to do. You know that property we're negotiating about on behalf of Major Hampole?"

"The Dorsetshire property?" answered Simmons. "Yes?"

"I'm not at all satisfied about the reports we've had of it," continued Shelmore. "I'd like to have it personally inspected. I want you to go off at once—this morning—and have a thorough look over it. You can catch the eleven twenty—eight, can't you?—that'll enable you to get the twelve—fourteen for Dorchester at Portsmouth."

Simmons glanced at his watch.

"Oh, yes, I can catch that," he answered. "Plenty of time. No time to see much this afternoon, though. It's a four or five hours' run to Dorchester."

"Of course not!" agreed Shelmore. "You'll get down there today, and look round tomorrow and the following morning. I'll write a cheque for your expenses. There's no need to get home tomorrow—I want you to make a thorough inspection of that farm. See what state of repair it is in as regards buildings, fences, roads, and all that—the letters about it are vague. Keep your eyes open to everything about it—Major Hampole will be calling in a few days, and I want to be able to tell him the precise facts about the condition of the property he's proposing to buy."

"I understand." answered Simmons. "I'll see to it."

He presently took the cheque which Shelmore wrote out and went away to cash it at the neighbouring bank, and to hurry to his rooms and pack a bag. He had no objection to a mission of this sort; it meant staying at a good hotel, eating and drinking of the best, seeing new places and new people, and generally having a good time. True, he had an appointment with Miss Pretty for that evening, but he would send her a wire from Portsmouth saying that he was called away on business for a day or two; as for his other plots and plans they must wait until he came back. With every intention of enjoying himself on the liberal amount of expense money in his pocket, he went off to the station and bought his ticket.

Five minutes later Simmons wished that he hadn't bought a ticket at all—or that he had only taken one to Portsmouth instead of booking right through to Dorchester. This wish came into existence by his looking out of the window of his compartment at the very last moment, in quest of a newspaper boy. There was no newspaper boy handy—but Simmons saw and recognised a man who had evidently just left the train—a London to Portsmouth express—and who was giving the porter instructions about his suitcase. A well—fed, rosy—cheeked, substantial—looking man, with a professional air: a stranger, observant people would have said, by the way he looked about him, and the questions he was asking. But Simmons knew him—and muttered his name in accents of anxious wonder. Mr. Palsford, solicitor, of Normansholt!—head of the firm on which he, Simmons, had waited recently, at the time when Swilford Swale told him the mysterious story of Arradeane and his disappearance. Palsford, of course!—no mistaking him. What was he doing there—in Southernstowe?

But Simmons' ready wit supplied the answer to the question as soon as it was asked. The dispute between Sir Reville Childerstone and his tenant at Normansholt was still going on; it was indeed more of a dispute than ever; Palsford had probably thought it well, on behalf of his client, to come and see Shelmore personally about it. For that Simmons cared nothing: Palsford, or his partner, or his clerks could come to Southernstowe and jaw about legal matters as much as ever they liked for all it mattered to him. But Palsford was a Normansholt man; Palsford would know all about the Arradeane case of many years ago. Supposing, while he was in Southernstowe, he saw

Mrs. Champernowne, who was always a good deal about the town, and recognised her as Mrs. Arradeane?—a not unlikely thing? What would happen?—Where would he, Simmons, be?—where would his rapidly-maturing schemes of personal profit get to? What had seemed half-an-hour ago a bit of luck now seemed a misfortune. He ought to be on the spot—ready for any eventuality.

But—he had not gone far. Nor did he go far. He left the train at Portsmouth, and instead of catching the twelve—fourteen to Dorchester, went to an hotel and lunched. He thought, and thought—and could not decide what to do. Eventually he decided to stay in Portsmouth for the night, and to consider matters more deeply. Dining early in the evening at his hotel, he subsequently went out for the theatre. And going theatre-ward, Simmons got a further shock. There, on the other side of the street, he saw Bartlett—in company with Superintendent Mellapont.

COIL WITHIN COIL

The comfortable and prosperous looking gentleman whom Simmons Hackdale had recognised as Mr. Palsford, solicitor, of Normansholt, having made due enquiry at Southernstowe railway station as to the best hotel in the place, left his luggage to be sent on there, and walked slowly away into the streets. In so small a town he had little difficulty in finding the office he wanted, and before Simmons had travelled half way to Portsmouth, Mr. Palsford was climbing the stairs which the clerk had so lately descended. He opened the door of the anteroom in which Simmons usually sat, and finding it empty, rapped on the table: Shelmore poked his head out of the inner office.

"Mr. Palsford, of Normansholt!" announced the caller, with a bland smile. "Mr. Shelmore, I presume?"

Shelmore looked his surprise and hastened to get his fellow-solicitor inside.

"My clerk's away for the time being," he remarked, as he drew forward an easy chair. "I only run one at present, Mr. Palsford—early days. But what brings you into these parts?"

"I had business in London," replied Palsford, with a benign smile. "And I thought, when it was over, that being within sixty miles of your interesting city, I would kill three birds with one stone, Mr. Shelmore. The first—I would see Southernstowe, which I have often heard of and never seen. The second—this affair between your client, Sir Reville Childerstone, and my client, his tenant. The third—possibly—I say possibly—the most important of the three."

"And what's that?" asked Shelmore.

Palsford, with an enigmatic smile playing about his lips, produced a long cigarette holder, a cigarette case, and a box of matches. He continued to smile while adjusting a cigarette to the holder; he was still smiling when he had lighted the cigarette and puffed at it a little. There was something sly, confidential, and humorous about the smile, and Shelmore began to be inquisitive.

"You are a Southernstowe man, Mr. Shelmore?" suggested Palsford. "Native?"

"I am!" admitted Shelmore. "Born and bred here."

"Then you know everybody. Do you know a lady here who calls herself Mrs. Champernowne?"

Shelmore stared in astonishment.

"Calls herself?" he exclaimed. "That implies—but yes, certainly I know Mrs. Champernowne! Who doesn't? She's Mayor of Southernstowe, a very smart and capable business woman; and very wealthy. What about her?"

Palsford smiled again, and producing a pocket book, drew from amongst a quantity of papers a cutting which he laid on Shelmore's desk. Shelmore found himself looking at a reproduced picture of Mrs. Champernowne, beneath which were a few lines of print.

"That she?" asked Palsford, laconically.

"To be sure!" said Shelmore. "A recent photograph!"

"Very good!" remarked Palsford. "Mrs. Champernowne, Mayor of Southernstowe. But I knew that lady as—somebody else!"

Shelmore started again. His eyes grew incredulous. But Palsford only smiled.

"As—somebody else!" he repeated. "I knew her as a Mrs. Arradeane, she lived in my own town some twenty years ago. I have no more doubt that Mrs. Champernowne of Southernstowe and Mrs. Arradeane late of Normansholt are one and the same person than

I have that that is the eminently graceful spire of Southernstowe Cathedral which I see through your window!"

Shelmore was feeling as a man might feel who has been brought nose-close to a curtain which is just about to be drawn up. What lay behind? Before he could speak, Palsford went on, tapping the scrap of paper.

"I happened to pick that up on my wife's table," he said. "I mean the paper. I cut it from—a fashionable society paper. You see, Shelmore, what it announces beneath the picture?—that Mrs. Champernowne is shortly to marry Sir Reville Childerstone—your client. Is that so?"

"That is so—oh, yes!" assented Shelmore.

Palsford waved his cigarette holder.

"All right." he said. "But—if she's the woman I'm confident she is—she can't marry Sir Reville Childerstone nor any other man. That's flat!"

"Why?" asked Shelmore.

"Because her husband's alive!" answered Palsford drily. "That's why."

"You mean that—that, if Mrs. Champernowne is really Mrs. Arradeane, there's some man named Arradeane, her husband, actually alive?" asked Shelmore. "That it?"

"Some man? A man!—the man!" said Palsford. "James Arradeane, the husband of the woman I knew as Mrs. Arradeane, and whom I believe to be identical with your Mrs. Champernowne is, I tell you, alive. Or," he suddenly added, "he was, four months ago!—and I haven't heard of his death."

Shelmore sat staring alternately at the photograph and at his caller. He suddenly turned on Palsford, with an abrupt question.

"Had your Mrs. Arradeane a brother who lived with her who was known as—"

"As Mr. Alfred?" laughed Palsford. "Precisely! Has—"

"She has!" said Shelmore. "Good Lord!—this is worse than ever!"

"What's worse than ever?" demanded the visitor.

Shelmore rose from his chair, thrust his hands in his pockets and began to pace the room, evidently deep in thought. Palsford fitted another cigarette in his holder and went on smoking quietly. At last Shelmore came back to his chair.

"Look here!" he said. "Have you read, in the papers, about what has been called the Southernstowe, or the Sand Pit mystery—a murder case?"

"No!—not that I remember," answered Palsford. Don't read murders—no interest in 'em—not even professionally. Not my line, Shelmore."

"Nor mine," said Shelmore. "But one's sometimes forced into things. Well—it's this. A stranger—a well—to—do man, calling himself James Deane—"

"Eh!" exclaimed Palsford, sharply, "James—Deane?"

"James Deane," repeated Shelmore, "—came to stay at the Chancellor Hotel here for a few days not very long ago, and was murdered—shot—on the very midnight of his arrival. His dead body was found in a disused sand pit behind Mrs? Champernowne's grounds. Up to now, the mystery of his death hasn't been solved, but I may tell you that there are serious grounds for believing Mrs. Champernowne to have had, if not active participation, at least complicity in the murder. Now this Deane."

"Who was he?—where did he come from?" asked Palsford.

"Camborne, in Cornwall," replied Shelmore. "He was part—proprietor of a tin mine; his partner, a nice girl, is staying in the town now, at the Chancellor Hotel—you'll be sure to see her, while you're here. She says that this man—James Deane, who'd been her father's partner, and was her guardian, was by profession a mining engineer."

Palsford's countenance, usually inclined to a benevolent jollity, had become very grave. He was rubbing his chin, thoughtfully.

"Odd, odd, odd!" he muttered. "A small world, after all! Deuced odd! And—murder?"

"You don't think this man James Deane could be the James Arradeane of whom you spoke just now?" asked Shelmore.

"No!" answered Palsford, with decision. "I'll tell you straight out, Shelmore. James Arradeane, the husband of the woman we're discussing, is in Australia, and has been for over twenty years. But I'm in communication with him four times a year—he has some property here in England which I manage. No!—this man wouldn't be James Arradeane. But—I've a pretty good idea who he was."

"Who, then?" asked Shelmore.

"My man had a cousin of the very same name," replied Palsford. "Another James Arradeane who lived in London—he was a mining engineer—they both were. I've met the London man—just once. Twenty—one—or two years ago. But I've never heard of him since. I guess that's the man, Shelmore! He must have changed his name to Deane, left London, and gone to Cornwall. Good heavens!"

"Why should he be murdered?" asked Shelmore.

Palsford threw away his cigarette, put the holder in his pocket, and gave the younger man a keen, suggestive look.

"Probably," he answered in low tones, "probably because he knew that the other James Arradeane was alive and was threatening to stop what would have been a bigamous marriage! That's about it, Shelmore. But look here—this thing is assuming much more serious aspects than I'd any idea of. After what I've told you, and after what you've told me, it'll have to be gone into. But—let me be certain, absolutely, positively certain that I'm not mistaken about the woman! I'm as confident as man can be that your Mrs. Champernowne is the Mrs. Arradeane who left Normansholt some twenty years ago and if I could set eyes on her-"

"You can do that within five minutes," interrupted Shelmore, glancing at his watch. "The City Council is sitting now close by—come away, and we'll just look in."

He led his visitor up the street to the City Hall and into a dark corner in the public gallery of the Council Chamber, where Mrs. Champernowne was at that moment presiding over a debate. Within five minutes Palsford nudged his guide's elbow.

"Yes!" he whispered. "Oh, yes! that's the woman! Let's get out of this."

Shelmore was only too glad to get out. The disclosures of the last few hours were beginning to confuse him: he wanted to start on the job of straightening them out. And when they left the Council Chamber he sheered Palsford away in the direction of Mellapont's office at the police station.

"She's very little altered," remarked Palsford, as they went away. "Wonderfully well preserved woman—always a smart, clever woman. Well!—I'd no idea that I was going to be cast into a maze of this sort! Has this superintendent of yours got hold of any thread that will lead us out of it?"

"I want you to tell him all you've told me," answered Shelmore. "Of course, there's a great deal that's happened here that I haven't told you of, yet. You, Mellapont, and I had better have a regular consultation."

Mellapont heard all that Palsford had to say—listening in absorbed silence. In the end he asked a direct question.

"You say that this man James Arraneane, whom you knew at Normansholt as the husband of the woman whom we, here, know as Mrs. Champernowne, is still alive?" he said. "You're sure of it?"

"He was alive four months ago," replied Palsford. "That was when he last wrote to me. I could establish this fact of his being alive within forty—eight hours, by cabling to him. He lives in Melbourne."

"What are your relations with him?" enquired Mellapont.

"When he left Normansholt," answered Palsford, "he left some property in my hands. I remit the receipts from it—rent, you know—to him, every quarter."

"Under what circumstances did he leave Normansholt?" asked Mellapont. "According to what you say, he left suddenly, leaving his wife behind him, and disappeared. You aren't suggesting that it was in collusion with her?"

"No," replied Palsford. "I'll tell you all about it—I believe, indeed, I'm sure, I'm the only person who knows the truth. To this day, people in Normansholt talk about the extraordinary disappearance of James Arradeane, but nobody but myself knows anything about it. The facts are these—Arradeane, who wanted to get interested financially in coal mines in our neighbourhood, came to live in Normansholt with his wife and her brother. He and his wife, it was soon well known, were both persons of considerable means—very well off. But it was also soon well known that they didn't get on together. There were various reasons. His tastes weren't her's—her's weren't his. They had no children—so there was the absence of that particular bond. He objected to her brother, from whom she wouldn't be parted—a weak, good-for-nothing idler, born to be a parasite on anybody who would keep him! Altogether things were neither smooth nor pleasant. And I very well remember that Arradeane at last came to me, and said, in confidence, that he'd had enough of it, and was quietly going to clear clean out. He told me that all his affairs were in order; all his accounts squared: a certain sum of money—considerable—was paid in to his wife's separate account at her bank, and that she had plenty of money of her own— which I already knew. He further said that he should make no fuss, no bother, no announcement, but just walk off. He did—without notice to me, and the next I heard of him he was in Melbourne, where he's been ever since."

"In his correspondence with you has he ever mentioned her?" asked Mellapont.

"Never!—never once," replied Palsford. "The notion was that there should be a clean cut. And, as I tell you, it certainly was so on his part. He just—vanished!"

"Did she ever make any effort to find him?" enquired Shelmore. "Was any search instituted?"

"Not while she remained in Normansholt," said Palsford. "But that was not for long. Within a very short time of his disappearance she had cleared everything up there, sold all her effects, and gone—her brother with her. And, as far as I'm concerned, I never heard anything of her until I saw that portrait in the lady's paper and recognised it. I'd no doubt about my recognition, and now that I've seen Mrs. Champernowne in the flesh I know she's the woman I knew at Normansholt as Mrs. Arradeane."

"Twenty years is a long time," remarked Mellapont, musingly. "A very long time!"

"Oh, well!" said Palsford. "If you doubt my being right, just contrive for Mrs. Champernowne to see me suddenly! If she doesn't recognise me at once, I'll eat my hat! But she will!—I haven't changed much in twenty years."

"I didn't mean that you aren't right," replied Mellapont. "I think you are—I've no doubt you are. What I meant was that a lot can happen in twenty years. She's been here most of these years, and has built up a big business, made a pile of money, become mayor of the city, and is contemplating marriage with a baronet!"

"She can't marry him!" said Palsford. "Her husband is alive! That's probably what her cousin, the other James Arradeane, whom I take to be the murdered man Deane, told her, or wanted to tell her. He would know."

101

Mellapont glanced at Shelmore and shook his head.

"Worse and worse!" he muttered. "I'm afraid there's going to be some illumination of all this that'll be a bit—dazzling, eh? Mr. Palsford, you'll be staying at the Chancellor? Yes, well, don't say a word of all this to the young lady you'll no doubt see there—Miss Pretty. Mr. Shelmore—I suppose that clerk of yours went off? All right—let me have another consultation this evening. I may—I hope to have more information by then."

"Where are you going to get it?" asked Shelmore.

"I'm going to find Bartlett and get it out of him," answered Mellapont, with a grim look. "Bartlett, I'm certain, knows a lot! Let me convince him that it's in his interest to keep in with me—and Bartlett will talk. Take Mr. Palsford away, Mr. Shelmore, and post him up in every detail of the story as far as we know it. Then, tonight, eh? In the multitude of counsellors."

Chapter

21

BARTLETT'S HEARTHRUG

While Mellapont, Shelmore, and the north country solicitor were discussing matters in the superintendent's private office at Southernstowe police station, Bartlett, all unconscious that he was one of the subjects of their debate, was comfortably eating his dinner at Portsmouth. He had gone back there with his thousand pounds in his pocket and with the highly satisfactory knowledge that from that time forward John Hackdale would send him five pounds every Friday evening. He lodged the thousand pounds in his bank, and had a little talk with the bank manager about investing his capital, now two thousand. But it was only a preliminary talk—"there was no hurry," said Bartlett: "he would consider matters and study the market lists in stocks and shares." He went to his lodgings and ordered his dinner—an unusually good one, and when it was served to him, he ate it with the appetite of a man who feels that he has thoroughly deserved the good things of life.

Dinner over, he mixed his mid—day allowance of rum, lighted his pipe, took up the newspaper, and got into his easy chair before the fire. "Life!" said Bartlett to himself, "was henceforth going to be very pleasant, blissfully comfortable." These were good lodgings; the landlady was capable and obliging; the situation quiet and respectable. He had a vision of an orderly and placid existence—as one day was, so should the next be. He would breakfast leisurely, dawdling over his eggs and bacon and the morning paper. Later, he would take his constitutional; it would end at his favourite house of call; there he would have a glass or two, and exchange political speculations with his fellow habitues of the bar parlour. He would go home to dinner at one o'clock and dine well. He would have a nap before the fire; he would wake to a dish of tea. The evening would find him at the favourite tavern again: there was good company there of an evening, and as good talk as you would find anywhere. At half past nine he would go home to a hot supper—yes, it must be hot, every night—and then, after a night cap of his habitual beverage—the best old Jamaica—would come bed. An ideal existence for Bartlett.

He dropped asleep over these day dreams and the newspaper, and slept soundly in his padded chair. And suddenly he awoke to hear a voice—the landlady's voice—which seemed at first far off and then unpleasantly near.

"Mr. Barton—Mr. Barton—there's a gentleman to see you!"

Bartlett turned confusedly, unable to remember that to his landlady and his new found world he was Barton and not Bartlett. Before he realised this he was aware of something more pertinent—his caller, already in the room, was Mellapont. And somehow or other, Mellapont, in mufti, and looking like a highly respectable gentleman, a retired Army officer or something of that sort, seemed more formidable than Mellapont in his dark blue, black-braided uniform. But Bartlett's wits rose to the occasion and he put a good face on things.

"Oh, how do you do, sir!" he exclaimed, rising hurriedly from his chair. "An unexpected pleasure, sir, I'm sure. A little refreshment after your journey, Mr. Mellapont. I've a drop of very good whisky in the sideboard, sir—Mrs. Capper, a clean glass or two if you please."

"Well, I've no objection, thank you," answered Mellapont. He came forward as the landlady left the room and gave Bartlett a meaning look. "All right, my lad!" he murmured. "Just want a bit of a talk with you—that's all. Nice situation you've got here, and very comfortable rooms, eh?" he went on as the landlady returned with a couple of glasses and a syphon of soda—water. "Make yourself at home here, no doubt?"

"Oh, we're quite at home here, sir—aren't we, Mrs. Capper?" responded Bartlett, with a jovial air. "Oh, yes—allow me to help you, sir," he continued, bustling about. "Excellent whisky this, I'm told, Mr. Mellapont—never touch it myself. I'll take a little rum with you." He handed a glass over to the visitor and gave himself a rather larger allowance of his own spirit than usual. "My respects, Mr. Mellapont." Then, as the landlady having left them and closed the door, he turned sharply. "Nothing wrong, I hope, sir?"

Mellapont took his glass, nodded over its brim, remarking that the contents were good, old, sound, and relapsed into a chair, waving his host back into the one he had just vacated.

"There's a great deal wrong, Bartlett!" he said. "And I've come to see you because I'm certain you know things. You can help to clear up. Now I'll tell you straight out. I know a good lot about you. You've been behind the scenes in this murder affair at Southernstowe—it's no use denying it, Bartlett."

Bartlett's nerves, shaken by Mellapont's sudden descent upon his retreat, were tightening again under the stimulus of the rum. He began to grow wary.

"I may have seen a bit, known a bit, Mr. Mellapont," he said. "The watch, for instance-"

"You can leave all that out," interrupted Mellapont. "That part of it's cleared. There's no doubt we got at the truth of that in Shelmore's statement before the magistrate. Kight and the chambermaid got Deane's jewellery under the circumstances they confessed to, and in due course they'll be tried, convicted and sentenced. But—they'd nothing to do with the murder. Now, Bartlett, I'll put it straight to you—have you any idea whatever, any suspicions as to who had?"

"Suspicion's neither here nor there, Mr. Mellapont," answered Bartlett. "You might suspect a dozen people—without cause. I don't know who murdered that man!—I've no idea whatever."

"Very well!" said Mellapont. "Then I'm going to ask you something—after telling you something. And the last first. The other night, Bartlett, you and John Hackdale went together to Mrs. Champernowne's house, Ashenhurst. You were admitted. You waited in a small room in the hall while John Hackdale went to see Mrs. Champernowne in her drawing room. He fetched you to her—after a while. Mrs. Champernowne talked to both of you. Eventually she wrote out a cheque, which she handed to John Hackdale. He and you then left. But… "

Mellapont paused, purposely. He was watching his man with keen, searching eyes. He saw that his first words astonished Bartlett, but he also saw that after the opening stage of astonishment had passed it was followed by an expression of almost smug and confident assurance; it was as if Bartlett were saying to himself, "Yes, he may know that much, but that's all, and that all's nothing?' And he went on, watching his listener still more closely.

"But there's more," he said. "Next morning, Hackdale cashed that cheque at Mrs. Champernowne's bank in Southernstowe. It was for a thousand pounds, and he took the money in notes. And you, Bartlett, have just paid a thousand pounds into a banking account that you've started here in Portsmouth, in the name you're now living under— Barton. You paid it in in the identical notes which Hackdale received at the Southernstowe bank—I have the numbers in my pocket-book. Now, Bartlett, my question—be careful and think about your answer! Why did Mrs. Champernowne pay you a thousand pounds?"

Bartlett was astonished enough, and in a bad way, by that time. His hand shook as he set down his glass.

"We—we all have business, private business, of our own, Mr. Mellapont," he faltered. "I don't see-"

"Don't fence with it, Bartlett!" interrupted Mellapont. "You'd no business with Mrs. Champernowne! If you had business with her it wouldn't have been done in a hole-and-corner fashion. Now come—I've approached you in friendly fashion—be reasonable and let's get at the truth—it'll pay you in the long run. Far better keep in with the law, and with us, the police, than turn to crooked ways, Bartlett! Now, honestly, wasn't that thousand pounds given you as hush-money?"

"I would like a definition of that term, Mr. Mellapont," said Bartlett. "Your definition!"

"Money paid to prevent exposure," answered Mellapont, brusquely. "You know!"

"I don't know that I could expose anybody,'" retorted Bartlett. "I couldn't!"

"Then you tell me what the money was paid for," said Mellapont. "If for a genuine business deal of which you're not ashamed, tell me in confidence—it'll go no further."

"I've no permission to do that, Mr. Mellapont," replied Bartlett. "There's always two parties to a transaction. Supposing I am one in this case, there's still another. If I'm willing to tell you, perhaps the other party isn't."

Mellapont leaned forward across the hearthrug.

"Look here, Bartlett," he said earnestly. "Let me tell you something. You're in a very risky position; a very dangerous position. I'm not afraid of being candid with you, and I'll just tell you how things stand. You know that Deane was found murdered, shot by a revolver, in a sand pit just behind Mrs. Champernowne's house and grounds—now I'll tell you of certain facts—facts!—that are in our possession. Deane was with Mrs. Champernowne in her grounds that night—he was seen talking to her. The revolver with which he was probably shot has been found in Mrs. Champernowne's orchard. Mrs. Champernowne holds a police certificate for a revolver—this revolver so found may be hers. There's a prima facie case, for according to evidence put into my hands this very morning she'd good reason for wishing to rid herself or to silence the murdered man. Now, Bartlett, you listen to me!—more carefully than ever. If Mrs. Champernowne is arrested on this charge, and if she's found guilty, and if it's found that she gave you hush—money to keep you quiet about something you know, you'll let yourself in for—do you know what, Bartlett?"

Bartlett was listening more carefully than ever, and he was conscious that Mellapont was gradually scoring points against him in this verbal encounter. But he still strove to affect a polite indifference.

"Can't say that I do, sir," he answered. "I'm not a lawyer, you know, Mr. Mellapont."

"No doubt!" agreed Mellapont. "But that plea wouldn't stand you in any stead. Every Englishman is supposed to know the law, and he can't plead ignorance as a defence. Bartlett!—do you know what an accessory is?"

"Not in legal parlance, sir, not in legal parlance!" said Bartlett.

"Then I'll tell you!" continued Mellapont. "An accessory is one, who, though not the principal in a felony, and even absent at the time of its committal, has nevertheless been concerned with the crime, either before or after the fact. After!—mind that, Bartlett—after, as well as before. Now what is it to be an accessory after the fact? It's to be one, who, knowing that a felony has been committed, assists, relieves, or protects the felon. Just get that into your head!"

"I don't know of any felony having been committed," said Bartlett. "And I've neither assisted, relieved or protected anybody!"

"Not by silence?" asked Mellapont, sharply. "Come!—why did Mrs. Champernowne give you a thousand pounds? Bartlett!—you'd better be careful! Think again!"

Bartlett thought—for a good five minutes.

"Do you really mean," he said at last, "do you really mean—no bluff, Mr. Mellapont, if you please!—that if Mrs. Champernowne were found guilty of this, and it was discovered that I knew, well, just something—some little thing—I should be liable to—what you're talking about?"

"I do!" answered Mellapont. "Most certainly! If you know anything—anything, however small—against her, and conceal it from us, you're assisting and protecting her. That's so?"

"You think things will come out against her?" asked Bartlett, uneasily.

"From certain facts put before me this very day—yes!" replied Mellapont.

Once more, Bartlett assumed his thinking cap. After all, if Mrs. Champernowne were convicted, which now seemed likely, his weekly stipend would come to an end. On the other hand, if he told Mellapont what he knew, his information would qualify him for the reward offered by Miss Pretty—and a bird in the hand…

"Mr. Mellapont?" he said suddenly. "' If I tell you all I do know—all!—will it be confidential?"

"As far as justice will allow, yes," answered Mellapont. "Certainly!"

"I don't know that my name need be brought in," remarked Bartlett. "But another thing—if I do tell you, will you back me up in putting in for that second reward of the young lady's—Miss Pretty's? She offered a thousand pounds to anybody who saw and spoke to Deane on the night of the murder."

"Don't mind doing that," said Mellapont. "I'd as soon see you have Miss Pretty's money as anybody else—she's a bit of a fool, in my opinion. Why, Bartlett, did you see and speak to him?"

"I did!" answered Bartlett, readily enough at last. "I did, sir!—and that's literally all I know. He met me near North Bar just about midnight and asked me to tell him where Ashenhurst House, Mrs. Champernowne's residence, was. I told him. He went in that direction. Two nights later, I heard of the murder, and knew that the dead man must be the man who'd stopped me—the description tallied. Just after I'd heard, I met John Hackdale, on his beat as special constable. I told him what I've told you. He begged me to keep my mouth shut, and gave me—I should say, all the money he had in his pocket. Next day—night—he came to me with a hundred and fifty pounds and told me that if I'd go to America with it and stop there he'd cable me the same amount as soon as he heard that I'd landed in New York. I promised. He'd no sooner gone than I heard of Miss Pretty's offer of a reward. That roused me. Instead of going to Southampton, I came here and waited and watched the papers. Mere chance gave me that opportunity as regards the watch and those two people from the Chancellor—Kight and Sanders. I got the reward from Miss Pretty for that—the thousand offered about the jewellery. When I sent to Southernstowe about that affair, John Hackdale saw me and was taken aback, because I hadn't gone to America. He took me to Mrs. Champernowne's house—I saw her, with him, as you say. But she never mentioned anything to me, Mr. Mellapont—I mean as regards why I was to keep my mouth shut. All she did was to give me—through Hackdale—that thousand pounds and the promise of a weekly pension. And that's all—all!"

Mellapont was thinking—thinking hard. His thoughts were chiefly on John Hackdale. He remembered that the sand pit and its surroundings were in John Hackdale's beat; that it was John Hackdale who found the dead man; that John Hackdale had concealed the fact that he knew a man, Bartlett, who had met and spoken with Deane; altogether, it was obvious, John Hackdale had played a double game. And then he suddenly remembered, too, that John Hackdale held a police certificate for a revolver. Altogether...

"Um!" he said, waking out of his reverie. "So—it was John Hackdale who acted as principal in all this, Bartlett, until that last interview, eh? And that's really all you know—all?"

"All, Mr. Mellapont!" protested Bartlett. "Doesn't seem much, does it?"

"Um!" murmured Mellapont. "That remains to be seen." He pulled out his watch. "I must get to the station and back to Southernstowe," he said. "Walk with me—I want to ask you a few more questions."

Bartlett went with him. Simmons Hackdale, lounging around, saw them together. He saw them part at the entrance to the station. And once Superintendent Mellapont had taken a seat in the next train for Southernstowe, Simmons also took one—further back. It seemed to him that an astute general like himself should be on the battlefield in the thick of things.

22

CHECKMATE

All unconscious that Simmons Hackdale was on the same train and only a few yards away along its corridor, Mellapont went back to Southernstowe, plunged in thought. He had an instinctive feeling that Bartlett had told him the truth and revealed all that he knew. What did it come to? In Mellapont's opinion, to this—that if there were any people who knew more about the sand pit murder than anybody else, these people were Mrs. Champernowne and John Hackdale. Obviously John Hackdale was hand-in-glove with his employer in the effort to silence Bartlett.

Bartlett seemed to incline to the opinion that John Hackdale was merely a go-between; a medium between Mrs. Champernowne and himself. But Mellapont felt by no means sure of that. It seemed to him that he had grounds for suspicion that Mrs. Champernowne and John Hackdale shared a darker secret. There was a fact within his knowledge which obtruded itself again and again. Ashenhurst House, its grounds, the adjacent lanes, and the disused, grown-over sand pit, were all within John Hackdale's boat as special constable. What more likely than that he was around that part on the night of the murder and became privy to its commission—by Mrs. Champernowne, who certainly possessed a revolver, and, in Mellapont's opinion, was just the sort of woman to use it effectively? It might be, and, undeniably, it would be in John Hackdale's interest to shield the woman upon whom his living depended, and who had it in her power to advance his interests.

The more Mellapont thought of this, the more he was convinced that he was on the right track—that Mrs. Champernowne murdered Deane, for reasons of her own, and that John Hackdale knew it. He saw how it could be done. She might be looking round her own grounds and out-houses with the revolver in her pocket (he had already ascertained from one of his subordinates that the reason Mrs. Champernowne gave in applying for permission to keep a revolver was that her house lay in a lonely situation and that tramps had a trick of getting into her sheds and conservatories): then she met Deane. She might easily lure Deane away into the sand pit and shoot him, trusting that suspicion would fall on the rag-tag and bob-tail always left behind in the town on fair day. And John Hackdale might be close at hand, and hear the shot and go up to the place from whence the sound came, and find—Mrs. Champernowne. Possible— all of it!—and in Mellapont's opinion, John Hackdale was just the sort of man likely to enter into a conspiracy of silence.

Anyway, now that he knew all that he did know, both John Hackdale and Mrs. Champernowne had got to be seen—and talked to. Hackdale first, certainly; and alone; there were—questions—all-important questions—they must be put at once. And then the woman. Mayor or not, wealthy or not, Mrs. Champernowne would have to go through it.

It was dark when Mellapont reached Southernstowe. Looking neither to right nor left, he went quickly away to the police station and sought out Nicholson, one of his plain—clothes men. After a few words, he took Nicholson away with him, and went straight to the house in which Hackdale lodged. Leaving Nicholson outside, in a corner of the square from which he could see without being seen, Mellapont knocked at the door, asked for Mr. John Hackdale, and, on learning that he was in, went, unannounced, to the brothers' private sitting room. John sat there alone, over the tea—table. He had a cup of tea in one hand, and a newspaper in the other; he set down both as the superintendent strode in, and Mellapont was quick to notice that his hand shook and his face paled.

Mellapont closed the door, turned, and slipped into a chair close by Hackdale's—all in—silence. He looked keenly at the man he had come to see.

"Hackdale!" he said in a low voice. "I've come to see you on serious and important business. I won't beat about the bush. I'll put my cards on the table. I've just come from seeing James Bartlett at his lodgings at Portsmouth. I may as well tell you—Bartlett made a clean breast to me! Of—everything! Now then, Hackdale, why have you and Mrs. Champernowne been paying Bartlett hush-money to keep him from telling that Deane stopped him, on the night of the murder, to ask his way to Ashenhurst House? Why?"

Hackdale was pale enough now, and his colour showed no sign of returning. He was struck all of a heap—and Mellapont saw it.

"Take your time, Hackdale," he said, not unkindly. "That's hit you!—but you can't be surprised. Men like Bartlett are never to be counted on. But I'm sure he's told me the truth, now, and—you'd best do the same. Why did you square him, from the first? Think! First, you gave him all the ready money you had on you; then, a hundred and fifty pounds with the promise of a similar amount if he'd go to America, to be paid as soon as you knew he'd arrived; then, when he didn't go, a thousand! Looks bad, Hackdale—very bad! Now—what do you say about it?"

Hackdale knew by that time that Bartlett had split. He was astonished, amazed, stupefied. And he could only stammer.

"I—I—" he began. "You see—you see, Mellapont—Mrs. Champernowne-"

"Well?" demanded Mellapont, sharply. "Mrs. Champernowne—"

"Her name—of course—to be kept out of it," stammered Hackdale.

"Why?" asked Mellapont. "Do you know?"

"Upon my honour, I don't!" protested Hackdale. "I—I know no more than—than Bartlett knows. No more than that—that Deane met him and asked his way, and that—that—" He checked himself, remembering the episode of the safety pin. But no one, no, not even Mellapont, he decided, could find out about that. "I—I don't know anything!" he concluded lamely.

"You don't know who shot Deane?" demanded Mellapont.

"Before God, no!" exclaimed Hackdale. "I do not!"

"And you mean to tell me that Mrs. Champernowne was willing to pay all that money—a thousand cash down, and a pension for life—to Bartlett, just to keep him from telling that he'd met a man in North Bar?" asked Mellapont. "What reason had she?"

"I don't know," protested Hackdale. "She has, anyway. Her affair!"

Mellapont sat silently regarding Hackdale for a minute or two.

"It's well known in the town, Hackdale, that the very day after the murder was discovered you were advanced to a very superior post at Champernowne's," he said at last. "Now, had that anything to do with this? Were you squared as Bartlett was squared?"

Hackdale was recovering himself a little. He shook his head.

"I—I deserved any advancement that my principal could give me, superintendent," he answered, not without some dignity. "I'd expected it! My promotion was the result of my long and faithful service."

Mellapont rose from his chair.

"You hold a police certificate for a revolver, Hackdale," he said in precise, official tones. "Show me the revolver!"

Hackdale stared, reddened, looked annoyed, but rose instantly. He turned towards a door.

"Certainly!" he answered. "It's in a drawer in my bedroom there—I'll fetch it."

"No—I'll come with you," said Mellapont.

Hackdale stared at him again. But he opened the door, switched on the electric light, and followed closely by Mellapont, walked across to a chest of drawers and drew one out. He slipped his hand under a neatly—folded stack of linen—to withdraw it with a sharp exclamation.

"Not there!" he said. "I—I'm dead certain I put it there—that's—where I've always kept it. Who—?"

He began to search and rummage, pulling out drawer after drawer, and turning the contents here and there in his haste and agitation, while Mellapont, coldly silent, stood by and watched. But no revolver came to light, and its owner turned a white, astonished face on the watcher.

"It's—it's gone," he said. "It was there, not so long since—a month. Simmons must have—"

Mellapont turned to the door.

"You'd better think things over, in the light of what I've told you," he said severely. "You'll probably think of more you can say to me, and if and when you do, you know where to find me."

With that he left the room and the house, and went across to the shadow amongst which his man lurked.

"He's in there, Nicholson," he whispered. "If he goes out, follow him. Keep an eye on him all through, until you hear from me. You know what to do if there's anything to report."

The plain-clothes man nodded, and Mellapont, leaving him, walked rapidly to Shelmore's private house, a little distance away. Learning there that Shelmore was dining with Mr. Palsford at the Chancellor Hotel, he went there, and walking unannounced into the coffee room, found the two solicitors just finishing dinner. Within a few minutes he had whispered to them an outline of all that he had learnt since seeing them at noon.

"What next?" asked Shelmore.

"Mrs. Champernowne," said Mellapont, with decision. "I want you both to go up there with me—now. It's only ten minutes' walk. When you're ready-"

The three men presently walked up the streets towards Ashenhurst House in silence. No one spoke, indeed, until they were at Mrs. Champernowne's door. Then Palsford whispered:

"Over twenty years since she saw me, you know! Will she—"

"I'm thinking of that," said Mellapont. "Leave it to me."

Jane Pratt opened the door and at sight of Shelmore seemed inclined to start and to exclaim. But Mellapont was quickly at her side and whispering to her, and within a moment she had shown all three into an adjoining room and left them. Mellapont nodded at his companions.

"I told her to give my name only," he said. "Mr. Palsford, stand there, in full view of the door! I want Mrs. Champernowne to see you first—"

The door opened before he could say more; Mrs. Champernowne was already there. And she saw Palsford first, and except for a slight increase in colour, showed no particular interest in his presence. Her gaze swept Shelmore and Mellapont and settled on the superintendent with anything but pleasure.

"Well?" she demanded with some asperity. "What is this, Mellapont? Why do you—"

"Business of the highest importance, Mrs. Champernowne," interrupted Mellapont. "Grave business, to which I must ask your attention. But first—I think you knew this gentleman when you lived as Mrs. Arradeane, at Normansholt, some twenty-odd years ago?"

Mrs. Champernowne gave Palsford another look. But she made no response to his bow; instead, passing all three men, she seated herself at the head of a centre table, and pointed to chairs.

"Now, Mellapont," she said. "What do you want? Drop your mysteries and come to the point."

"Willingly!" answered Mellapont, as he took a chair facing the table. "Nothing will be more agreeable to me, Mrs. Champernowne. And it'll save time if I do go straight to the point. I may as well tell you that James Bartlett has admitted to me this afternoon that you have been paying him hush-money to keep his tongue quiet about a curious fact. Now, why, Mrs. Champernowne?"

Mrs. Champernowne gave him a hard look.

"My business!" she answered.

"Police business, if you please, Mrs. Champernowne," retorted Mellapont. "Don't let us get at cross-purposes. I know more than you think. John Hackdale has also made some confessions. Mr. Palsford there has posted me up as regards your life at Normansholt, your husband's disappearance, and so on. Now, Mrs. Champernowne, let me be frank. We'll call the man who came to the Chancellor Hotel, and who was murdered in the sand pit behind your grounds, what he called himself, James Deane, though we believe that he was James Arradeane, your husband's first cousin. James Deane left the Chancellor late at night and went out. He asked his way to your house, mentioning you by name. Later, he was seen in your grounds, in company with you—you may show surprise at that, but I have the proof. He never returned to the Chancellor, and he was found dead, murdered, forty-eight hours later. Then you begin to square people to say nothing—you certainly squared Bartlett, and I have a strong suspicion that you squared John Hackdale. Things look very black, Mrs. Champernowne, and I think you ought to speak; I ask you to speak! Why not speak and let us at at the truth? Come, now, Mrs. Champernowne, you, as a magistrate, know—"

"And supposing I won't?" asked Mrs. Champernowne.

Mellapont threw out his hands.

"Think of my position," he said. "All this information before me! What does it look like, Mrs. Champernowne? What would anybody say? Here are two legal gentlemen!—I'm sure, if you asked their advice—"

But Mrs. Champernowne showed no intention of turning to either Shelmore or Palsford. She kept looking from the rings on her fingers, which she was turning over mechanically, to her questioner; from him to the rings. There was a silence, broken abruptly at last.

"Well!" she said. "The man certainly was the other James Arradeane—the cousin! He did come here—I did talk to him, in the grounds. He had a reason for coming here. He'd seen and recognised me at the picture house."

"What was his reason, Mrs. Champernowne?" asked Mellapont, quietly.

"He'd heard that I was to be married—to Sir Reville Childerstone. He—he wanted to tell me, in case I didn't know it, that the other James Arradeane, to whom I was once married, and who ran away from me at Normansholt, was dead."

Mellapont turned to Palsford. Palsford was staring at Mrs. Champernowne.

"Dead?" he exclaimed. "When? Where?"

"At Melbourne, in Australia, three months ago," replied Mrs. Champernowne. "He gave me the proof—a cablegram. I have it—safely put away. That was all—when he'd told me that, he went away, out of the grounds. I never saw him again—I don't know where he went—I don't know who killed him. I'm quite sure that John Hackdale doesn't either. That's all I know."

The three men looked at each other, wonderingly.

"But if that's all, Mrs. Champernowne," asked Mellapont, "why all this extraordinary precaution to ensure silence from—a man like Bartlett?"

Mrs. Champernowne gave him a queer look.

"My business!" she said for the second time. "I have reasons for not wishing the past to be gone into—good reasons. My own reasons!"

"Because of your marriage with Sir Reville?" suggested Mellapont.

"Sir Reville Childerstone has known everything from the beginning," said Mrs. Champernowne quietly. "And now you know all that I can tell you. I don't know anything whatever about anything that happened to James Arradeane after he walked out of my gate!"

Presently Mellapont and his companions went away from Ashenhurst House. They had passed North Bar before anyone spoke.

"That's a sort of checkmate!" said Mellapont at last. "I don't know what I think. However, there's no use in giving up, and I've more to do tonight. I want to ask some questions of Miss Pretty. Come with me, you gentlemen."

The chambermaid who was Jane Pratt's friend led all three to the door of Miss Pretty's sitting room, and with no more announcing than a preliminary tap, threw it open. There, seated side by side on a sofa before the fire, were Miss Pretty and—Simmons.

MELLAPONT'S EXHIBIT

Of the four men in that room, the quickest to grasp the situation was Simmons.

He saw at once what had happened during his absence. Palsford had not only gone to Shelmore about Sir Reville Childerstone's business, but had told him all about the Arradeane mystery at Normansholt, and had probably seen Mrs. Champernowne and recognised her as the Mrs. Arradeane he had known in his own town. And Shelmore had taken him to the police—and here was Mellapont with both of them, obviously wanting Miss Pretty. Why? Clearly, he must act, and act quickly, if he wanted to be first.

But Shelmore was already speaking. He and Mellapont had exchanged glances at sight of Simmons. Shelmore hastened to translate the meaning of those glances into words.

"What are you doing here, Hackdale?" he demanded sharply. "You ought to be in Dorsetshire! What—"

"Missed the noon train," answered Simmons, readily and with some show of defiance. "Had to wait till night for another. And hanging about, I happened to see Superintendent Mellapont there, with Mr. Bartlett. I knew what that meant—and I came back!"

"Why?" asked Shelmore, still more sharply.

"To safeguard my own interests!" retorted Simmons. "And—Miss Pretty's!"

He turned to Miss Pretty as he spoke, and Miss Pretty, who seemed anything but pleased at the unceremonious invasion of her privacy, blushed a little.

"Mr. Hackdale has been very persevering in pursuit of my interests," she murmured. "He's worked very hard—"

"He'll be consulting his own if he comes away for a little talk with me!" interrupted Mellapont, eyeing Simmons significantly. "You'd better come, my lad—now."

"As I please!" answered Simmons. "Not at your bidding, Mellapont! You've no charge against me. And you've no right to walk into this lady's parlour, unannounced, either— you, or any of you!"

"I shall speak to the maid—and the landlord—about that!" murmured Miss Pretty. "Very rude, I think."

Mellapont glanced at Shelmore. Then, taking a step forward, he touched Simmons on the shoulder and motioned him into a corner of the room. Simmons went—and the others, watching, saw the superintendent bend and whisper a few words in his ear. What they were, none of them knew—but Simmons started, flushed, looked angrier than ever and, as Mellapont added another whispered communication, grew sullen of countenance. "Well—where, then?" he growled. "Not here, anyway! Nor at your place!" Mellapont turned to Shelmore.

"Suppose we go across to your office?" he suggested. Then, as Shelmore nodded, he looked at Miss Pretty. "I have two or three questions to ask you. Miss Pretty," he added. "I'll look in later. And as to being unceremonious, or rude—when murder's abroad even policemen may be allowed a little license. Now, Hackdale!"

Simmons muttered something to Miss Pretty about returning speedily, but he went away readily enough, and with a semblance of meekness. The fact was, Mellapont, in that whispered communication, had told him that Jane Pratt had given him away— unreservedly. That had knocked out the foundations of Simmons' elaborate structure, and he was now eager to know if he could do anything to prop up the walls before they came tumbling about his ears. He preceded the other three across the street, unlocked the office-door with his private key, and turned on the lights in his own and his employer's room—all as if he were performing an agreeable duty.

The four men seated themselves around Shelmore's desk, and Mellapont turned on the clerk with a judicial air.

"Now look here, Hackdale," he began. "You've been playing a nice game, all to yourself, for the purpose, of course, of getting the reward which that rather foolish young lady across there offered. But when you come to affairs with young ladies you should remember that there's a wise old saw which tells you that it's well to be off with the old love before you are on with the new! Jane Pratt heard on Sunday night about your philandering with Miss Pretty in the wood on Sunday afternoon—oh, yes, she heard, my lad, for you were watched!—and Jane Pratt's a jealous young woman. She gave you clean away to Mr. Shelmore last night—and now we know everything. Yes—even to the finding of the revolver in Mrs. Champernowne's orchard. You'd better make a clean breast, Hackdale."

"Not to you!" said Simmons.

He had listened closely to Mellapont, and his spirits had risen in consequence. If they only knew all that Jane Pratt could tell, he cared little. His chief concern now was with Miss Pretty. He could get round her. And, with a slight laugh, he repeated his defiance, adding a word or two.

"Unless I like!"

"I think you will like," remarked Mellapont, quietly. "You'll run a big risk if you don't!"

"What with?" asked Simmons, with a sneer. "Do you think I'm a fool? You've nothing against me! It's at my own pleasure that I'm here, and I can snap my fingers at all of you and walk out of that door this minute if I choose!"

He rose from his chair and moved towards the door as if to make good his threat, staring impudently at the superintendent. Mellapont nodded.

"Do so, my lad!" he said. "Do so—and you'll walk into a cell at the police station within five minutes! Do you hear that?"

Simmons stopped—staring again, but with a different expression.

"What d'you mean?" he demanded.

"I mean that I suspect your brother John of being concerned in the murder of James Deane, and you of being an accessory after the fact!" answered Mellapont. "Now, my lad—how does that strike you? And you sit down again in that chair, and answer my questions or I'll arrest you now!"

Simmons had turned unpleasantly pale, and his close-set eyes began to twinkle curiously. But he tried to smile.

"That's all damned rot, Mellapont!" he began, with an attempt to bluster. "You know-"

"I know that the revolver you picked up last night is your brother's, my lad, and that you're aware of it," said Mellapont. "Now then, sit you down, and answer what I ask, or else—"

Simmons re-seated himself, on the edge of his chair, thrust his hands in his pockets, and became sullen.

"I'm not going to say or do anything that'll do me out of that reward!" he muttered. "I've worked hard for that, and—"

"If Miss Pretty's ass enough to fling her money broadcast into your hand, young fellow, you're welcome to it for all I care, privately or officially," said Mellapont. "I don't care what you tell Miss Pretty, or how you bamboozle her—you seem to have got round her pretty well, already! What I want is information that you can give. You may save your own brother by it, though from what I've seen and learnt of you, you don't seem to care much about that."

"Every man for himself!" growled Simmons. "I've myself to think about."

"Then you'd better think about yourself now," said Mellapont, "and save yourself from unpleasantness. Now, you answer my questions. Did Jane Pratt tell you that on the night of the murder she saw a stranger in the grounds of Ashenhurst House with Mrs. Champernowne?"

"She did—certainly," replied Simmons.

"Did she tell you that your brother and Bartlett went there the other night, and that she saw Mrs. Champernowne hand John Hackdale a cheque?"

"She did."

"Was Jane Pratt with you on Sunday night, when you picked up a revolver in Mrs. Champernowne's orchard?"

"Yes, she was! And she's told you all this already, damn her!" said Simmons. "So what's the use."

"You answer my questions, Hackdale! Where is that revolver?"

"Safely put away—where no one but myself can find it," growled Simmons.

"All right!—you'll have to produce it. Now then—do you know to whom that revolver belongs?"

Simmons withdrew his hands from his pockets, folded his arms, and tilting his sharp chin, stared at the ceiling. There was a spider, a big, fat spider up there; he watched it walk right across from one corner to another before he spoke. The three men watched him curiously. He brought his eyes to the level of their faces at last. "Yes, I do!" he said.

"Whose is it, then?" asked Mellapont sharply. "Come!"

"It's my brother's, John Hackdale's," answered Simmons. "I knew it at once—that is, as soon as I turned a light on it. It has his initials scratched or cut on it. But I don't see that that proves, or could prove, that he shot Deane! Not it!"

"Well?" said Mellapont. "Why doesn't it—why shouldn't it?"

"He may have lent it to somebody," suggested Simmons. "He may have sold it to somebody. What use was it to him?"

"Where did he use to keep it?" asked Mellapont. "Do you know?"

"Oh, I know! In a drawer, in his bedroom; under some linen."

"When did you see it last?"

"Can't say! Months ago."

Mellapont remained silent for a moment or two.

"Do you remember anything about your brother's movements on the night of the murder?" he asked. "A Monday night."

"I remember the night—fine, dry night," replied Simmons, "but nothing particular about him. He was on special constable duty at that time and always out late. It was generally one or two o'clock in the morning when he came in."

"Let me put a definite question to you, Hackdale," said Mellapont. "Have you been suspecting your brother?"

"Not directly," said Simmons. "I've thought he knew something about it. I was taken aback when I found his revolver in that orchard. I thought he might be accessory after the fact. I did think that!"

"Let's be frank," suggested Mellapont. "Whom do you think of as the actual murderer of Deane? Come, now?"

Simmons laughed. There was a note of confidence in that laugh, the significance of which was not lost on his companions.

"Why, Mrs. Champernowne, of course!" he said. "Mrs. Champernowne!"

"Your grounds?" asked Mellapont. "What are they?"

But Simmons shook his head. "I'm not going to give away my chances of that reward—" he began.

"I've told you already you're heartily welcome to Miss Pretty's reward, and to her and her fortune!" interrupted Mellapont. "It's up to you to convince her that you're entitled to it—I shall do nothing against you. And this—now that you've been amenable and spoken—is between ourselves. What made you suspect Mrs. Champernowne?"

Simmons put out a long, thin finger, poking it through the air towards Palsford.

"I reckon he knows!" he said, with a sardonic smile. "Mr. Palsford knows, well enough. You see, Mellapont, Shelmore sent me down to Normansholt to look over some property which Sir Reville Childerstone has there. Now I knew—never mind how—that Deane had been at Normansholt, and had a picture postcard of a part of it, on which he'd marked a particular house. Well, that struck me as odd to mark one card out of hundreds! When I went to Normansholt, a chap named Swale, one of Mr. Palsford's clerks, showed me round the town. I saw the house I'm speaking of, and Swale told me a romance concerning it. It had been tenanted some twenty odd years ago by a Mr. and Mrs. Arradeane. The man made a mysterious disappearance; the woman left the town. There was more—but I came back to Southernstowe convinced that this James Deane who came to the Chancellor was the James Arradeane who used to live at Normansholt; that the Mrs. Arradeane of Normansholt was our Mrs. Champernowne, and that she murdered him, her lawful husband, so that she could marry Sir Reville Childerstone!"

"And you still think so?" suggested Mellapont.

Simmons looked from one to the other of his listeners.

"I should like to know who did, if she didn't!" he said, meaningly. "Why did she pay Jim Bartlett hush-money?—that cheque she handed to John, in Bartlett's presence, was for Bartlett, of course—though I guess you know more about that than I do, as you've been in touch with him. And why—if this is all in confidence—why, the very morning after the murder was discovered, did she give John a new post, worth more than twice, nearly thrice, what he was getting—why, but to keep his tongue still? She's hushed things up all round—for that reason. John knows a lot—a lot!"

"You're giving your brother away!" said Shelmore, speaking for the first time, and in tones of deep disgust. "You might keep his name—"

"He said—in confidence," retorted Simmons, pointing to Mellapont. "And—every man for himself! I've myself to think of. And I can do with that three thousand pounds reward. It'll help me to a career."

The three men looked at each other. There was silence for a while—and it was Simmons who broke it.

"I want to go," he said abruptly.

"A moment!" replied Mellapont. "That revolver? You have it—in safety?"

"Safe enough," answered Simmons, grimly. "So safe that nobody could find it."

"You've no doubt about it being your brother's?"

"None!"

Mellapont seemed to be considering some proposition that was suggesting itself to him in the secret recesses of his mind. Suddenly, rising to his feet, he took out his pocket book, and producing from it a small package done up in tissue paper, slowly unfolded the wrappings, and turning to Simmons, showed him, before the other two, the fragment of broken cuff-link which he had once shown to Shelmore.

"Do you know anything of that?" he asked, quietly. "Ever seen it before?"

But even as he spoke he knew that Simmons had recognised the thing he was exhibiting. The colour came and went in the clerk's face; his lips parted, his eyes flashed, his long fingers began to work excitedly.

"Good Lord!" he muttered. "Where—where did you get that?"

"In the sand pit, close by where Deane's body was found!" answered Mellapont. "Do you know it?"

Simmons suddenly clapped his hat on his head and turned to the door. But before he had taken two steps he paused.

"Stop here!" he said, with a queer eagerness. "Here—or be at your office, Mellapont. An hour—two hours, perhaps—and—and I'll ring you up. I—I see the whole thing!—I know who did it! Good Heavens! to think—but—wait... "

Before they could stop him, he had darted from the room, through the outer office, and was pounding down the stair. Mellapont, the broken cuff-link in his palm, turned, inquiringly to the other men. Palsford spoke.

"That chap knows." he said, quietly. "He knows—at last!"

Simmons hastened across the street and hurried into the Chancellor Hotel. But instead of going straight to Miss Pretty's private apartments, he turned aside to a quiet and snug smoking room, reserved as a rule for commercial travellers. Just then, however, there were no commercial travellers to be seen there; such as were staying in the house were either lingering over the supper table or gathered in the billiard room. And Simmons made for the one writing table in the room, and finding some blank note paper there, sat down, reflected a moment, and then quickly wrote out two documents, the wording identical in each case, save that in the second a convenient blank was left. With these neatly folded, and bestowed one in the left and one in the right pockets of his coat, he sped upstairs and walked into Miss Pretty's sitting room without as much as a tap at the door.

For the second time that evening. Miss Pretty let out a gasp of astonishment. But Simmons slipped his arm round her waist and kissed her—breathlessly.

"All right—all right!" he said. "Me!—back again!"

"What did those fellows want?" asked Miss Pretty.

"Never mind them!" answered Simmons. "All bluff and bluster—trying to get things out of me. No good—I'm a darned sight too clever for either police superintendents or country town lawyers! You don't know how clever I am—yet."

"I think you are clever!" murmured Miss Pretty. "Very clever!"

"Ain't I?" assented Simmons, with another kiss. "And I'm going to show you—and the whole town—how clever I am, this very night. Listen—don't scream—don't exclaim—don't do anything but just listen. I've solved the mystery!"

Miss Pretty, who was still within the encircling arm, twisted her slender figure round and stared, full face.

"You—you don't mean—" she began.

"Steady!" said Simmons, warningly. "Now—I know who killed James Deane!"

Miss Pretty gasped. And Simmons nodded, once, twice, thrice, at her parted lips and dilated eyes.

"I know," he repeated. "Dead certain! Nobody else knows. Nobody else could know. Nobody else could have found out. The culprit hasn't the least idea that I know. All my work! Alone!"

"Who is it?" whispered Miss Pretty.

"No!" said Simmons. "Not yet! Mustn't spoil things or run risks—even walls, especially hotel walls, have ears. Things to do yet—last arrangements—final plans. But before midnight—perhaps sooner—done! The whole town will ring with it tomorrow morning. And—you won't forget that your Sim did it, will you?—worked and schemed and spent toilsome days and sleepless nights to—to succeed? You won't?"

"Of course I shan't!" protested Miss Pretty. "And I do think you're most amazingly clever, Sim—I do, really. That you should succeed where that big, fat Mellapont—"

"Pooh!" said Simmons. "Mellapont! Brains of a rabbit?—he's no good—fool him, any time. But look here—the reward? You'll take care it comes to me?"

"Oh, of course!" asserted Miss Pretty. "It would be mean not to take care of that! Besides, how could I forget that it's—you?"

"Angel!" exclaimed Simmons, rapturously. "But look here!" he continued, growing very grave. "Don't be afraid, but there's, well, considerable danger in what I've got to do to—night—personal danger. I might get—"

"Oh, don't run any risks, Sim!" entreated Miss Pretty. "Don't get yourself—"

"Impossible to avoid risk in an affair of this sort," said Simmons, sternly. "I'll run 'em—for your sake. Do my best, of course, to avoid 'em, you bet! But still—the risk is there—queer company I've got to go into. And in case anything happens—or that somebody else should chip in and say that he's entitled before me, just—mere form, you know—just put your name to that paper, there's a love!—and then I shall be safe. Due to me, that, you know, angel!"

The angel would have stood on her head to oblige Simmons, with whom by that time she was fatuously in love, and she hastily scrawled her name to the first of Simmons' two documents. She made no attempt to read it, but Simmons re-read it over her shoulder as she signed it with his fountain pen, and he once again admired its neat wording:

"Simmons Hackdale, having informed me that he has now found out who it was that shot James Deane, and that he can produce undoubted proof of the murderer's guilt, I hereby promise to pay the said Simmons Hackdale three thousand pounds as soon as he gives the guilty person into the hands of the Southernstowe police."

"Please—please don't—don't get shot—or—or anything of that sort!" pleaded Miss Pretty, as Simmons refolded the signed document and put it safely away. "I don't know where you're going, but can't you take somebody with you?"

"Impossible!" said Simmons, still stern and immovable. "Secret matters need secret treatment! Hope for the best, angel!—and look here, there's just one thing you can do. You have, somewhere about "-here he assumed the air of great mystery which profoundly impressed Miss Pretty—"the dead man's walking stick! Give it to me!—I need it!"

Miss Pretty drew away from him, shuddering. But she retreated into her bedroom, through a door in the corner—and as soon as she had gone, Simmons, glancing rapidly over the table by the fire, strewn with books, magazines and newspapers, caught up a slim, faded volume and thrust it into an inner pocket. When Miss Pretty returned, he was standing with folded arms, a monument of resolution.

"Here!" said Miss Pretty, faintly, holding out gingerly a stout oak staff. "I—I was almost afraid to touch it!"

Simmons took the stick, threw the other arm round Miss Pretty's shoulders, and kissed her forehead. He pulled his cap over his brows.

"Now for it!" he said.

The next instant he had left the room, and Miss Pretty, her heart fluttering and her pulses throbbing, went to the window and, drawing the blind, looked out on the gas-lighted street below. Simmons came into view for a second or two—then he vanished. As he went round the corner, the great clock in the cathedral struck ten heavy, booming strokes.

Before the strokes died away, Simmons was half way up the street that led towards Ashenhurst House; very soon he was at the gates of that desirable residence. He opened them softly and stole into the grounds—stole in so quietly that he startled a man just within, who made a sudden bolt for the adjacent shrubbery. Simmons, who could not afford such expensive luxuries as fear or diffidence, made a spring after the retreating figure and caught its clothing. He dragged his captive into the feeble light of the lamp above the gates.

"Hullo, Nicholson!" he exclaimed—recognising the plain clothes man. "What's your game?"

"What's yours?" retorted Nicholson surlily, as he released his arm from Simmons' grip. "That's more like it."

"Pretty much the same as yours, I should think," answered Simmons. Just then he caught sight of another man, half hidden amongst the laurel bushes. "Oh!" he exclaimed, with a laugh. "Two of you, eh? I've a good idea of what you're after, too. My brother, John. Eh, Nicholson?"

"That's our business!" growled Nicholson. "And if you're going in there—"

"I am going in there, and I shall be in there for a while, and then I'm coming out!" declared Simmons. "And there's no need for you to be so dark and secret with me. I've just left Mellapont—and I know more than you do!"

"We know nothing—except to keep an eye on—him!" said Nicholson, impressed by Simmons' reference to the superintendent, and nodding at the lighted house. "That's all—we followed him here."

"How long has he been in there?" enquired Simmons.

"Ten minutes, maybe," replied the plain-clothes man.

"Anybody go in with him?"

"No!"

"Well, I'm going in!" said Simmons. "And when I come out, I'll very likely tell you something. There's going to be big doings tonight, Nicholson, You'll perhaps come in at them!"

Without further parley he hastened up the drive to the front door. It was flanked by plain glass panels; through one of these Simmons made an inspection of the hall inside. Empty!—not a soul to be seen—not even a glimpse of Jane Pratt's black gown, smart apron and coquettish cap. He quietly opened the door, stole into the hall, and, tiptoeing his way along, made straight for Mrs. Champernowne's drawing room; a second later and he was within and had shut the door behind him and turned, a finger raised warningly, on its occupants.

Mrs. Champernowne sat in an easy chair by the hearth; John Hackdale stood near her, leaning against the mantelpiece. Simmons saw doubt, anxiety, perturbation on their faces; John started erect at sight of him, and Mrs. Champernowne frowned angrily.

"What—" she began. "What—"

"H'sh!" whispered Simmons, stealing softly across the thick carpet. "Do you know what's outside?" He paused, to give dramatic effect to his inquiry. "I'll tell you! A couple of detectives!"

He saw Mrs. Champernowne flush, and John start. But neither spoke, and Simmons, again making mysterious signs, went across the room and officiously drew blinds and curtains.

"Anyway—plain-clothes men!" he said, coming back. "Nicholson and Burbidge! In the shrubbery. Followed you, John! With a purpose, too. Look here!—it's no use beating about the bush, Mrs. Champernowne—you and John may as well know how things stand. I've just come from Mellapont—been through it with him—hot time, I can assure you! But I got away—and hurried here, to warn you both."

"Warn us of—what?" demanded John.

"Mellapont's going to arrest both of you!" whispered Simmons, with a comprehensive wave of his thin fingers. "Both!—on a charge of murder! That's why I'm here. Also, it's why these chaps are outside. House watched back and front. You're up against it—both!"

John Hackdale glanced at Mrs. Champernowne; Mrs. Champernowne was staring at Simmons. She began to turn and turn the rings on her fingers—a sure sign, as John knew, of nervous agitation.

"That's—absurd!" said John at last in a voice that he himself recognised as strained and dry. "What evidence-"

120

"Absurd nothing!" exclaimed Simmons. "You don't know all I know!—Mellapont's been rather more than open with me. Look here. Your revolver has been found—found in Mrs. Champernowne's orchard! What do you make of that?"

John started unmistakably. He felt rather than saw Mrs. Champernowne's astonished eyes on him.

"Then it was thrown there by somebody who stole it from me!" he declared. "I missed it—missed it tonight. I—"

"There's no use in all that," said Simmons. "Do you think the police are going to believe that sort of stuff? It's your revolver, and you were up and round here about the time that Deane was shot, after being seen with Mrs. Champernowne in these grounds. And Mellapont's got it firmly into his head that either you or Mrs. Champernowne actually shot Deane, and that you're partners and accessories—and he's going to arrest you—both! Then—however it goes—there will be a fine making public of—all sorts of things!"

He looked meaningly at Mrs. Champernowne, and Mrs. Champernowne again turned to John Hackdale. John was pale and nervous; his eyes kept turning to the door; he looked as if he were listening intently.

"Yes—without any mistake!" said Simmons, interpreting his thoughts. "But—I can stop it!"

The two listeners turned on him sharply, eager inquiry in their eyes.

"You?" exclaimed John. "What—"

"I!" answered Simmons. "I can stop it! Stop—everything!"

"How?" demanded John.

Simmons nodded first at one, then at the other.

"I know who killed Deane!" he said. "Do you hear that? I know!"

John drew a sudden sharp breath, and stepped nearer to his brother.

"You—know!" he said. "Then—why didn't you tell Mellapont? Why haven't you told it before, instead of—"

"That be damned!" retorted Simmons. "My business! Self first!—didn't you teach me that? I've got myself to think of! I didn't tell before because I've only just learnt the exact truth this very evening; I haven't told Mellapont because—I want paying for my knowledge! Let Mrs. Champernowne there make it worth my while, and I'll take those men outside away to put the handcuffs on the real culprit-"

"And if she won't?" said John, with a sneer.

"Then I shall keep my knowledge to myself!" retorted Simmons. "But she will," he continued, as he produced his second document and laid it before Mrs. Champernowne, "she will!—for her own sake. If I say nothing, you and she'll be in Southernstowe police cells before midnight; if I speak, you're both safe. Let Mrs. Champernowne fill up that blank space there in her own handwriting with the words two thousand pounds, and then sign the whole, and—I hand the guilty person over to Mellapont! If she won't—silence!"

"Extortion!" exclaimed John. "It's—"

"Never extorted anything from her yourself, did you?" retorted Simmons. "No!—of course not! And never let her be fleeced by Jim Bartlett?—no! Better fill up and sign, Mrs. Champernowne—it'll pay you! When people want to draw a thick curtain over the past—or a slice of the past—they can afford to spend a bit, eh? Fill up—and sign!"

Mrs. Champernowne obeyed him. And while John muttered something like a disgusted curse on his knavery, Simmons calmly folded the paper and turned to the door.

"One word to both of you," he said. "Don't leave this house! Stop here, John—don't you go out, Mrs. Champernowne. By midnight—before, indeed!—I'll send you word that

James Deane's murderer is safe within four walls! And then—you'll breathe easier, and sleep easier than you've done for a good while, eh?"

He stole out again, fearful of meeting Jane Pratt, and rejoined Nicholson and his companion in the drive. Taking Nicholson by the arm, he led him aside and made a whispered communication—at the end of which the plain—clothes man jumped.

"Good God, Mr. Simmons!" he exclaimed, "You don't mean it?"

"Fact!" said Simmons coolly. "Now then, off to Mellapont and tell him, and insist on his doing just what I've told you! Then—you see."

He left the two men outside Ashenhurst House and went home by a short cut across the top part of the city. Arrived in his private sitting room, and leaving the door partly open, he turned the light on to the full, and getting out a bottle of whisky, and a syphon of mineral water, and glasses, he mixed himself a drink, and lighting a cigarette, sat down to wait and to read the evening newspaper.

Some time passed; at last he heard a heavy step on the stairs. And at that he rose and looked out of the half—open door to see who was coming up. Ebbitt appeared—home from his managerial duties at the Picture House.

Ebbitt's gaze, going past Simmons into the lighted room, fell upon the whisky and the tumblers, and he laughed.

"Hullo, laddie!" he exclaimed. "Having a night of it?"

"Come in!" responded Simmons. "No!—just having a drink before bed time. Help yourself!"

Ebbitt lounged slowly into the room, took off his big cloak and hat, unwound the white silk muffler from his neck, and again rubbing his hands together with the remark that it was getting precious cold o'nights, proceeded to mix himself a stiff drink and to carry his tumbler to the easiest chair.

"Well, here's towards you!" he said, drinking; and nodding at his host. "The best of 'em! Where's John?"

"Out!" answered Simmons.

"Courting?" suggested Ebbitt with a leer.

"Not that I know of," said Simmons. "Never heard of it."

Ebbitt fumbled in his waistcoat pocket, brought out a cigar, and proceeded to light it.

"If I'd been your brother John, laddie," he remarked presently, "I wouldn't ha' let an elderly roue like Sir Reville carry off the widow Champernowne. I'd ha' taken that vessel in for myself—good—looking fellor like John!"

"Old enough to be his mother, she is!" said Simmons. "Guess she's fifty!"

"What's that to do with it?" sneered Ebbitt. "Fifty? Lor' save you, a woman's just at her prime at fifty, nowadays, if she's taken care of herself—as that one has. Fine woman, Mrs. C.—and got the dibs, too. And there's worse things than money in this world, Sim, my laddie—much worse!"

"Ain't things good at that show of yours?" asked Simmons. "Thought you were turning money away every night."

"Frequently happens that we do," assented Ebbitt, with an air of indifference. "But that doesn't affect me, laddie. I'm a salaried man. So much a week—full or empty."

"Well, it's a certainty, anyway!" said Simmons. "Better than being—well, a strolling player, eh?"

"Yes, I was that once," replied Ebbitt, musingly. "Strolling? God; I should think so!—often with a half-clothed back and an empty belly! But I'd more fun out of those times, laddie, than I get out o' these!"

"Doubtful!" said Simmons. "Not me, anyhow! Give me a fixed position and money at the back of it; none of your haphazard business for me! Where did you do most of your strolling, then?"

Ebbitt's eyes grew dreamy. He took a pull at his tumbler, balanced it in his hand, and stared thoughtfully at the fire.

"All over the place!" he answered. "Through the mill from the beginning. I've seen it all. I've played in a fit—up, and I've played at the T.R., Drury Lane. I've played Hamlet in a booth, and done a no-line, walk-on show to Henry Irving in the same part. I once had a benefit that fetched in three hundred pound, and I've recited in a wayside inn and been glad of the hat-full of coppers I got for doing it. Experience, laddie!—and there was adventure in it. And—now I wear a dress suit and an opera hat o' nights and superintend—pictures! Pictures!—thrown on a screen out of a blinking magic—lantern! Bah! Give me living men and women and the human voice! If you'd only known the men and women I've known—ah, we could act in my day!"

"Must have known a lot of actors in your time," suggested Simmons.

"Crowds!—multitudes!" assented Ebbitt. "Yes. Good fellows!—dear boys!—gone, now, most of 'em. No such nowadays—poor lot on the boards is there."

Simmons pushed the whisky nearer to his guest. And as Ebbitt replenished his glass, his host glanced at the clock on the mantelpiece, which he had set by the City Hall time when lie came in.

"Actresses, too?" he said, as Ebbitt once more pledged him. "You'd know plenty of actresses?"

"Aye, laddie, no end of 'em!" answered Ebbitt. "From way back in the 'sixties, when I started. Bless you!—I've played with Madame Celeste—knew her well enough at the old Lyceum. Actresses—hundreds of 'em—good, bad indifferent."

Simmons remained silent for a moment or two. He was keeping an eye on the clock and an ear on the stair outside. And as the minute hand of the clock pressed slowly forward he spoke again.

"Ever know an actress called Nora Le Geyt?" he asked quietly.

Ebbitt lifted his face sharply from the glow of the hearth. A frown shot across its upper half and his lips parted in something like a snarl.

"Nora Le Geyt!" he repeated. "What the devil do you know about Nora Le Geyt?"

"Heard of her," retorted Simmons, steadily. "Why not? Lots of actresses' names are remembered—long afterwards."

Ebbitt continued to stare at him. His lips were still open, showing his teeth, and his eyes were suspicious.

"Not likely that you'd ever hear of her!" he growled. "Where did you—a mere lad!—ever hear?"

Simmons glanced again at the clock; listened again for a sound on the stair. He turned to his guest with a half—cynical, half—impudent laugh.

"Lawyers—like me—get to know a lot, Ebbitt," he retorted. "We're never surprised at anything. I know a good deal about Nora Le Geyt. She married a man named Arradeane, James Arradeane, who subsequently called himself James Deane—the James Deane who was murdered in the sand pit behind Ashenhurst House. There," he continued, pulling out and opening at its title-page the book which he had picked up from Miss Pretty's table, "there's a book of Nora Le Geyt's, with her autograph—recognise it? But of course you do!—I think you were an old flame of Nora's, and that she jilted you for the other man, and that—" he gave a swift glance at the clock and strained his ear towards the door—"and that—that," he went on, bending forward with a steady stare at Ebbitt's startled eyes, "was—why you shot him!"

A dead silence fell on the room—save for the slow ticking of the clock. It was broken by Ebbitt's movements. He set down his glass and rose, staring at Simmons, and as he stared he backed towards the door. But he got out a word—one.

"What-"

"What nothing!" exclaimed Simmons, disdainfully. He knew that the door was open, though but a mere crack, purposely so by himself when he asked his visitor in, and he raised his voice. "What indeed? Shall I tell you what I know, Ebbitt? You recognised Deane as the man who'd supplanted you that night he went to your show; you resolved to have your revenge, and you came home and stole John's revolver out of an open drawer in the next room and went out with it; you had an idea that Deane would go to Ashenhurst House that night to see his relatives there—you knew all about it!—and you hung about for him. You did see him; you got him, somehow, into that sand pit and shot him, and flung the revolver into Mrs. Champernowne's orchard—where it's been found—

I found it. And something else has been found—you dropped the enamel facing of a cuff-link in that sand pit, Ebbitt, and that's been picked up. Why, man, you're wearing the rest of that cuff-link just now—look at it! And it's all up, Ebbitt—the police know everything—and what do you say to that, what do you—"

Ebbitt's eyes dropped sharply from his accuser's face to the right—hand wrist of his finely-laundered shirt. He looked for a second at the damaged cufflink, and he muttered something under his breath. Simmons laughed—and Ebbitt's hand stole suddenly and quickly round to his hip. Within the second and before Simmons' laughter had died, the accuser found himself staring into a levelled revolver.

"No need to steal or borrow a revolver, now!" said Ebbitt. "This is mine, and this time—you!"

It was a big cry, rising to a shriek of agonised fear that Simmons let out as he leaped back behind the table, thrusting out his hands.

"No!" he shouted. "Ebbitt!—put it away—away!—Oh, my God!—Mellapont!—Nicholson!"

The revolver spoke sharply, and Simmons withe a groan, toppled back, clutching at anything and nothing. And then, as the police, with Mellapont at their head, came tumbling up the last few stairs and into the smoke-obscured room, Ebbitt turned his weapon upon himself, and without a sigh or a cry went out of the world.

According to all the moral principles and precedents as laid down in melodrama, Simmons ought to have been picked up dead, shot through the heart. Maybe his heart was so tough that the bullet glanced off it; maybe it was so small that it didn't extend over the area at which Ebbitt aimed. Anyway, instead of being mortally wounded, Simmons was found to be shot through the shoulder—a nasty and unpleasant injury, but not one that was likely to deprive the community of his services. He was unconscious when Mellapont and his men laid hands on him; when lie regained consciousness he found himself in a private ward in the Southernstowe Infirmary, with doctors and nurses in attendance. And within forty-eight hours Miss Pretty was admitted to his bedside, and she hung over him and wept tears on his red poll, and told him, in whispers, that he was a hero—her hero.

There are queer people everywhere in this world, and Southernstowe was not without its percentage of them. The Simmons Hackdale cult, engendered by Miss Pretty, spread and flourished. Truth and fable were mingled in it, as in all cults. While Simmons lay in his white bed, men in bar-parlours magnified him. All alone, unaided, young Hackdale had quietly, slowly, persistently, ferreted out the truth about the sand pit murder, and, bold and unafraid, had tackled the murderer single handed, and nearly lost his life in ministering to justice. A fine, sharp, resourceful young fellow! said the wiseacres of pot and pipe, and certain sure to go far—yes, even to being Lord Chancellor. Brains!—yes, almost more brains in his little finger than all the slow—witted solicitors and pesky policemen in the city or the county—didn't he do quiet and unostentatious, what they couldn't do with all the machinery of the Law? True it was!—and well deserving was that there smart young fellow of the rewards and what not. In Simmons' case, skill undoubtedly won favour.

He recovered, slowly at first—more rapidly when, beneath his pillow, he placed the cheques which duly came in from Mrs. Champernowne and Miss Pretty. Miss Pretty gave him hers to play with, as she put it—it seemed silly, she whispered to him, during one of her twice-a-day visits, to give him this mere bit of the whole which was presently to be his—said whole consisting of herself, her hand, her heart, her fortune. But Simmons considered a cheque of any sort as a good soothing plaster, and he slept better after the receipt of this and the other. And in the end, thanks to careful doctoring, nursing and feeding, he arose and went forth. Everybody wanted to shake hands with him, and did; Alderman Bultitude, ex-mayor, thanked him publicly in High Street, for clearing the city of a stain on its fair name. On the strength of everything, and in view of his approaching union with Miss Pretty and emigration to her tin-mine, Simmons took more pretentious rooms and ordered several new suits of clothes from his tailors. In one of these, a smart frock suit, set off by a silk hat, he took Miss Pretty to the afternoon service at Southernstowe Cathedral one Sunday afternoon soon after his return to convalescence. The Canon-in-Residence selected as the text of his sermon the thirty-fifth verse of the 37th Psalm: "I have seen the wicked in great power and spreading himself like a green bay tree." He discoursed upon this with great clarity and force and with a wealth of illustration in which reflections and animadversions upon such things as deceit, craft, subtlety, hypocrisy, lying and selfishness were plentiful and pointed. Had Simmons ever been taught to search his heart and examine his conscience he might have felt uneasy under that sermon. But he was quite comfortable and well satisfied—very largely because there were plenty of vacant chairs around him in the nave, and he was able to place his new silk hat on one of them, and thereby ensure its not being kicked by his own or anybody else's feet—and he ceased not from spreading himself when he went forth from the venerable fabric. He considered himself a very smart and clever fellow, and Miss Pretty was of his opinion. The truth was that neither Simmons nor his Cynthia had any sense of humour. They will probably do very well.

Printed in Great Britain
by Amazon

26308259R00071